Emmy hadn't known Ben for long, but she sensed he was out of sorts the whole day.

It was almost as if Ben was jealous of Adam—but that would be preposterous. Ben had never intimated that his feelings were more than platonic.

"Is something wrong, Emmy?" Ben took a step toward her, concern clouding his eyes.

"I—I was going to ask you the same question."

For a moment, he didn't say anything, and when he looked up she saw the old Ben reappear. "Nothing is wrong."

"Then why the sullen mood today?"

"I'm sorry I've been so moody. There's no excuse for it."

"Maybe not, but is there a reason?" The question came of its own accord, as if her heart longed to hear that his feelings did run deeper while her mind begged her to walk away—nay, run—before he answered.

He studied her for a moment, as if he, too, wanted something he knew he shouldn't want, but then he shook his head and started toward the door. "Good night, Emmy."

Ben's actions were ... didn't know what to th... ere not what conc... scared her even more.

Gabrielle Meyer lives in central Minnesota on the banks of the Mississippi River with her husband and four young children. As an employee of the Minnesota Historical Society, she fell in love with the rich history of her state and enjoys writing fictional stories inspired by real people and events. Gabrielle can be found at www.gabriellemeyer.com, where she writes about her passion for history, Minnesota and her faith.

Books by Gabrielle Meyer

Love Inspired Historical

Little Falls Legacy

A Family Arrangement
Inherited: Unexpected Family
The Gift of Twins

A Mother in the Making

GABRIELLE MEYER

The Gift of Twins

Recycling programs for this product may not exist in your area.

LOVE INSPIRED BOOKS

ISBN-13: 978-0-373-42553-2

The Gift of Twins

This edition published by arrangement with Love Inspired Books.

www.Harlequin.com

Printed in U.S.A.

Therefore shall a man leave his father
and his mother, and shall cleave unto his wife,
and they shall be one flesh.

—*Genesis* 2:24

To Beka Swisher, Sarah Olson, Lindsay LeClair and Jessica Janski. Thank you for being some of the first people to read my stories and believe in my dream. Your friendship is a gift from God.

Chapter One

Little Falls, Minnesota
October 15, 1858

Reverend Benjamin Lahaye was usually a man of patience, but tonight he felt like a caged bear, pacing up and down the room. He stopped in front of the fireplace and placed another log on the blazing flames to give himself something to do. When he stood, he glanced out the window at the raging blizzard and started to pace again.

The new schoolmaster, Mr. Emery Wilkes, should have arrived on the stagecoach hours ago, but the temperature had dropped steadily all day and an unseasonable snowstorm came out of nowhere. Maybe the stagecoach driver had stopped to find shelter. At least, that's what Ben hoped. He'd hate to think the schoolmaster was stuck in a snowdrift, freezing to death.

A knock sounded at the front door, bringing Ben's worries to rest.

He sprinted across the room to the front door where a lantern sat on a table near the window. He kept it lit every night to welcome friends or strangers who might need a warm home, a listening ear or a bit of counsel. Tonight, the lantern would welcome the first male schoolteacher to Little Falls—a much-needed change after the three previous female teachers had all married before their contracts were fulfilled. In a town that boasted over two hundred bachelors, women were in high demand. As a school board member, it had become a tiresome task to refill the position, so Ben had been adamant about hiring a man. He'd also offered to let the new schoolmaster board with him, since he lived alone.

Ben opened the door, a smile at the ready. "Welcome, Mr.—"

A young woman stood on his front porch, shivering and hugging her body as she blinked up at him with snowflakes clinging to her long lashes. Her cheeks and nose were pink, making her blue eyes more brilliant under the light of the lantern. "H-hello," she said through chattering teeth. "A-are you Reverend Lahaye?"

He stood there, speechless at the sight of her.

"I'm M-Miss Wilkes," she continued as a shiver moved through her body. "Th-the new schoolteacher."

She couldn't be. He'd reviewed the application himself. It had clearly said "Emery A. Wilkes."

She stared at him for a moment, a frown creasing her brow. "Y-you are R-Reverend Lahaye, aren't y-you?"

He finally found his voice. "Yes."

"May I—I come in?" She took a step toward the warmth of his home. "I—I've never been s-so cold in m-my life."

Where were his manners? He couldn't let her continue to freeze on his front porch. He opened the door wider and let her come over the threshold. "Yes, of course, come in."

She moved past him and shook out her full skirts,

snow falling to the ground in a perfect circle around her gown. "Is there s-someone to help with my l-luggage? The driver p-practically tossed me off the s-stage in his quest to find suitable lodging."

He looked out at the swirling storm where three trunks sat haphazardly collecting snow. Ben couldn't very well bring her trunks into the house—what would people think? But he couldn't leave them out there to get buried, either. If he did, they might not dig them out until spring. "I'll see to them."

He grabbed his coat off the hook and slipped it over his shoulders, his mind whirling with unanswered questions. "Go on over to the fireplace and warm yourself."

Miss Wilkes didn't wait for a second invitation, but walked to the fire and extended her hands to the heat, closing her eyes with a sigh.

Ben stood for a minute, his confusion mounting. Who was this little bit of a thing and how had this mistake happened? Nowhere on the application did it hint that Emery Wilkes was a woman.

He stepped into the biting wind and hefted the first trunk onto his shoulder. It was surprisingly heavy, and he suspected it was full of books. He brought it into the house where the ring of snow was now melting into a puddle.

He dropped it to the ground and shoved it to the side. As soon as he had a place for her to go, the trunks would need to leave. But where would he take her? The Northern Hotel? It seemed the best place, though it could be dangerous trying to get there in this storm. He'd known people lost to wander in the blinding white, freezing to death without finding shelter. Maybe he'd take her to the Coopers. They were his closest friends and they'd never turn away a young lady in need. Their house was full, but it had been fuller.

He contemplated his choices as he brought in the other trunks. When he finished, he closed the door against the frigid wind and stood for a moment to shake off the snow. Miss Wilkes had removed her coat and bonnet and pulled a chair up closer to the fire, her back to him.

Firelight danced and flickered over her face as she surveyed his home. Her gaze went to the mantel where he kept his snowshoes from his circuit preaching days, reminding him that God's plans were not always his own. Next, she looked toward the piles of books he had stacked on the floor. The stories had been his boon companions these three years, and he suspected that if her first trunk was filled with books, then she fully understood why he had so many.

She must have sensed him, because she stood and clasped her hands in front of her. "Thank you for bringing in my things." Her voice had an eastern ring to it that he didn't hear often. It reminded him of Mrs. Ayers, the woman who had raised him when his father had abandoned him at the mission in Pokegama when he was six.

"It was my pleasure." Ben slipped off his coat and hung it on the hook, uncertainty in his movements. What would she say when she learned about the mistake?

The young lady looked around the parlor, an uncomfortable smile forming on her pretty face. "It's awfully quiet. Is Mrs. Lahaye at home?"

Ben took a tentative step into the room—but paused. "There is no Mrs. Lahaye."

Her smile fell and she took a step back, putting the chair between them. "No Mrs. Lahaye?"

"I think there's been a mistake."

She swallowed, her gaze darting around the room as if mapping out her escape. "What kind of a mistake?"

"You're not who we expected."

She frowned, her expressive eyes filling with dismay. "What do you mean?"

"Are you Miss Wilkes of Springfield, Massachusetts?"

"Yes."

"Miss Emery Wilkes?"

"Yes. Miss Emery Anne Wilkes of Springfield, Massachusetts."

Ben groaned. "We thought you were a man."

She let out a relieved breath. "Is that all? It's an honest mistake. I was named after my maternal grandfather, Emery Anthrop, though my parents have always called me Emmy."

He took another step toward her. "But you don't understand. We didn't want to hire a woman—we were specifically looking for a man."

Her frown deepened as the truth settled over her. "I'm just as capable and hardworking as a man."

"I'm sure you are, but every woman we've hired has been married within three months of arriving and then we're forced to look for another schoolteacher. We want more consistency for our students."

She swallowed and lifted her chin a notch, though her quiet voice didn't match her determined confidence. "You have nothing to fear on that count. I have no intentions of marrying."

"Neither did the others."

"You have my word." She looked pained, clearly expecting him to believe her.

He wanted to, but experience had taught him otherwise. "I don't think your word will be good enough for the school board." They were just as adamant as Ben. They had better things to do than replace their teachers every three months.

Her shoulders drooped and she shook her head. "I'm not wanted?"

The simple question was laced with a deeper pain—one Ben knew all too well. He'd spent his entire childhood believing he wasn't wanted.

He didn't answer. Couldn't.

"Surely the school board won't turn me away after I've come so far." She looked at him with uncertainty. "They won't…will they?"

Ben wished he could offer some hope. She *had* come a long way after all, and according to her application, she was more than qualified. But Mr. Samuelson, the newly appointed superintendent of the Little Falls school, was a hard man and once he had his mind set, it was difficult to change. Ben could just about imagine what he'd say to this attractive young lady. It wouldn't take long for a line of beaus to come knocking on her door.

"We need to find somewhere for you to stay." Ben started toward the kitchen. "But, first, I'll get you a cup of hot coffee to warm you up."

He entered the cozy kitchen and grabbed a mug, glancing at her when she stepped over the threshold. She was so young and defenseless, he wondered how her family felt about her coming all the way to Minnesota. If he had a daughter, he doubted he'd let her go so far alone—especially if she was so pretty.

"We'll need to face the weather and go down the hill to my friends, the Coopers." He handed her the mug of coffee, taking note of her long, slender fingers and her clear skin. "They're friends of mine and the best chance we have of getting you somewhere safely tonight. They'll put you up for a few nights until we can get you back on the stage Monday morning. The school board will pay for your trip home."

"I'm not going home." She held the coffee mug in both her hands, her back straightening with determination. "I've come west to teach and that's what I intend to do."

He crossed his arms. "Then I'm afraid you'll have to do it somewhere else, Miss Wilkes. The school board decided to hire a man, and we won't be happy until one is found."

It looked like the school board would need to start looking for another teacher, and Ben would need to find a new boarder—one who wasn't as fetching as Miss Emery Anne Wilkes.

Emmy was not going back east—not after she had come so far and sacrificed so much to leave Massachusetts. There was nothing holding her to the east, nothing but dreadful memories and angry words.

The hot coffee didn't set well in her stomach as she stood near the front door in Reverend Lahaye's home a few minutes later, a bag of necessities by her feet, tying her bonnet strings in preparation to go to the Coopers' home. She watched Reverend Lahaye wrap a long scarf around his neck and then put mittens on his large hands. He was not what she had expected—but then, nothing was as she had expected. If it wasn't snowing, she'd already be at the superintendent's home, begging him to give her a chance. As it was, she'd go to him as soon as possible and assure him she was there to stay. She had no intentions on marrying—ever. After William's unexpected death two days before their wedding, she had vowed to never love again. She refused to put herself in a position to suffer through the same heartache twice.

Surely, they wouldn't turn her away once she gave her word that she didn't plan to marry.

Reverend Lahaye glanced at her with his dark brown eyes as he put a knit cap on his equally dark hair. He was much younger and far more handsome than she had expected. When he'd answered the door, she had thought she'd arrived at the wrong house. In her mind, Reverend Lahaye was old and married—nothing like the man standing before her.

Kindness and gentleness radiated from his countenance, though she'd had a moment of panic when she realized they were alone in the house. But what woman wouldn't?

"Do you have a scarf?" he asked.

"I'm afraid not."

"What about mittens or a warmer coat?"

She shook her head. She hadn't anticipated such weather for several months—time enough to buy the needed items.

"You'll freeze to death in that bonnet and coat." He took the lantern from the ledge near the window and walked to a door on the right side of the parlor. He opened the door and stepped inside, the shadowed light revealing a bed and a bureau in the large room. His bedroom?

She stood patiently and waited until he returned. When he stepped into the parlor again, he had a large item draped over his arm. It looked like the skin of an animal, but she'd never seen anything like it.

"What is that?"

"It's my old buffalo robe. I used to wear it when I was a circuit preacher." He set the lantern on the ledge again and held the robe out for her.

She blinked at him. "What am I to do with it?"

"It'll keep you warm. Much warmer than that." He nodded at her fashionable winter coat. "Trust me," he said. "You'll thank me when we're in the midst of the storm."

He held it open with the fur toward the inside and the skin on the outside. She turned to let him put it on her shoulders.

She swam in the heavy material and it dragged on the floor. She could easily wrap it around her body two or three times. "I don't know that I can trudge through the snow in this thing."

His expression softened and a bemused smile tilted his wide mouth as he looked her over. "It's a little bigger than I remember, but I'll help you." He handed her a cap, scarf and mittens. "You'll need these, too."

The buffalo robe engulfed her and she could hardly raise her arms. "I don't think I can manage to put them on."

He took the robe off again, which allowed her to remove her bonnet. She placed it in her bag and then put on the winter items.

Without warning, he draped the robe over her shoulders again. Its weight almost knocked her down.

"Your boots are impractical for this weather, as well," he said.

"I can't possibly wear your boots." His feet were much larger than hers.

"I suppose you can't." He looked at her, the smile returning to his eyes. "I can hardly see you under all that gear."

She felt ridiculous, but she appreciated the added protection against the cold and snow.

He lifted her bag. "We'll go out the back door."

She followed him through the parlor, tripping over the buffalo robe, and entered the kitchen. He glanced out the window, squinting as he looked uncertain. "I hate to take you into this storm—but we have little choice." He turned to study her. "You'll need to hold my hand at all times. I'm familiar with the trek to Abram and Charlotte's, so I'll rely on my instincts. If, for some reason we're separated, don't move. Stay where you are and I'll find you."

Apprehension wound its way around Emmy's heart as she thought of the consequences of being lost in a blizzard. She simply nodded, thankful that he seemed so confident—but wondering if she could trust his instincts.

He opened the door and then reached his hand toward her.

She took it without hesitation and followed him into the storm. The wind bit at the exposed skin of her cheeks and nose. It stole her breath with its intensity and she clung to Reverend Lahaye's hand with all her might. Somehow, it was even worse now than it had been when the stagecoach dropped her off.

He closed the door and then bent into the storm, tugging her along with him.

The snow whipped about them in every conceivable direction. She didn't know if it was coming or going. Though she held his hand, she could hardly make out his shape in front of her and it hurt to look into the swirling wind and snow.

There was no sunshine to mark the way—just darkness and bitter cold wind.

They didn't go more than ten yards before Reverend Lahaye stopped and she bumped into his back. She didn't dare move as he turned to face her. He bent forward and spoke, but she couldn't make out his words in the howling wind.

He didn't move and she feared they were lost. Panic began to creep up her legs. It hit her heart with a thud, making her want to run—yet she didn't dare.

Again, he leaned forward and spoke into her ear, but she couldn't hear. What was wrong? Why had they stopped?

Finally, he tugged on her hand again—but if they were going forward or backward, she didn't know. It was impossible to know anything.

They didn't walk very far when she made out the shape of a building and he stepped through an open door.

When she followed, and her eyes adjusted, she realized they were back in his kitchen.

He shoved the door closed against the raging wind, breathing hard. "It's madness out there."

Emmy swallowed hard, trying to catch her breath, her fingers and toes numb. "Why are we back?"

He shook his head and took off his cap and mittens. "We would never have made it alive. We could have very well ended up in the river, or wandered out of town. I didn't know my right from my left out there." His eyes filled with concern. "I'm sorry, Miss Wilkes. I couldn't risk your safety. We'll have to stay here for the night."

Emmy stood motionless in the buffalo robe, the reality of their situation hitting her. "I must choose between my safety or my reputation?"

He took a step away from her, as if sensing her dismay and put some space between them. "We can try again in the morning when there is a bit of sun. Maybe the storm will cease by then." He went to the stove and put more wood inside. "Are you hungry? I can make you some flapjacks and sausage."

She hadn't eaten since lunch, but she didn't think she could swallow a bite now. "Where shall I sleep?" If she'd sleep at all.

"There are two bedrooms upstairs. I had one prepared for Mr. Wil—" He paused. "You should be comfortable there. I'll sleep in my room down here."

She nibbled her bottom lip. Would sleeping unchaperoned in the pastor's house make it more difficult to convince the superintendent to let her stay? What would the community say? It was vital that they think highly of her.

"I'm sure everyone will understand." He put an iron skillet on the stove and gave her a reassuring smile, as if he could read her thoughts. "This is a small community, but no one would fault us for staying safe. I'll explain everything."

Emmy wasn't so sure, but what choice did they have? They were stuck in the parsonage until the storm subsided.

Chapter Two

The next morning, Ben stood near the cast-iron stove scrambling eggs for breakfast. Snow and ice blew against the house with a vengeance, as if winter was shaking its angry fist at the world, daring it to lay dormant. He'd never seen a blizzard so early, and it didn't bode well for the lonely months ahead.

A floorboard creaked and Ben turned to find Miss Wilkes fidgeting uncomfortably in the doorway. In the light of day, he found her to be even prettier than he'd first thought by the glow of the lantern. Her blond hair was twisted in a becoming knot, with tendrils curling around her face. Blue eyes, the color of wild forget-me-nots under a warm prairie sun were fringed with those long lashes, and she had the tiniest waist he'd ever seen. She didn't look as young and defenseless as he'd first thought, either. He guessed her to be twenty-three or twenty-four, though she carried herself as if she had a fair share of life already behind her.

"Good morning," Ben said as he nodded to the table. "I'll have some eggs for you in a minute. Help yourself to bread and jam. The coffee's hot."

She took a tentative step into the kitchen as if afraid

of being in the same room alone with him. Last night, they'd gone to their bedrooms immediately after they ate their flapjacks. It had been awkward and she'd fled the moment he'd said good-night. He didn't blame her. It was a difficult situation she'd found herself in, but he'd do all he could to protect her reputation.

"Will I find a more suitable place to stay this morning?" she asked as she picked up a mug and filled it with coffee. "I'd also like to see the superintendent as soon as possible."

Ben glanced out the window, but all he could see was snow and more snow. "I think the storm is worse today than last night." He shook his head. "I don't feel right about taking you out there again. At least not now. We'll go later, if it lets up."

She sighed and set the coffeepot back on the stove. "I suppose the damage is already done."

Ben put the eggs on the table and motioned for her to take a seat. He also sat and then he bowed his head. "For this meal, and our lives, Lord, we are eternally grateful. Amen."

"Amen," she echoed.

Ben dished up her plate and she took a piece of bread and lathered it with strawberry jam. There was so much he'd like to know about her. He was always fascinated when a young lady braved the frontier and set out on her own—this one especially. She seemed so vulnerable, yet he suspected there was steel-like determination under that delicate exterior.

She glanced up at him. "Thank you for your hospitality. I'm sure this isn't what you expected, either."

He laughed. "I was definitely expecting *Mr.* Wilkes."

She smiled, revealing a row of beautiful white teeth. "Do you take in many boarders?"

"He would have been my first."

She laughed, and the sound was the merriest thing he'd ever heard. "*He* doesn't exist."

"I suppose you're right." Ben scooped some eggs onto his own plate. "I was looking forward to a roommate for the winter months. I used to be a circuit preacher and I would go from home to home, rarely alone for more than a night or two. Before that, I lived at three different missions, which were always busy with people coming and going. It's been a hard transition to living alone."

Miss Wilkes studied him with unabashed curiosity. "You're a very interesting man, Reverend Lahaye. I'd like to hear more about your life and travels one day."

He didn't mind her honest assessment. Welcomed it, actually. "Feel free to call me Ben."

She lifted her eyebrows and took a sip of her coffee. "I hardly know you."

"I don't sit on pretenses or eastern manners," Ben said. "Life's too hard and too short to worry about all that."

She set her mug down, sadness filling her countenance. "Life *is* too short."

What had this young lady experienced that would sit so heavily upon her? He had always been good at reading people, and he could sense she had a great deal of pain in her past.

She pulled herself from the sadness and squared her shoulders. "I suppose you should call me Emmy, then, since I intend to stay."

Ben paused as he spread his jam over his bread. "I have it on good authority that the superintendent will send you home on Monday."

"And I have it on good authority that I won't let him."

He liked her willpower, even if it was misguided. "The school board wants a man."

"Don't you need a teacher? At least while you look for a man? Why not give me a chance?" Her eyes filled with such passion, he couldn't look away, even if he wanted to. "Allow me to prove to you that I am here to stay. I want this job more than anything—and I assure you, I have no intentions on marrying now or in the future."

What a pity. It wasn't hard to imagine her in a snug home, surrounded by children.

"As a school board member," Emmy continued, unaware of Ben's wayward thoughts, "could you speak on my behalf? I promise you won't regret keeping me in Little Falls."

It wouldn't take long for suitors to come calling on Emmy Wilkes—despite her declaration to remain single. It would be impossible to keep the men away. But didn't they owe her the benefit of the doubt? "I will do what I can to help."

She let out a relieved sigh. "I'm in your debt."

A knock at the front door brought both their heads up.

"Who would brave this storm?" Ben wiped his mouth and looked out the window. Sure enough, the wind had finally calmed and the snow lessened so he could actually see his backyard again. He had hardly noticed as he spoke to Emmy.

Should he invite her to join him in the front room? The last thing he wanted was a neighbor to see them alone together—yet, he didn't want to hide her and lie. Everyone would eventually know.

"Would you care to join me?" he asked.

She also wiped her lips, but shook her head. "I'll stay here and finish my breakfast."

He left the kitchen, being sure to close the door behind him, and entered the front room.

The knock came again, this time with more force.

Ben pulled the door open and found Mr. Samuelson on his front porch.

"Ahh, Reverend Lahaye." Mr. Samuelson walked into Ben's house without invitation and clapped his mitted hands together. "Is Mr. Wilkes here? Did he arrive safely?"

"Come in, Mr. Samuelson." Ben closed the door behind him, glancing toward the kitchen. The superintendent lived about two blocks east of Ben. He was a widower with five children, though his two oldest daughters were old enough to see to the needs of the younger ones.

"I came the moment the snow started to let up a bit." Mr. Samuelson's dark eyebrows were caked with ice. "I wanted to meet the man who will teach my children."

Ben was uncertain how he should proceed. No matter what he said, it would still come as a shock to Mr. Samuelson, and there would be no way around the truth.

The kitchen door squeaked open and Emmy spared Ben the discomfort of deciding.

She stepped out with confidence and grace. "I'm afraid there's been a mistake, Mr. Samuelson."

Dennis Samuelson spun on his heels at the sound of the lady's voice.

Emmy walked across the front room and extended her hand. "*I* am Miss Emery Wilkes. It's a pleasure to meet you."

Dennis didn't move a muscle to welcome the new teacher.

Ben squared his shoulders, ready to fight on Emmy's behalf. They had made the mistake in hiring her, and they owed her a chance to prove them wrong.

The superintendent stared at Emmy much longer than she felt necessary.

Ben came to stand beside Mr. Samuelson, though his gaze was on her. "As Miss Wilkes said, there's been a mistake."

Mr. Samuelson stood in all his outdoor gear, mouth and nose covered by a thick scarf. Emmy was only able to see his hazel eyes as he took her in, head to foot. "What's the meaning of this?"

"Apparently, you thought I was a man."

"Of course we thought you were a man. Your name is Emery, is it not?"

"She was named after her maternal grandfather," Ben told the superintendent.

He'd remembered that little detail?

"I don't care if she was named after the president of the United States." Mr. Samuelson unwrapped his scarf with more force than necessary. "We don't want another female."

"I realize that," Ben said, coming to her defense. "But what's done is done."

"It must be undone." Mr. Samuelson was younger than Emmy first thought, now that she could see the rest of his face. He was a pleasant-looking fellow, though his face was contorted in anger. "She'll have to go back posthaste."

Emmy took a step forward, unwilling to let these two men determine her future without some say in the matter. "I came in good faith that a job would be waiting for me. I'm not returning home until I fulfill the contract."

"She's right, Dennis." Ben put his hands in his pockets and nodded in her direction. "She came because we hired her—"

"We didn't hire *her*." Mr. Samuelson motioned toward her like she was a pesky fly. "We were expecting *him*."

"I realize you're upset," Emmy said. "But you have to understand how I feel." It had been five years since William died, and it had taken her that long to get the courage to fulfill their dream to come west. She couldn't let one little mistake send her back. "Reverend Lahaye explained to me why you're seeking a male teacher—and I've assured him you have no fear of losing me. I don't plan to marry, nor will I in the future. I am committed to staying in Little Falls as long as the Lord sees fit." She smiled and added quickly, "Which I hope is a long, long time."

Both men studied her. Mr. Samuelson with a calculating, unhappy look, and Ben with an approving, tender one.

"I suggest we let her stay on at least until we can find a replacement," Ben suggested. "We did guarantee her a contract for the first term, which ends at Christmas. Surely she'll stay unmarried until then."

Mr. Samuelson crossed his arms and let out a discontented grunt. "I thought we were done with looking for a teacher once and for all."

Emmy offered up a silent prayer, hoping her journey was not over before it had begun. She wanted desperately to stay and serve the children and families of Little Falls. It was all she had thought about this past month after she'd received the acceptance letter. She had fought so hard to come on her own, defying her parents' wishes, her friends' concerns, and putting up with the tittle-tattle of neighbors who thought she was ruining her life. She couldn't return now, not like this.

"Fine," Mr. Samuelson said. "She can stay—but only until Christmas. In the meantime, I will continue searching for a male teacher and have him ready to take her place the first of the year."

Emmy let out the breath she'd been holding. It wasn't what she'd hoped for, but it was a start. "If I can prove to you that you have nothing to fear, and that I have no intentions on ever marrying, will you allow me to stay?"

Mr. Samuelson squinted at her. "How would you prove that?"

"On Christmas Day, if I have made myself invaluable to the school and community, and I've shown myself above reproach, will you allow me to stay?"

Mr. Samuelson looked at Ben, who stared back at him without expression.

The superintendent threw his hands in the air. "Fine. But I'm warning you, *Miss* Wilkes—" he pointed at her, his finger shaking "—I will watch you closely, and if I see even a hint of romance, I will immediately terminate your contract and find a new teacher. Do I make myself clear?"

Hope bubbled in Emmy's chest for the first time since her arrival. She had no doubt she'd prove herself to the superintendent. No doubt at all. "You've made yourself clear."

"Now." Mr. Samuelson turned to Ben. "Where is she staying?"

"I haven't decided."

Mr. Samuelson eyes grew wide as he swung around to face Emmy. "Where did you stay last night, Miss Wilkes?"

"She stayed here," Ben said quickly. "We tried to

go to the Coopers, but I turned back, knowing it would have put her life in jeopardy if we had continued."

"Here? Unchaperoned?" Mr. Samuelson's face filled with disapproval.

"There was nothing untoward about last night," Ben said with authority in his voice. "Neither one of us expected the mistake and we did our best to rectify it. Miss Wilkes slept upstairs, while I slept down. I hope my character and reputation will speak for itself."

Mr. Samuelson balled his scarf in one hand. "I don't like it, but what's done is done." He addressed Emmy. "It is your upmost priority to ensure that your reputation stays untarnished, do you understand?"

"Of course." Her reputation meant more to her than almost anything.

"I want you to bring her to the Hubbards immediately," Mr. Samuelson said to Ben. "It'll be cheaper to board her with the Hubbards than pay full price at the hotel, and her meals will be included."

"But don't you think she'll have more privacy at the hotel?" Ben asked. "The Hubbards' boardinghouse is always full."

"Pearl will make room for her." Mr. Samuelson's voice suggested the debate was over. "And she'll be across the road from me, so I can keep an eye on her."

Emmy suspected that was the real reason he wanted her at the Hubbards' boardinghouse.

"I'll help you with your things," Mr. Samuelson said to Emmy. "We'll leave right now."

"We haven't finished our breakfast," Ben said.

"Now."

Emmy smiled at Ben, offering him a quiet thank-you with her eyes. He had done more than he needed, and she was grateful.

Without prompting, Emmy entered the enclosed stairway near the front door and went up to the room she'd slept in the night before. It was a spacious bedroom with a large bed, a bureau and a generous window. The bed had been warm and comfortable, and she'd had the best night sleep since leaving Massachusetts, given the circumstances. She gathered up her things as quickly as she could and placed them in her bag, and then she went back downstairs where the men were waiting.

"Feel free to borrow the cap and scarf and mittens," Ben said. "You'll need them."

"Thank you." She dressed for the outdoors, and when she was ready, she instructed them to bring the two trunks she needed most. She'd leave the one full of books at Ben's to be picked up later. She lifted her bag and then followed them out into the snow.

The cold air took her breath again, but this time she could see where she was walking. It was hard to get a good look at Little Falls with all the snow, but there would be time enough for that later.

She followed close behind Ben, thinking of the evening before when he'd held her hand. He was a kind man and she could sense that they would be friends. It didn't surprise her that he was a pastor. No doubt his parishioners loved him. She looked forward to attending church the following morning to hear him preach. She imagined he was good at that, too.

Ben led her and Mr. Samuelson across the road and down a block. A large, brown house appeared in the falling snow. It was quite impressive, and not what she would have expected on the frontier. Where Ben's home was modest and simple, this structure was overbearing, if not ornate. It was styled after the Greek Revival architecture and reminded her of some of the homes back east.

"Timothy and Pearl Hubbard are one of the founding families in Little Falls," Ben explained as they drew near the house. "You'll like Pearl. She runs a respectable home. They have three children. They'll be some of your students."

Excitement raced up Emmy's spine at the prospect of meeting some students, despite the frigid air. She had taught for several years back east, but she suspected it would be much different in the West.

A picket fence ran around the property and Ben unlatched the gate, allowing Emmy and Mr. Samuelson to pass by. Mr. Samuelson then went to the front door and opened it without knocking.

Emmy stepped over the threshold and into the foyer. She was instantly met with the smell of warm spice cake and fresh coffee. A wide staircase ran straight up the right-hand wall, curving to the left at the top. Two archways flanked the foyer. The one on her left went into a front parlor and the one on her right looked into a dining room. Noise at the back of the foyer suggested a kitchen was in that direction.

"Hello," called a woman from the kitchen.

"Hello, Mrs. Hubbard." Mr. Samuelson set the trunk down with a thud. "We have a boarder for you."

A plain-faced woman entered the foyer, her middle thick with child. She wiped her hands on her apron as she came down the hall. She was a bit older than Emmy would expect to bear children, but she looked healthy and robust, if a little frazzled. Her dark hair was split down the center and dropped to cover her ears, before being secured at the back in a bun. She smiled a welcome to Emmy and offered Ben a fond glance, but she squared her shoulders when she met Mr. Samuelson's gaze. "I'm sorry, but I'm full at the moment."

As if summoned, five boisterous men plodded down the wide stairs. They stopped short when they glimpsed Emmy, the ones in back plowing into the ones in front. All but one grinned like an idiot in her direction.

"Is there nowhere to put her?" Mr. Samuelson asked, as if she was a piece of furniture to be stored.

"Mrs. Hubbard," Ben said graciously. "May I introduce you to Miss Wilkes, the new schoolmistress?"

Pearl's eyes lit and she took Emmy's hand in a gentle squeeze. "The new teacher? Why didn't you say so to begin with? It's a pleasure to meet you, Miss Wilkes. I'm so happy you've come to teach our children."

"For the time being," Mr. Samuelson amended. "Now, can you board her or not?"

The men passed by and entered the parlor, though they didn't make any noise, suggesting they were listening to the conversation in the foyer.

"I suppose I can make room." Mrs. Hubbard sighed. "We always have space for the teacher. You'll need to room with Rachel, my serving girl. She sleeps in the room off the kitchen."

It wasn't ideal. Emmy liked to spend her evenings studying and reading in solitude—but if it was all that was available to her, and meant she could stay in Little Falls, she'd make do. "Thank you."

Mrs. Hubbard eyed her two large trunks. "We'll have to store your things in the attic. There won't be any space in your room with Rachel."

"Store my things? Will they be safe?"

"It's just until another room becomes available," Mrs. Hubbard assured Emmy.

"When will that be?"

"There's no way of knowing. We have men in and out all the time."

"I'll go home and retrieve your other trunk," Ben said to Emmy.

"There's more?" Mrs. Hubbard asked.

"All my books." Emmy felt bad that she'd packed so much, but she couldn't bear to leave anything behind.

Mrs. Hubbard shook her head. "There's not much room in the attic, either, I'm afraid."

"I'd be happy to store them for the time being," Ben offered. "You could come for them anytime you'd like."

The thought of not having her books at her disposal made her uneasy—but one look at Mr. Samuelson suggested she leave well enough alone. "Thank you, Reverend Lahaye."

"If this storm passes, we'll expect school to begin at eight o'clock sharp on Monday morning," Mr. Samuelson said. "See that you're there and ready on time."

"I will."

Mr. Samuelson tipped his hat at Mrs. Hubbard, and then at Emmy, though she suspected he did it out of habit and not a desire to be a gentleman, and then he left.

"I'll bring the trunks to the attic," Ben said to Mrs. Hubbard. He turned to Emmy. "It's been my pleasure, Miss Wilkes. I hope you'll be happy here."

"Thank you." She wanted to say more than *thank you*, but she couldn't find the words to express her gratitude. If he had been any other man, she probably wouldn't have a job right now.

"Do my ears deceive me?" One of the men exited the parlor and put his hands over his heart. "Is this beautiful creature going to abide under the same roof as me?"

"Mr. Archibald, remember your manners," Mrs. Hubbard said. "Miss Wilkes is a lady."

"How could I forget?" Mr. Archibald took Emmy's hand and bent over it. "It's a pleasure to meet you, Miss Wilkes." The other men followed Mr. Archibald out of the parlor. They circled her like a hungry pack of wolves, and she their prey.

It would be quite a feat to hold them at bay—of that she was certain—but it was vital if she wanted to keep her job.

Chapter Three

Ben returned home, disliking the way the men had surrounded Emmy. He'd seen it countless times before. As one of the only single females in town, she would be hounded incessantly. He didn't doubt she could resist their charms—but it wouldn't be an easy task.

He trudged through the drifting snow, his thoughts full of the young lady and all that had transpired since last evening.

A sleigh sat in front of Ben's home. It was piled with furniture and household belongings. A man waited on the front bench, reins in hand, while half a dozen children sat huddled in the back. They looked as if they were just passing through. People often stopped by the church and parsonage for one thing or another, and he tried to accommodate everyone to the best of his ability.

"Hello," Ben called as he drew near the parsonage. Snow continued to fall, but it was letting up and would probably stop soon. Activity had begun to commence on Main Street, though most would still be home, digging out from the storm.

A woman stood by Ben's front door, two small children by her side. She turned when she heard Ben and grabbed each child by an arm. "Are you the pastor?"

"I am."

The man on the buckboard gave Ben a cursory glance, but his attention was soon snagged by one of his children.

"I need to talk to you, quick," the woman said.

"Would you and your husband like to step into the house?"

"Norm will stay outside with the children, if it's all the same to you. We don't have much time and I'd like to get this over with." The woman had brown hair with strands of wiry gray at the temples. She looked tired and worn—but there was grit in the way she held her thin shoulders.

"Please step inside," he said, opening the door.

The lady walked into Ben's home with heavy footsteps, pulling the two children with her. Now that he was close enough to see, he noticed they were little boys, about the same age, if he were to guess.

Ben closed the door behind them, but didn't make a motion to remove his hat, or invite her farther inside. "How may I help you?"

"These here are my sister's boys, Zebulun and Levi. They're twins, five years old." She grasped each one's wrist. "Their ma died when they were three and their pa wasn't fit to raise them, so she sent 'em to me." She let them go and gave a decided nod. "My husband and me ain't got the means or the energy to raise 'em no more. I've got six of my own, and one more on the way, and we're just plumb wore out."

"I'm sorry to hear that." Ben stood there expectantly, wondering why she'd come. Did she need money? He kept some on hand for situations like this one. "If there's anything I can do to help, please let me know."

"You can take 'em off my hands." She started to move to the door. "That's why I've come and now I'm heading out with my man. We're going north and want to get a move on before another storm takes us by surprise."

Alarm rang inside Ben's head as he looked down at the two little boys. They clasped hands and looked up at him, their eyes round with fear.

"I can't take them."

The lady grabbed the knob. "I can't take 'em, neither. Do what you want with them. I did what I could, and now I'm handing them off to you. I told my man that the first church we come across we'd drop 'em off, so here we are." She turned the knob to leave.

"Wait." Ben reached out to put his hand on the door to stop her departure. "I don't have a wife, or the means to raise them."

"Then find a family who needs a couple extra hands."

"But—I don't even know their last name, or their kin. How am I to find their father?"

She snorted. "That good-fer-nothing shouldn't be found."

"But he deserves to know where his sons have gone."

"The name's Trask—Malachi Trask—but I don't know where he is. Last I heard, he was in St. Paul, but I suspect he moved on. Probably lying in a saloon somewhere west of here, I'd wager."

"Malachi Trask." Ben repeated the name.

"They're not my problem anymore," the lady said. "I did what I could, but I can't do no more." She nodded at the twins. "Goodbye, boys. I hope the pastor'll do right by you."

She opened the door and Ben moved back, knowing he couldn't keep her from leaving. He followed her out of the house, his pulse speeding up as she walked toward the sleigh.

"How will I contact you?" Ben asked.

"I don't aim to be contacted," the lady said, climbing into the sleigh. "I told my sister not to marry that man, but she went against my wishes. I don't hold no responsibility for them boys she bore."

"Giddyup," the man said as he hit the horses' rumps with the reins.

Neither one looked back as they pulled north, out of town.

Ben stared after them, helpless to stop them and make them return for the boys. He didn't know the name of the lady or her husband, but he suspected that was intentional. They didn't want to be known.

Ben turned back to the house, scratching his head with his mitted hand. What would he do with twin boys?

He entered his house and found them exactly as he'd left them.

Ben closed the door, apprehension making his back tight. He tried to smile, to reassure them that he was trustworthy, but they continued to look at him with those sad, fearful eyes.

"You're twins?" Ben asked, uncertain what else to say. They didn't look like twins—didn't even look like brothers, really. One had brown hair and round green eyes, while the other one had blond hair and almond-shaped green eyes. The brown-haired boy was shorter, but he was the one who nodded at Ben in answer to his question.

The blond-haired boy just stared.

"Which one of you is Zebulun?" Ben asked.

The brown-haired boy raised his hand, just enough for Ben to acknowledge him. "And this is my brother, Levi." He spoke with a bit of a lisp.

"It's nice to meet you both." Ben slowly took off his coat, not wanting to frighten them with quick movements. Memories of the day his father had left him at the mission at Pokegama came rushing back unbidden. He hadn't been much older than these two, and he'd been just as scared. Above all else, he remembered how hungry he was that first day, but he'd been afraid to ask for a thing. "Would you like something to eat?"

The boys looked at one another, and then Zebulun nodded. "Yes, sir."

"Let's see what we can find." He didn't bother to ask if they'd like to take off their coats. He remembered feeling safer keeping his meager belongings with him when Father left. These boys didn't even have a bag—just the clothes on their back, and threadbare clothes at that. Where had they sheltered the night before? Had they been cold? Scared? He hated to think that they had suffered through the storm, only to be abandoned today. But he suspected their suffering had started long before now.

They slowly followed him, not letting go of one another, their eyes roaming his home.

The breakfast he'd enjoyed with Emmy only an hour before was still on the table, cold and half-eaten. Ben cleared away the dishes and set them to the side, then he stoked the fire and put the frying pan over the heat. "Do you like eggs?" he asked.

Zebulun nodded, but Levi shook his head. Ben smiled to himself. It was the first response he'd gotten out of Levi. "What do you like, Levi?"

The little boy looked around the kitchen, his gaze resting on the bread and jam. "I like toast and jam."

"Then that's what you'll get." Ben sliced a couple pieces of bread and looked at Zebulun. "What about you? Do you like toast, too?"

Zebulun nodded.

"Why don't you two have a seat at the table. I'll get some milk for you while we wait for the food."

The boys did as he suggested, needing to let go of each other to take their seats.

"Do you know your names are from the Bible?" Ben asked as he placed the bread on a pan to put into the oven.

"Yes, sir," Levi spoke up, confidence in his answer. "We're tribes of Israel."

Ben's eyebrows rose, impressed that a boy so young would know about the Tribes of Israel. Someone must have taught him.

"My name is Benjamin," Ben said, trying not to pay them too much attention, lest they get nervous, but trying to hold up the conversation to keep their minds preoccupied. "It's also a Tribe of Israel."

Zebulun looked impressed, but Levi didn't show any response to the revelation.

Ben grinned. "We just need to find Asher, Judah, Naphtali, Reuben, Simeon, Issachar, Gad, Dan and Joseph, and then everyone would be here."

The boys looked at one another, clearly confused at the string of strange names he'd just said.

Ben's smile fell and he took a deep breath. What would he do with these boys? He wasn't equipped to care for them, yet he didn't know who could. Abram and Charlotte Cooper had just welcomed their fifth child less than three weeks ago, and Jude and Elizabeth Allen had their hands full caring for their twin girls, only two months old. With the national recession, and troubles closer to home, he could think of no one eager to take in two extra children. Ben had the financial resources—he just lacked the skill and experience, not to mention the help.

The only thing he could think to do was go back to the Hubbards and ask Pearl for advice. She had become a surrogate mother in the community. An honorable woman of wisdom and discernment. If anyone could help, it would be Pearl.

The bedroom was smaller than Emmy anticipated, and there was only one bed she'd have to share with the girl named Rachel. There were four hooks on the far wall, a single window looking out at a snow-covered world, and a rag rug on the floor. The space was so tight, it would be almost impossible to dress properly without bumping the walls. She thought of the large room she'd slept in the night before at Ben's home and sighed. How would she get the privacy she craved, or the necessary space to study here? A cursory glance around the house had suggested there were generous public areas—but those rooms would also hold men. Lots of men. Too many men for Emmy to get anything done if she took her books to the parlor or dining room to study. Maybe there was another space she wasn't aware of. She'd be sure to ask Mrs. Hubbard.

Her trunks were now in the attic, with two long flights of stairs in between. She'd taken only the necessary items she'd need, but she suspected she'd make that trek up the stairs several times a day.

With a final glance around the room to make sure her

few items were in their place, she entered the kitchen at the same moment as a young lady she'd yet to meet.

"Hello," Emmy said. "You must be Rachel."

"And you must be Emmy." Rachel set a pile of folded towels on a worktable and smiled. "Welcome to Little Falls."

Rachel was not a girl, after all, but a young woman in her midtwenties with shiny black hair and large brown eyes. If Emmy wasn't mistaken, she, like Ben, had Indian heritage, though her English was flawless and lacked any hint of accent. She was a beautiful woman, and Emmy wondered for a fleeting moment why she wasn't married.

"I'm sorry to intrude on your space," Emmy said, indicating the small room.

"I don't mind. It's nice to have another lady in the house again." She opened a cabinet door and placed the towels inside. "They come and go so fast."

"Is Mrs. Hubbard close at hand?" Emmy moved through the kitchen, not wanting to intrude on yet another room Rachel occupied.

"She's in the parlor, setting her feet up." Rachel smiled. "I told her to take a little break with that baby coming any day."

"Thank you." Emmy left the kitchen and walked down the long hall to the foyer. She didn't want to bother Mrs. Hubbard if she was resting, but it was important to find a room to work, and the sooner the better. With school starting in two short days, she needed to prepare.

The parlor was beautifully decorated with floral wallpaper, wide plank flooring painted blue and a large piano in the corner.

Mrs. Hubbard sat in a chair near a window, a sewing project in hand, while three men sat at a table in the opposite corner, a card game between them. When Emmy entered, the men immediately stood.

"Sit yourselves down," Mrs. Hubbard said to the men. "She probably didn't come to see you."

Emmy smiled at Mrs. Hubbard and nodded an acknowledgment to the men, who listened to their landlady and stayed on their side of the room.

"What can I do for you, Miss Wilkes?"

The front door opened, letting in a gust of wind and snow. A man walked over the threshold with two boys in tow, holding hands.

"Ben?" Mrs. Hubbard rose from the chair, holding the small of her back as she stood.

Ben ushered the boys into the house and then closed the door behind them. They stood like little statues, their eyes wide beneath the felt brims of their flat caps.

The pastor took off his knit cap and held it in his hand, nodding a greeting to Emmy before turning his attention to Mrs. Hubbard.

"Who are these lads?" Mrs. Hubbard asked.

Ben glanced at the boys, and then stepped around them, coming into the parlor. He spoke quietly. "Their aunt just left them with me."

"Are they your relation?"

Ben shook his head, his eyes filled with concern. "I've never met them or their aunt before. She left them with only their names and the clothes on their back. I don't know who she is, or where she is going. The only thing I know is the name of their pa."

"Well, I'll be." Mrs. Hubbard looked around Ben. "They're cute little ones."

Emmy caught the eye of the blond-haired boy and

smiled. He looked at her with soulful eyes, but didn't return her smile. How frightened they must be.

"What will you do?" Mrs. Hubbard asked.

"I don't know." Ben clenched his cap and glanced from Emmy to Mrs. Hubbard. "That's why I came here."

"It seems the good Lord is full of all kinds of surprises today," Mrs. Hubbard said with a smile in Emmy's direction. "Never a dull moment in these parts."

"What *will* you do?" Emmy asked.

Ben swallowed and looked at the boys again. They glanced up at him, quiet as mice. "I'll need to find them somewhere to live."

"I wish I could help," Mrs. Hubbard said. "But Timothy and I have more than we can manage now."

"I understand." Ben nodded. "I wouldn't ask you to care for them, but is there anyone else you can think of?"

Mrs. Hubbard pursed her lips as she looked from one boy to the next. "I don't know of a single family who could take the pair of them—and I don't think they'd like to be separated."

The boys locked hands even tighter than before.

Ben shook his head. "I would never separate them."

Mrs. Hubbard sighed. "Then there's only one thing to do."

Ben watched her, waiting.

"Keep them yourself."

Emmy's eyebrows rose as she looked to Ben for his reaction. She didn't doubt his capability—but was his life conducive to raising a family?

"What?" Ben asked.

"Widow Carver was by here last week," Mrs. Hubbard said. "Since Stan passed, she's been mighty lonesome in that house by herself. Her oldest daughter is expecting her first child come New Year's, and Mrs. Carver plans to go to her—but she's not needed until then. Perhaps she'd consider keeping house for you, until you can create a more permanent arrangement."

Ben frowned, his eyes hooded as he studied the boys, deep in thought. "I visited Mrs. Carver a couple weeks ago and sensed she was lonely." He took a step toward the boys and they looked up at him. They didn't warm to his nearness, but they didn't cower, either. It would take them some time to come to know and trust this unexpected guardian.

"I think I'll visit with Mrs. Carver again and ask if she'd consider such a request." Ben nodded, lifting his shoulders. "That might be just what we all need—for now."

"If she's willing, it will give you some time to think and plan for the future." Mrs. Hubbard smiled at the boys. "Give you all time to pray."

Ben continued to nod, as if he was trying to wrap his mind around this change of events. "Thank you for your advice, Pearl."

"You're always welcome."

Emmy took a step forward, eager to meet the boys and try to put them at ease. "I'm Miss Wilkes, the new teacher," she said in her kindest voice. "Have you been to school?"

The boys shook their heads, but it was the one with blond hair that spoke up. "I know all my numbers and letters, and I can spell Zeb's name."

Zeb smiled at his brother, admiration in his eyes. "Levi's smart."

"I'm sure you're both smart." Emmy bent to look them in the eyes. "I'd love to see you at school on Monday. We'll have fun learning how to read and write. Would you like that?"

The boys looked at each other, and then Zeb glanced up at Ben, a question in his eyes.

"I think school's a fine idea." Ben put his cap back in place, his handsome brown eyes filled with appreciation. "We'll see you first thing Monday morning."

"Hopefully you'll see me at church tomorrow first." Emmy straightened and gave him a reassuring smile. "I'd be happy to sit with the boys during the service."

Relief washed over his features as he put his hands on the boys' shoulders. "We'll plan on that."

Ben said his goodbyes and then left with Zeb and Levi.

"Well, what do you think about that?" Mrs. Hubbard shook her head. "Ben Lahaye, raising a set of twin boys."

"It is a strange turn of events," Emmy conceded, wishing she could help the pastor in some way. "I imagine he'll have a lot of adjusting to do in the coming weeks."

"He'll need help, that's for sure."

Emmy glanced out the window and watched Ben walk away with the boys. One slipped on the ice, but Ben reached out and grabbed him before he fell.

As she watched them, her heart tugged at the tender scene. If things had gone differently with her and William, perhaps they would have had children close to that age by now. Instead of Ben, she would be watching William walking in the snow with their children.

Tears threatened to gather in her eyes, but she forced them away, nibbling on her bottom lip to keep it from trembling. It had been almost a year since she'd given up the melancholy of losing her fiancé. At that time, she'd set her mind to fulfilling their dreams, even if William was not there with her—and that's what she was doing, she was living her life in the West. She just prayed it would be everything she'd always hoped and imagined.

Chapter Four

On Monday morning, Ben trudged through the snow before the sun had crested the eastern horizon. His breath billowed out in a cloud of white as he turned and glanced at Zeb and Levi who followed behind, their mitted hands clasped together. Levi's pants were about an inch too short, and a hole in Zeb's pants showed his knobby knee. Ben wished he had found proper clothing for them before they started school, but there hadn't been time. Sundays were always a busy day for him, and especially so with two little boys in tow. If Mrs. Carver came to live with them, he'd ask her to sew them a new set of clothes immediately.

The school was only three blocks up Main Street from Ben's front door, but with the snowdrifts and the boys lagging, it took much longer than he'd anticipated.

"We're almost there," Ben said over his shoulder.

The boys didn't respond. They had been quiet since their aunt had left them and they only spoke when spoken to. Ben had used every conceivable idea to draw them out and so had the ladies in the church. When Charlotte and Abram had invited them to lunch yesterday, the boys had sat in the kitchen with the grown-ups, while the Cooper children played in the other room.

More than anything, Ben wanted them to feel safe in his care—but he knew better than to expect too much, too soon. It had taken him months, years really, to get used to his life at the mission when Father left. And, as soon as he'd come to accept the Ayers as his guardians, there had been an ambush by the Dakota and the Ayers had fled for their lives, leaving Ben with the Chippewa missionary, John Johnson. He'd felt abandoned all over again, and it had led him to rebellion and the darkest moments of his life.

He shook off the memories as he spotted the schoolhouse just ahead. A lantern was lit within the white clapboard building and smoke puffed out of the chimney. He'd hoped to get to the school before Emmy to start the fire and haul in wood for the day, but he wasn't surprised to find her already there.

A movement behind the school caught Ben's eye. Emmy was wrapped in the scarf and cap he'd lent her, and she was filling her arms with wood.

Seeing her again sent a warm sensation straight through Ben's chest. It had been a pleasant, if somewhat unnerving, experience to see her shining face in the congregation yesterday. His gaze had returned to her several times, and each time he'd looked at her pretty face, he'd had a hard time concentrating on his sermon.

He smiled now as he watched her determination. She tried to pile the wood high, but she'd have to return to the pile three or four times to have enough wood for the school day.

"Come, boys," Ben said. "Let's help Teacher bring in the wood."

The boys followed obediently around the schoolhouse and into the back lot where a pile of wood had been stacked earlier that fall by members of the community.

Emmy didn't notice their arrival as she continued to stack the wood precariously on her arms. She turned, and swayed under the cumbersome weight, but Ben reached out and put a steady hand on her elbow.

"Whoa, there," he said.

"Oh, my!" She startled at his touch and the wood cascaded from her arms.

"I'm sorry." Ben still held her arm to steady her. "I didn't mean to frighten you."

She was breathing heavy and her cheeks were pink from exertion. Her free hand came up and rested over her heart. "I was so preoccupied with my chore I didn't hear you arrive."

Ben reached down and picked up the wood one piece at a time. He could carry three times as much as her, but he didn't want her to feel incompetent. "The boys and I are here to help. I should have made our presence known a bit sooner."

She straightened her cap and smiled at the boys. "Good morning."

Ben handed a stick of firewood to Zeb. "Hold out your arms."

Zeb obeyed and Ben stacked three pieces in his grasp.

"Your turn, Levi," Ben said.

"I can hold more than three." Zeb puffed out his chest.

"Zeb's strong," Levi said to Ben. "He's stronger than anyone I know."

Emmy smiled as she started to gather more wood.

"One more piece, then," Ben said with a serious nod,

though he caught Emmy's eye and smiled. "Now you, Levi."

Levi took a few pieces and then Ben filled his own arms.

"Thank you," Emmy said to all three of them. "But you didn't need to bother."

They followed her into the back of the school and filled the wood box near the door.

"We'll plan to get here before you tomorrow and have all the chores done," Ben said. "It's the least we can do."

Emmy's eyes showed her appreciation as she shook her head. "I don't expect such treatment. I'm capable to do the work required of the teacher."

"We'd like to help." Ben looked at the boys, who stared at the schoolroom with a bit of awe. "Wouldn't we like to help, boys?"

Zeb glanced toward Ben and nodded, but Levi didn't seem to hear Ben. He took a step away from his brother and looked at the shelf full of primers.

Emmy's gaze followed Levi and she watched him for a moment, a knowing look on her face.

"I'll fetch more wood and then bring in fresh water," Ben told her.

Emmy looked his way. "I'd be happy to fetch more wood."

"No need." Ben stepped outside before she could protest and returned to the woodpile.

The sun peeked over the horizon when Ben entered the school with the last load of wood. He filled the water buckets and then put more wood in the stove as the first children arrived outside the schoolhouse, their conversation and laughter filling the air.

"Boys, you'll need to go outside until Miss Wilkes

rings the school bell," Ben said to the boys. "You can join the other children in their games."

Zeb and Levi looked at one another, apprehension in their green eyes.

"It won't be long." Emmy stood in front of the chalkboard, a piece of dusty chalk in hand. "I'll ring the bell in about fifteen minutes."

The boys walked quietly toward the door, in no apparent hurry.

"I'll be back to pick you up at the end of the day," Ben said as they slipped outside. Zeb glanced at Ben before he closed the door, his sad eyes filled with uncertainty.

Ben let out a sigh. "It'll take them time to trust me."

"I'm afraid you're right—but you're off to a great start."

He turned and met her gaze. "I'm heading to Mrs. Carver's to see if she'll agree to keep house for me."

"I hope she'll say yes." She smiled, and the light in her eyes made him want to stay right where he was for the rest of the day, but she looked at her pocket watch and then glanced out the window, and he knew it was time to leave.

"I need to get going," Ben said quickly. "I'll see you later this afternoon."

"Goodbye."

Ben left the school, looking around for Zeb and Levi. They stood off to the side, alone, as they watched the other children laugh and play. He hated to see them excluded, but there was little he could do. They weren't like the other children, nestled into warm and loving families. They were twice abandoned, living with a man they didn't know, in a town they'd probably never heard of. The other children didn't seem to notice them, and the boys didn't try to join the games.

Maybe, given time, they would warm up to the other students—but by then, they'd probably be back with their father and need to readjust all over again.

That evening, Emmy wanted nothing more than a quiet corner, a comfortable chair and a good book. Instead, she sat awkwardly on the bed she shared with Rachel, her feet hanging off the edge, and her back against the hard wall. In place of a good book, she held a large tome titled: *A School Atlas of Physical Geography*, while balancing a piece of paper on another book on her lap to take notes. Her handwriting was wobbly and her patience waning.

Supper had been an exhausting affair filled with eager young men all clamoring for her attention. They begged her to stay in the parlor afterward, but she had returned to her room to study. Though she was in the back of the house, she could still hear the piano music and boisterous laughter from the front.

"What is the point in studying?" she asked herself as she closed the atlas with a thud.

"Miss Emmy?" Rachel opened their door and peeked inside. "There's coffee and cookies if you'd like some refreshment."

"What I'd like is to prepare my lessons for tomorrow."

"I'm sorry, I'll leave you in peace," Rachel said, closing the door.

"Oh, no!" Emmy scrambled off the bed and opened the door, embarrassment warming her cheeks. "I'm sorry, Rachel. I didn't mean for you to think you're the problem." It had been a long first day of school and things had not gone smoothly. From Mr. Samuelson's daughters, who treated her like an imposter, to the Trask twins who had been teased by the other children, she'd had her hands full just dealing with discipline. It had taken most of the day to test the children and see where their strengths and weaknesses were, and she'd been disheartened to realize they were farther behind than most their age. Was it because they hadn't had consistent teachers? "Maybe I do need some refreshments."

Rachel gave her a reassuring smile. "You'll find it in the front parlor. I'd bring you some, but Mrs. Hubbard is feeling poorly and she asked me to fetch her another blanket."

"The baby?"

"Not yet, but soon."

Emmy thanked Rachel and left the kitchen, taking a deep breath to prepare herself. Maybe, if she was quick, she could get her refreshments and return to her room in peace.

At least a dozen men sat in the parlor. Some were playing cards, others were singing around the piano and still others were sitting on the furniture engaged in conversation.

The one named Mr. Archibald was the first to notice her. He stood near the piano, his boisterous voice louder than the others, but he stopped singing and let out a whoop. "She's here, gents!"

Everyone paused what they were doing, and for a heartbeat, there was complete silence—then all of them started talking at once. Mr. Archibald rushed across the room and took her by the elbow. "This way, Miss Wilkes."

He practically pulled her to the piano. "Do you sing?

No matter. Everyone sounds good around Mrs. Hubbard's piano."

"I only came for the coffee," Emmy protested, trying to pull away. "I have work to do this evening."

"Ah, work," Mr. Archibald said it like it was a dirty word. "We work during the day and play at night, right boys?"

A chorus of agreement rang in the air.

"How about a little dancing?" someone yelled from across the room. "I get the first dance."

"No." Emmy shook her head. She had no desire to spend the evening in frivolity. "This was a mistake. I shouldn't have come."

"You're here now." A man with red whiskers pulled her into his arms, as if he was spinning her in a waltz.

Emmy yanked out of his hold and straightened her skirt. "Gentlemen," she said in her sternest teacher's voice. "I have no intention to dan—"

The piano music started again, drowning out her objection, while all the furniture was pushed to the edges of the room.

"Really," Emmy said. "I don't want—"

"Come on, Aaron," Mr. Archibald said to the man who had suggested the dance. "You're up first."

Emmy shook her head while the man named Aaron climbed over a chair, his eager gaze focused on her, his mouth in a lopsided grin.

She dashed behind a table and shook her head, out of breath. "No!"

"Ah, come on." Aaron circled the table like a cat on the prowl. "Just a little fun is all we want." He lunged for her, but she was fast and dodged his advance.

"The lady said no." A firm male voice filled the parlor.

The piano music came to a jarring halt, and all the men turned to stare.

Ben stood under the archway, still in his outdoor clothing, his brown eyes full of authority.

"We were just funning her, Reverend," Mr. Archibald said. "No harm done."

Emmy still stood behind the table, her hands braced, her feet ready to take flight, her chest rising and falling with deep breaths.

Ben looked her over. "Are you all right, Miss Wilkes?"

She stood straight and ran her hand over her hair, tucking a wayward curl back into place. "Yes."

Ben surveyed the room, looking at each man with intention, and nodded at Aaron. "See that all of Mrs. Hubbard's furniture is put to rights." He then looked at Emmy. "Could I have a word with you?"

She almost sighed in relief. "Of course."

"Ah," Mr. Archibald whined. "We got to her first."

"Miss Wilkes is not a prize to be won," Ben said to the other man. "She is a lady who is to be respected. Now leave her in peace and quiet."

Emmy took a tentative step away from the security of the table and kept her eyes on the men as she stepped out of the parlor, across the foyer and into the dining room. A lantern had been left on, but dimmed, making the room intimate. Thankfully it was quiet.

Emmy sank into one of the chairs, her legs wobbly.

A smile quirked Ben's lips as he sat near her. "That was quite something to watch."

"How long were you standing there?"

"Long enough." He couldn't hide his grin.

Emmy sighed and shook her head. "I just want a quiet, comfortable place to study. I suppose I'll have to stay late at the school to get things done."

"It's not safe for you to be there so late alone." Ben's smile disappeared. "Little Falls is a lawless town, thanks to our sheriff, and there's no telling how long it will take for the men to discover you're at the school alone."

"What will I do? I have to study."

Ben was quiet a moment. "You could always come to my home in the evenings. With Mrs. Carver there, she'd act as chaperone, and the boys are not loud."

"Mrs. Carver agreed to stay with you?"

"She's there now getting to know the boys and putting her things in place."

Emmy smiled, truly relieved for him. "I'm so happy she could come."

"So am I."

"Do you know what you'll do once she leaves?"

Ben looked down and fiddled with his cap. "I plan to find their nearest kin as soon as possible. I'm going to Abram Cooper's this evening to see if he can help me locate their father. That's partially why I stopped here first. I wanted to make sure you were getting along and see if you needed anything before I go to the Coopers'." He chuckled. "It appears that you were in dire need, actually."

"Unfortunately, I was." She smiled, thankful he had come. "But I don't believe I have any other needs right now. You've done more than enough."

Ben stood and put his knitted cap back on. "I should go, but before I do, I'd like to reiterate my invitation." He looked at her, his brown eyes so warm and friendly. "You're welcome to come and study at my home whenever you'd like."

The prospect of being in Ben's snug home was appealing, especially with all the commotion at the Hubbards'. "I just might."

"Good." He glanced across the foyer, into the parlor. "Will you be okay?"

She stood. "I'll go back to my room."

"That's probably for the best." He pulled his mittens on and met her gaze. "Good night, Emmy."

"Good night, Ben."

He took his leave and Emmy stood in the dim dining room for a few moments, her thoughts full of Zeb and Levi, and their dashing guardian.

Chapter Five

Ben knocked on the Coopers' lean-to door, his hands cold and his thoughts swinging from Levi and Jeb to the image of Emmy being chased around that table in the Hubbards' parlor.

Charlotte Cooper greeted Ben with a big smile, opening the door wider for him to enter. She held baby Louise in her arms, swaddled in a blanket. "Why'd you knock?"

"Is that Ben?" Abram asked as he entered the kitchen from the front room.

"It is," Charlotte answered, closing the door behind Ben.

Abram paused on his way to the stove with his coffee mug in hand, a frown tucked between his brows. "Why'd you knock?"

Ben grinned at his friends, who were more like family. "I thought it the civilized thing to do."

Charlotte's brown eyes filled with mirth as she tried taking his coat with her free hand.

"I've got it." Ben slipped it off and hung it on the peg near the door.

"I remember the first time we met," Charlotte said with a shake of her head. "You came right on in—"

"And scared you half to death," Ben finished, thinking of that long-ago day when he'd walked into the cabin and learned that Abram's first wife, Susanne, had died and Charlotte had come to help raise Abram and Susanne's three boys. Back then, he'd dressed more like his mother's people and Charlotte had feared that he was there to do her harm.

"I thought Charlotte would be so frightened from the incident, she'd be on her way back to Iowa when I got home." Abram laughed as he took another mug off the cupboard and didn't even ask Ben before filling it for him.

"Come in." Charlotte gently nudged Ben out of the lean-to and into the warmth of her kitchen—but she paused. "Where are Levi and Zeb?"

"Mrs. Carver is with them."

Charlotte placed her free hand over her heart. "Oh, good. I'm happy that worked out for you."

"I actually came to talk to you about the twins." Ben took the steaming mug of coffee from Abram. "I need some help."

"Let's go into the front room," Abram suggested. "It's almost bedtime for the children, but they'll be happy to see you first."

Ben loved Abram and Charlotte's children. In all the ways that mattered, they were like his nieces and nephews.

The adults pushed through the door and entered the front room. The oldest boy, Robert, was eight and had been deaf for almost four years. He sat with his half-sister Patricia, who was only two years old, pointing to pictures in a book and making the signs for them.

Martin, at the age of six, was playing jacks on the floor with George, who would soon be four. Miss Louise had been a welcome addition to the growing family, and Ben marveled that Charlotte and Abram made parenting look so effortless.

In just two days, with two little boys who barely made a sound, Ben felt overwhelmed at the idea of parenting. Having Mrs. Carver to rely on had already made a big difference, but she couldn't stay with him forever. He needed to find the boys' father before Christmas. If he didn't, he would be raising them by himself.

Ben played with the children for a few minutes, and then Charlotte handed the baby to Abram before taking the children up to bed.

"Good night," the children called out to Ben.

Ben said good-night and signed to Robert.

"It's amazing how quiet it gets when they all go to bed," Abram commented as he looked down at his sleeping daughter. He glanced up at Ben. "Don't tell the children, but it's my favorite time of day, when I get Charlotte all to myself." He chuckled and began to rock as he looked back at Louise. "Well, almost all to myself. This one stays close to her mama most of the day."

Ben tried not to envy the happiness of his friends. There had been a time when Ben had been in love with Charlotte and he'd proposed, but the whole time he knew in his heart that she was in love with Abram. He'd stepped back when he knew he should, and he'd been truly happy to perform their marriage ceremony.

Two years later, he'd fallen for a young lady named Elizabeth, but she was in love with Ben's friend, Jude. Ben had performed their marriage ceremony, as well, leaving Ben to wonder if his time would ever come.

With so few prospects, and so many competitors, it didn't seem likely.

On its own accord, his mind turned back to Emmy—but he pushed thoughts of her aside as best he could, knowing she had no interest in marriage. Even if she did, there would probably be someone else she'd take a liking to.

"What'd you have in mind to discuss?" Abram asked as he studied Ben.

"I'd like help locating Levi and Zeb's next of kin. I thought if I spread the word, maybe someone would have heard of them. Their father's name is Malachi Trask."

"Trask." Abram continued to rock as he looked toward the floor, deep in thought. "The name sounds familiar, but I can't place it." He glanced up at Ben. "Would you like me to ask around?"

"That's exactly what I was thinking. At least it's a start. I'm hoping to go to St. Paul soon and see if I can find any leads there. The boys' aunt said their father was in St. Paul last she heard."

"Are you sure that finding their pa is the right thing to do?" Abram asked.

Ben had been thinking hard about the wisdom in finding Mr. Trask. The boys' aunt didn't speak highly of him, but Ben believed he needed to know where his children were. In Ben's opinion, everyone needed a second chance.

They spoke for some time about the boys and then Charlotte reappeared. She took a seat in her rocker and closed her eyes with a weary sigh—but when she opened them, and looked at Abram, they shared a contented smile.

"I don't want to take up more of your time," Ben said as he stood to leave.

"Nonsense." Charlotte put her hand on his arm. "I just sat down to visit."

Ben nodded and sat once again. "I really shouldn't stay much longer. I left Mrs. Carver with the boys quite a while ago to check on Emmy—Miss Wilkes."

Charlotte looked at Abram again, this time a knowing smile in her eyes before turning her attention back to Ben. "How is the new schoolteacher getting along? Robert and Martin said Mr. Samuelson's girls were giving her a hard time today, but it sounds like my boys like her."

"I stopped by the Hubbards' and found her in quite a predicament." Ben laughed just thinking about the scene he'd come across. "The boarders were trying to get her to dance, and Aaron Chambers had her cornered behind a table, ready to pounce."

Charlotte's mouth parted. "That's horrible. Those men should be ashamed of themselves."

"Things haven't changed much around here," Abram said. "I remember that first winter, when Charlotte was the only female for miles. It was a full-time job just keeping the men at bay. The only way to stop them was to marry her myself."

Charlotte chuckled. "I suppose that's true."

"Unfortunately, that's not an option for me," Ben said.

"And why not?" Abram asked. "It's about time you find a nice young lady and settle down."

"Miss Wilkes wouldn't be interested. The school board hired her to teach—and that's exactly what she needs to do." Not to mention that she already expressed her desire to stay single. Ben had been rejected more than he cared to admit, and the idea of pursuing someone again, just to be turned down, wasn't something he cared to do. He had come to terms with the idea of staying single while he served God, and that's how he intended to stay. Any time he had strayed from that plan, he had been heartbroken. "Miss Wilkes is struggling for other reasons at the boardinghouse. She needs a quiet place to work and study, and she'd like to have her books with her, but there's no room. She said she'd stay late at the school, but I said that would be foolish, so I invited her to study at my home in the evenings."

"Why can't she board with you?" Charlotte asked.

Ben frowned. "That would hardly be—"

"And why not?" Charlotte leaned forward, her eyes animated. "With Mrs. Carver there, it would be completely respectable. And, in my opinion, a better option. Living in a crowded house with over a dozen single men all vying for her attention doesn't sound like it's any more respectable."

The baby began to fuss, so Abram handed her off to her mama. "Charlotte's right. You have plenty of room, and with the housekeeper present, no one would have any issues with the arrangement."

Ben stood and paced to the fireplace. Would Emmy be amenable to the idea? "Mrs. Carver can only stay until after Christmas, then she's planning to move out to her daughter's farm to help with a new baby."

"At least the school board would have time to locate another place for Miss Wilkes to live." Charlotte held Louise up to her shoulder and patted her on the back. "And it would give Miss Wilkes time to get settled into the school without all the commotion at the Hubbards'."

Ben couldn't deny the surge of pleasure he felt at the idea of Emmy leaving the boardinghouse.

"There's no harm in asking," Abram added.

Ben supposed there was no harm in asking—only in being rejected, though he suspected Miss Wilkes would have no objections.

"Annabeth Samuelson." Emmy stood from her desk where she was listening to the first-year students recite their arithmetic. "Please come to the front of the class."

Annabeth gave a sideways glance at her sister, Margareta, and took her time leaving her desk. "Yes, Teacher?" she asked as she stopped in front of Emmy's desk.

Emmy pulled her shoulders back and inhaled a deep breath before addressing her pupil. The Samuelson sisters had been difficult from the moment the first bell had rung on Emmy's first day. Whether they believed they were above her authority because their father was the superintendent, or because they were grieving and missing their mama, they were bent on making Emmy's job miserable.

"I called for complete silence from the upper classes until the first-year students were through reciting."

Annabeth blinked in feigned innocence. "I remember."

"Why were you whispering to Margareta?"

The fourteen-year-old girl gave a pouty look. "Why are you picking on me, Miss Wilkes? Is it because my father doesn't like you and you're taking it out on me?"

Twenty students sat or stood around the room, all their eyes pinned to Emmy. Annabeth had tried bating Emmy every chance she could get—but Emmy refused to play her games.

"I want you to write on the board fifty times, 'I will not whisper in class.'"

"Fifty?" Annabeth's mouth fell open. "My hand will cramp, and my father will be very upset when he hears you're making an example of me. He doesn't like to be embarrassed."

"And I don't like disobedience. If you haven't finished by recess, you'll have to stay indoors."

Annabeth lifted her nose and walked to the chalkboard, stomping her feet all the way. She picked up a piece of chalk and scratched each word onto the board with deliberate strokes, causing the chalk to squeak in protest.

Emmy slowly sat in her chair and looked back at the younger students. Levi and Zeb stood quietly, their eyes fixed on Emmy's face, though Levi glanced at Annabeth from time to time.

"Now, where were we?" Emmy asked.

The door opened and a gentleman entered the schoolhouse with a gust of wind.

"What now?" Emmy asked under her breath, rising from her desk once again. "May I help you?"

The man took off his hat and clutched it in his hands, looking left and right at the students as he tentatively walked down the aisle between the desks. "Are you Miss Wilkes?" he asked as he stopped at her desk.

"I am."

He swallowed hard and turned his hat around in his hands. "I came to speak with you."

Emmy frowned. "Do you have a student you'd like to enroll?"

"No." He leaned forward, his greasy hair falling over his forehead, and lowered his voice. "This here is a personal matter."

Annabeth stopped writing and stared openly at the man while all the other children listened in.

"I'm sorry, but if you're not here on school business, you'll need to leave," Emmy said.

"But this can't wait. If I don't talk to you now, some other fella will swoop in and stake his claim."

"I don't know what you're talking about." Emmy came around the desk to show him to the door. "I have a school to run and I need you to leave."

"Will you allow me to call on you at the Hubbard home?"

Emmy walked with determined steps into the cloakroom and to the door.

"Miss Wilkes." He followed her. "Did you hear me?"

She opened the door. "I most certainly did, and I am not interested—"

"What is the meaning of this?" Mr. Samuelson stood on the stoop outside the door, his hand raised as if he had just reached for the doorknob. He looked between the strange man and Emmy.

Emmy's stomach dropped and she grappled for an explanation. "I was just showing this gentleman out."

"What is he doing here?" Mr. Samuelson demanded.

"I came to see if Miss Wilkes will let me call on her, but she hasn't given me an answer." The man looked at Emmy with great interest. "What do you say?"

Mr. Samuelson crossed his arms, his face turning red. "Well?" he asked. "What do you say, Miss Wilkes?"

"I've never met this man in my life," Emmy said to her superintendent. "I have no interest in accepting his invitation and I'd prefer if he left."

The man straightened his shoulders and shoved his hat back on. "I guess the lady has spoken."

Emmy lifted her chin. "Please do not return."

He stepped between her and Mr. Samuelson and

walked out of the schoolhouse without a backward glance.

Mr. Samuelson stared at Emmy. "Please put on your wraps and come outside with me. I'd like to speak to you."

Emmy let out a sigh as she grabbed her wraps and then poked her head back into the classroom. "Greta Merchant, will you please watch over the classroom while I'm speaking with Mr. Samuelson?"

Greta stood and nodded. "Yes, Miss Wilkes."

Annabeth gave Emmy a smug look at the front of the class, but Emmy chose to ignore the girl as she pulled on her mittens and stepped outside, closing the door behind her.

"How many men have come to the school like this?" Mr. Samuelson asked without waiting for her to explain herself.

"None. Like I said, I don't know—"

"Do you think it's proper to have men calling on you at the school?"

"Of course not—"

"I knew it was a mistake to keep you on. I should have gone with my first instinct and sent you back east."

"Please, Mr. Samuelson, listen to—"

"You leave me no choice but to start seeking another teacher to replace you."

Ben appeared at the edge of the school yard, his curious gaze latched on Emmy and Mr. Samuelson. "Is everything all right?"

"It is not." Mr. Samuelson shared the scene he'd just witnessed a moment ago. "I shouldn't have listened to you, Pastor Lahaye. I knew it would only be a matter of time before I caught her in an inappropriate situation—but I never thought it would be at the school."

Indignation rose in Emmy's chest. "I did not invite that man into the school!"

"You need to see reason," Ben said to Mr. Samuelson, his voice calm. "Miss Wilkes is not to blame."

"If she was a man, this would not have happened."

Ben chuckled. "I suppose you're right, but that's not her fault."

Mr. Samuelson straightened his shoulders, his jaw tight. "I can see it's impossible to discuss Miss Wilkes with you. I will bring up this matter at the next school board meeting." He spoke the words with finality. "I must get back to my store, and if I'm not mistaken, it's time to release the children for recess."

Emmy looked at her pocket watch, trying to calm the turmoil she felt in her gut. If she wasn't careful, she might say something she'd regret—but one look at Ben's gentle countenance and her emotions began to settle. "I made a promise to you and the school, and I intend to keep it."

Mr. Samuelson acted as if he didn't hear her. He gave her a curt nod and then strode away.

Ben shook his head. "That man has a knack for finding fault. I'm just sorry he's directed that particular talent on you."

Despite her frustration, she smiled. "I am, too." Her smile faded and she wrapped her arms around her body for warmth. "I thought I was safe from amorous men here at the school—but it doesn't look like I'm safe anywhere."

"That's actually why I'm here." Ben looked down and readjusted his footing, clearly uncomfortable with his mission. "I thought I could speak privately with you during recess. I can wait until you release the children."

"My whole day has been disrupted. The children can wait a few more moments if you'd like to speak now."

He met her gaze, uncertainty in his dark brown eyes. "My friend Mrs. Cooper made a suggestion that I thought I'd share with you."

"Go ahead."

"Since I have a housekeeper now, Charlotte thought you might be inclined to leave the Hubbards and board at my house." He went on quickly. "You'd have to share a room with Mrs. Carver on the second floor, but it's a big room, with plenty of space for your trunks. I could put a desk in there, and you could study to your heart's content each evening."

The thought of having more privacy to study made her want to cry in happiness—but then she paused. "Would it be seemly?"

"Charlotte assures me it would. With Mrs. Carver as a chaperone, no one would raise an eyebrow."

Emmy nibbled her bottom lip. Even if people did think twice about the arrangement, she couldn't deny its appeal. "I will accept."

He blinked twice before responding. "You will?"

"When shall I move in?"

"As soon as you'd like."

She reached out and shook his hand. "I will move my things immediately after school."

Ben's smile was wide and charming. "I'll be over to help."

A flutter filled her stomach at that handsome smile, but she pushed the silly notion aside and started to look forward to a quiet house after five days of chaos at the Hubbards'.

Chapter Six

Ben pushed the last trunk against the wall of the room Mrs. Carver and Emmy would share and stepped out into the hall. He wanted to make sure Emmy had everything she'd need to do her work and be comfortable with them, so he'd brought in a desk he usually kept in his front room and placed it near the window. After supper, he'd be sure to help Mrs. Carver clean the kitchen, giving Emmy plenty of time to study.

Laughter and conversation filtered up the stairs and he paused a moment to appreciate the sound. Not only were Mrs. Carver and Emmy getting along, but the boys were also joining in on the fun. He shook his head at the sound of one of the boys laughing. It did his heart good to know this little band of people who were in need of family for one reason or another had found each other. He could hardly believe that just a week ago, his house was quiet and empty.

Ben walked down the stairs, across the front room and into the kitchen where they were getting supper on the table. Mrs. Carver was a jolly old woman, almost as wide as she was tall. She had dark gray hair and kind blue eyes, which sparkled when she spoke. Life had thrown her more than her share of heartache, but she was resilient and faithful, and had always been one of Ben's favorite parishioners.

"Set the mashed potatoes over there, dearie," Mrs. Carver said to Emmy. "Right next to my chair." She laughed and the others laughed along, which made Ben suspect he'd missed out on a joke.

Zeb looked at Ben from where he was placing forks at the table and grinned. "Mrs. Carver says that potatoes help her keep her girlish finger."

Emmy and Mrs. Carver laughed, and Ben couldn't help but chuckle with them.

"Figure." Mrs. Carver enunciated the word with a nod. "And that, they do." She stood at the cast-iron stove, whisking up chicken gravy, and tilted her head toward Emmy. "We best put some by Miss Emmy's place, too."

Emmy's cheeks turned pink as she glanced up at Ben while setting a platter of sliced bread on the table.

"It looks like we're in for another feast." Ben walked over to the stove and inhaled the scent of roasted chicken. "Is there anything I can do to help?"

"You can have a seat," Mrs. Carver said. "I'll pour this gravy into a bowl and we're ready to eat."

"You did a wonderful job setting the table, boys," Emmy said to Zeb and Levi as she held out a chair for each boy to take a seat.

The boys glowed under her approval, and for the first time since arriving at Ben's, they looked comfortable to be there.

Mrs. Carver shuffled over to the table with the gravy and set it next to the potatoes. She stood for a moment, surveying the spread. "I feel like we're missing something."

"You!" Zeb said with a laugh.

"I think that's it." Mrs. Carver chuckled and took her seat closest to the stove.

Ben sat at the head of the table with the boys to his right. Emmy stood for a moment, as if she didn't know whether to sit in the empty seat near Ben, or take the seat at the foot of the table.

"Why don't you sit right here," Mrs. Carver said, patting the spot next to Ben.

Emmy walked around the table and took the seat Mrs. Carver suggested.

"Shall we say grace?" Ben asked.

Mrs. Carver reached across the table and took Levi's hand, and then offered her other one to Emmy, who sat to her right.

Emmy glanced up at Ben and their gazes met for a heartbeat before she slipped her hand inside his.

For a moment, Ben marveled at how soft and warm her skin felt, but then he reached for Zeb's sticky hand to his right and bowed his head, trying to concentrate on his prayer.

"For this meal and our lives, Lord, we are eternally grateful. Amen."

"And for Mrs. Carver's potatoes. Amen," Zeb added quickly.

Laughter filled the room again and Emmy gave Ben's hand a gentle squeeze before she let go, turning her attention to Mrs. Carver's savory food.

"It feels good to be cooking for a full house again." Mrs. Carver placed a drumstick on each of the boys' plates. "After my children grew up and moved away, and my husband, Stan, died, it was just me. I love to cook, but there was no one to eat my food, but me."

She smiled at the four of them. "Now look. Here I am, doing what I love most. I say this is a gift from God."

"I couldn't agree more," Ben said. "A gift for all of us."

"I'm also counting my blessings." Emmy took a piece of chicken and placed it on her plate before handing the platter to Ben. "Living here will be so much nicer than the boardinghouse." She smiled at the boys. "And I get extra time with two of my favorite students."

Levi's cheeks turned pink and Zeb dipped his head in embarrassment, clearly pleased by her words.

"I put the desk in your room and brought up all your trunks," Ben told her. "As soon as we're done eating, feel free to get to work."

Emmy looked around the table, sadness marring her features. "I would hate to miss out on all the fun we have planned."

"Fun?" Ben asked.

"We're going to make popcorn and hot chocolate with Mrs. Carver after supper," Levi said to Ben. "And Miss Wilkes said she would teach us a parlor game if we're good and help clear the table."

"It sounds like you have quite the evening planned." Ben took a bite of the fluffy potatoes, surprised by how creamy and smooth they were. "I can understand now why you love these potatoes so much, Mrs. Carver. I've never tasted anything like them."

Mrs. Carver grinned and Levi spoke up. "Her secret ingredient is love."

"Levi!" Zeb made a face at his brother. "That was supposed to be a secret!"

Ben tried to hide his laugh. "Love was the first ingredient I tasted, so the secret was out before Levi told me."

Levi looked relieved and the adults shared a smile.

"Do any of you play instruments?" Mrs. Carver asked the group.

"I play piano," Emmy offered.

"And I have a mouth organ, though I'm not very good." Ben took a bite of the tender chicken trying to concentrate on the conversation as his taste buds demanded attention.

"Maybe we can have us a little music this evening," Mrs. Carver said, tucking a napkin into her lap. "My Stan used to play the fiddle after supper and it was my favorite time of the day."

Emmy's soft gaze turned to Ben. "Would you play for us?"

"I suppose I could try—though I warn you, it's been a while since I played."

Mrs. Carver clapped and Emmy smiled. The boys cheered, though Ben suspected that they did it because the ladies seemed pleased, not because they were particularly excited to hear Ben play. But he didn't blame them for their joy. It felt good to bring a smile to Emmy's face and a fond memory to Mrs. Carver's mind.

But, best of all, it made him happy knowing this little makeshift family had found a home, as temporary as it was.

A week later, Emmy took advantage of the nice weather after school and walked around town to find help for an idea she had. The sun was shining bright, causing the snow to melt and puddle in the deep wagon ruts crisscrossing the streets. Dozens of clapboard buildings, some complete with false fronts and others fashioned in the Greek Revival style, lined every street, with wooden boardwalks connecting them together. It looked like many of the frontier towns she had passed on her way from Massachusetts to Minnesota—but unlike the others, it had the beauty of the Upper Mississippi River meandering alongside the town.

Emmy pushed open the door to the Northern Hotel and was surprised to find such an elegant interior. White wainscoting ran around the room, a wide staircase stood directly across from the main door and a generous counter took up the corner of the lobby to her right.

A tall gentleman stood there with a smile on his face. "May I help you?"

"I'm looking for Mr. Allen."

"I'm Jude Allen." He came out from behind the counter, his suitcoat pressed and his shoes shining. "How may I be of service?"

"I am Miss Wilkes, the new schoolteacher."

Mr. Allen extended his hand. "It's nice to meet you, Miss Wilkes. Rose has told us all about you."

"Rose Bell?"

"Yes. She's my wife's sister."

Rose was a sweet student with a bit of a stubborn streak. Emmy had taken a liking to her immediately. "She's been a very good student. So polite and kind to her classmates."

"Elizabeth will be happy to hear that." He glanced up the stairs. "She's tending to our newborn daughters at the moment, if you'd like to wait to speak to her."

"I won't take up more time than necessary." Emmy pulled a poster from her satchel and handed it to Mr. Allen. "I'll be hosting the first Friday Frolic at school next week and I am looking for volunteers."

He glanced at the poster. "Friday Frolic?"

"I thought it would be a nice diversion from the early winter." And a way to make herself indispensable to the school board. "Each week I'll host a social event at the school that the whole town is invited to attend. The first event will be a spelling contest."

Mr. Allen smiled. "I'll be happy to tack up this poster. It will be fun to hear the children compete."

Emmy smiled uncomfortably, because this was where she had lost interest from several others she'd already asked. "Actually, this will not be a student spelling contest. I am asking prominent members of the community to participate. Reverend Lahaye and Mr. Cooper have already agreed, but I need at least ten spellers. They told me to come to you." She quickly pulled another piece of paper out of her bag. "I have a list of four hundred words here for you to study ahead of time."

His eyebrows rose as he looked at the list—but didn't touch it. "I apologize, but I don't believe I'm the man for the job, Miss Wilkes."

"Nonsense, Jude." A beautiful lady appeared on the steps holding two infants in her arms. "It sounds like a lovely idea."

"Miss Wilkes, I'd like to introduce you to my wife, Lizzie, and our daughters, Virginia and Georgia."

"It's a pleasure to meet you," Emmy said to Mrs. Allen.

"It's nice to meet you, Miss Wilkes. Ben has told us so much about you."

She hated that her cheeks warmed at the mention of Ben.

Mr. Allen reached over and took one of the sleeping infants from his wife. "Lizzie would be a much better contender for the spelling contest."

"And who will mind the babies?" Mrs. Allen asked playfully.

"They'll sleep through the whole thing," Mr. Allen answered, just as playfully.

"I'd like to see that happen." Mrs. Allen bounced slightly as she looked down at her daughter fondly. "They like to take turns waking me up in the middle of the night."

Longing filled Emmy's heart at seeing those precious babies in their parents' arms. Thoughts of William came unbidden, and with them, the same sense of loss and regret that she would never have what these people had. She had dealt with years of bitterness and disillusionment after he died. She had buried more than her fiancé five years ago. With him she had buried her hopes and dreams for a family and a home.

She forced herself to focus on why she had come. "If you're worried about the words," Emmy said to Mr. Allen, "I can assure you they are fairly simple." She smiled at Mrs. Allen. "I don't want to knock out my contestants too early."

Mrs. Allen laughed and the sound made her husband smile.

"All right," he said. "You've convinced me—or rather, you've convinced my wife, so I guess there's no use fighting you now."

Emmy grinned. "Thank you. I promise I'll be kind to you."

"Don't you dare," Mrs. Allen said. "If I know anything, I know my husband can handle a little difficulty now and again."

Emmy smiled with the Allens. "I should take my leave. I need to find seven other participants before the day is through."

"Have you been by the bank?" Mr. Allen asked. "Mr.

Russell is new to town and he's eager to meet all the families. I think he'd be a good sport."

"And Mr. Hall, the attorney," Mrs. Allen said. "And there's always Timothy Hubbard and Mr. Fadling, the grocer, or Dr. Jodan. I'm sure if you ask around you won't have any trouble filling all ten places."

"Thank you for the suggestions." Emmy nodded goodbye and opened the door. "It was nice to meet you."

"And you, too," Mrs. Allen called as Emmy stepped outside.

The sunshine felt good on Emmy's skin and the warmth in the air reminded her of spring, though it was the end of October. She looked around town and read each sign making a mental note of the grocer, the lawyer, the doctor and the banker. She hated to think about returning to the Hubbards' boardinghouse to speak to Mr. Hubbard, but she would if she needed to.

Emmy stepped off the porch of the Northern Hotel and crossed the road to enter the bank. It sat on the opposite corner from the hotel, its large plate-glass windows and ornate door indicating its status in town.

She pushed open the door and wasn't disappointed with the plush furnishings. A caged area lined the back wall and a clerk stood there helping a patron. Emmy waited in line, admiring the leather furniture and walnut tables.

"May I help you?" A gentleman exited an office to her right and stood in the lobby with a smile on his face.

"Are you Mr. Russell?"

"I am. Won't you step into my office?"

Emmy crossed the lobby and passed by the handsome young man. His office smelled of ink and leather and was neat and orderly. A large walnut desk took up most of the space with shelves lining one full wall.

He left the door open and came around the desk. “Have a seat, Miss…”

“Wilkes, the new schoolteacher.”

His smile was quick and warm, not at all what she had expected from the banker. “It’s a pleasure to meet you.”

“And you.” She pulled out one of her posters and handed it to him.

His eyes lit up as he read it. “I’ve only just arrived in town and I’ve been looking for ways to meet everyone.” He looked at her, his green eyes filled with appreciation. “I’ll be there.”

She couldn’t help but smile at him. He seemed eager to please and genuinely happy to make a connection. “Our first event will be an adult spelling contest and I’m looking for prominent members of the community to—”

“I’ll do it.”

She laughed. “You don’t know what I’m asking.”

“Whatever you need, I’ll be happy to do.”

Her cheeks grew warm at the declaration. “Thank you.”

“I’m assuming you’d like me to be one of the spelling contestants?”

“Yes.” She fumbled to pull the list of words from her bag. “Here are the four hundred words you’ll need to study.”

He reached for them and glanced at them quickly before looking back at her. “Is there anything else I can do to help?”

“I don’t believe so.” She stood and he followed. “It’s been a pleasure meeting you.”

“Must you leave so soon?”

“I’m afraid so. I need to speak to several other people before I go home.”

"And where is home?" He looked embarrassed for a moment, glancing down at the poster before looking up at her again. "I'm sorry. That was a bit too forward. I simply asked because I was wondering where I might call on you, if you'll allow me to escort you to the spelling contest."

She shook her head and took a step back. "That won't be necessary."

"Then you already have an escort?"

She didn't have one officially, but surely Ben and the boys would walk with her to the school. "I do, thank you." She took another step toward the door.

"I look forward to seeing you again, Miss Wilkes."

"And you, Mr. Russell."

"Here. I'll walk you out—unless you have an escort for that, as well." He chuckled as he came around his desk and motioned toward the door. "Ladies first."

She hardly needed an escort to leave the building, but he walked her across the lobby and opened the front door.

"If there's anything else I can do for you, don't hesitate to ask," he said.

Emmy nodded as she passed by him on her way out, though she couldn't quite find her tongue to answer before he closed the door.

She took a steadying breath and turned her focus on the grocer, Mr. Fadling, trying to forget the gregarious banker.

Hopefully her spelling contest would be a success and Mr. Samuelson would have one less reason to get rid of her.

Chapter Seven

Ben paused his mare Ginger at the top of a hill and surveyed the countryside about thirty miles west of Little Falls. At the bottom of the hill, a tarpaper shack sat puffing black smoke into the clear blue sky. Not a cloud marred the expanse overheard, giving Ben a good look at the home of Reginald Trask, the man Abram believed was the boys' grandfather.

A soft wind blew across the snow-covered prairie and Ben pulled his coat tighter around his neck to prevent the chill from seeping inside. He nudged his mare into motion and followed the road down the hill, past a fence in need of repair and around a pile of discarded wood.

Knowing Levi and Zeb were tucked away safely at the school with Emmy, learning their numbers and letters, gave him the nudge he needed to approach this stranger.

His horse whinnied and he leaned down and patted her neck. "Feels good to be out again, doesn't it, Ginger?" Their days of circuit riding were over for now, but Ben would never give up on the idea of returning all together. He knew he was where he needed to be for the time being, but he was always willing to do what the Lord called him to do.

Right now, He was calling Ben to find the boys' kin.

A dog barked at Ben's arrival and the door to the shack opened. An older man stood at the open door in his stained long underwear and dirty socks. His stringy gray hair was in need of a cut and his whiskered face looked as if it hadn't seen a razor in months. "Who are you?"

"I'm Reverend Benjamin Lahaye." Ben stopped Ginger and dismounted. He held her reins and walked the rest of the way to the house. "Are you Mr. Trask?"

"I don't got no need for a preacher." He started to close the door.

"Please," Ben said quickly. "I'm here to ask about your son, Malachi Trask, and tell you about your grandsons."

Mr. Trask paused, his eyes narrowing. "My son?"

"Are you Reginald Trask?"

"How do you know who I am?"

Ben tried to be patient. "I have your grandsons in my care. Their mother died, leaving them with her sister who recently brought them to me."

"How do you know Clara?"

"Clara?"

"My son's wife."

"I didn't know Clara. Her sister brought the boys."

"Clara's dead?"

"I'm afraid so."

Mr. Trask looked beyond Ben for a second. "It's a pity. She was the only good thing that ever happened to Malachi."

Ben gave the man a moment to absorb all the information and then he continued. "Do you know where your son might be?"

Mr. Trask's attention came back to Ben and anger filled his face. "No, and good riddance. That boy was nothing but trouble from the moment his mama told me he was on his way. Took her life when he was born and hasn't done nothing respectable since—except marry Clara. I haven't seen him in six or seven years, not since he turned me out of his house when he was drunk and I tried to defend his wife."

"Did you know he and Clara had a set of twin boys?"

Mr. Trask studied Ben. "Who'd you say you were?"

"Reverend Ben Lahaye, of Little Falls."

Mr. Trask paused again and then said, "Care to get out of the wind, Reverend?"

"I'd like that." Ben tied Ginger's reins to the porch railing, hoping the mare wouldn't try to bolt. The lopsided porch looked like it could be pulled down with little effort.

Ben followed Mr. Trask into his home. The rotten stench of filth made Ben's eyes water. A small stove stood in one corner of the room, with dirty pots and pans stacked around it. In the other corner, a cot was held up by several logs and a pile of soiled blankets lay haphazardly on top.

Mr. Trask didn't seem to pay any of this too much attention as he pointed to a rickety bench against a wall. "Have yourself a seat. Can I get you some coffee?"

"No, thank you." Ben moved aside a pile of old newspapers to find a place to sit.

"Suit yourself." Mr. Trask sat on a rocking chair near the stove, scratching his whiskers. "What's this you say about Clara having twins?"

"They are five years old. Their names are Levi and

Zebulun. I've been trying to locate their next of kin. I learned about you through a friend who recalled doing business with you a while back. He said I'd find you here."

Mr. Trask rocked his chair. "And what do you want from me?"

"I'd like to find their father. The boys need a permanent home and I was hoping it could be with him."

The old man shook his head. "If Malachi's the same as before, the children are better off with someone else."

Ben glanced around the man's shack. If Reginald Trask made a claim on the boys, he'd have the right to take them from Ben—but Ben couldn't imagine them living in such squalid conditions. But what if their father was worse? The debate tore at Ben's conscience. He felt obligated to find the boys' father, yet worried that he wouldn't be fit to raise them. Malachi Trask needed to at least know where his boys were, didn't he?

"Do you know where I might locate your son?" Ben asked.

Mr. Trask continued to study Ben. "If I was you, I wouldn't go poking a rattlesnake and getting him all stirred up. Leave well enough alone and keep those boys as far away from their father as possible."

If it was that simple, Ben would agree—but it wasn't. Something compelled him to find Malachi. His voice became serious. "Do you know where he is, Mr. Trask?"

"You're wasting your time here, Reverend Lahaye."

Ben didn't say anything for a moment, and then he stood. "If you'd like to meet the boys, please come and see us sometime. I live at the parsonage next to the church."

Mr. Trask didn't bother to stand. "They're better off not meeting me, either. I'm not proud of my life and I wouldn't want to saddle those children with my baggage."

"My door is always open to you," Ben said. "Our church is full of sinners saved by grace. Not one of us is perfect or without sin."

"The only Christian I ever liked was Clara—and God saw fit to take her away from us. I figure He's like that. Takin' the good ones and leaving the bad ones here to cause heartache for everyone else."

Ben was disappointed that he felt that way, but he could see by the look in Mr. Trask's eyes that he had made up his mind and it wouldn't easily be changed. "Maybe one day I'll prove that theory wrong, Mr. Trask."

The man scowled and didn't meet Ben's gaze.

"Good day and thank you for your time."

His only response was a grunt.

Ben put on his hat and walked out of the shack. Ginger hadn't moved from her spot and Ben patted her shoulder when he reached her. "Sure wish I had more time to talk to him," he said to his mare as he stepped into the saddle. "If I was still on my circuit, I'd be sure to stop in and see him every chance I could get."

Ginger tossed her head and whinnied as if to agree.

Ben led her out of the Trask yard and pointed her toward home.

Frustration sat heavy on his chest. He was nowhere closer to finding the boys' father than when he had begun—yet, the revelation was bittersweet. From all accounts, Malachi Trask wasn't a good man, but Ben couldn't shake the feeling that he needed to know where his sons were.

Maybe, it was because Ben's father had never come looking for him. Ben had lain awake as a child, hoping and praying his father would one day return for him. When he had left the mission at Pokegama, he feared his father would never find him at Belle Prairie. He begged the missionaries to write to his father and tell him that he had moved, but his father never responded to the letters.

"Lord." Ben looked up into the clear blue sky. "You know the end from the beginning. You knew those boys would come into my home, and You know when they'll leave. Help me do Your will in this and all things. Amen."

He nudged Ginger into a gallop, eager to be home.

That evening, Emmy sat at her desk, a lantern offering a soft glow for her to read by. She had spent so much of her week planning the Friday Frolic, she had gotten behind on her personal studies. But tonight she feared she wouldn't get any studying done, either. She couldn't stay focused on *A Pictorial History of the United States* because her mind continued to wander to Ben and how quiet he had been earlier that evening.

It wasn't her practice to intrude on people's private thoughts, so she hadn't asked him what was wrong. But it still troubled her to see him so unsettled.

The door creaked open and Emmy turned to find Mrs. Carver entering the room. "I hate to bother you, dearie, but I have a sick headache and I need to lie down."

Emmy stood quickly. "Oh, it's no trouble at all. I wasn't able to concentrate tonight, anyway." She walked across the room. "Do you need help getting ready for bed?"

Mrs. Carver patted her hand. "Thank you, but no. I've had more sick headaches than I care to recount, and I know what I need is a dark, quiet room, and lots of sleep."

"Then I'll go and not bother you."

Mrs. Carver was already unbuttoning her blouse in preparation for her nightgown. "Thank you, dearie."

Emmy picked up her book and left the room, tiptoeing along the hall so she wouldn't disturb the boys who had already gone to sleep. Maybe she could get in some studying in the front room.

A lantern was glowing as she came to the foot of the stairs. Was Ben still awake? The thought of having a few moments alone with him was more appealing than she would have suspected. They hadn't been alone since that first day when she arrived by mistake.

She walked into the front room and found him sitting in a rocking chair near the fireplace, a book in his lap—but he wasn't reading. Instead, his gaze was lost in the flames.

He looked up at her approach, a genuine smile of pleasure tilting his lips. "Emmy."

Her heart filled with warmth at the familiarity in his greeting. "Do you mind if I join you?"

"Here, have my rocker." He stood, but she shook her head.

"You stay there. I'll pull up a chair."

"I insist." He turned the rocker toward her and offered such a welcoming smile, she couldn't refuse. She sat on his favorite chair and watched as he pulled another chair from the corner of the room.

The fireplace put off a gentle heat and filled the space with a warm light. It was a cozy room with a large rug, comfortable chairs and several stacks of books. The rocker looked well-worn and she couldn't stop herself from running her hand along the smooth armrests, wondering how many hours Ben had sat quietly in this room, passing the long evenings alone. It still puzzled her that a man as handsome and kind as Ben wasn't married—but then, there were so many unmarried men in town, it shouldn't be all that surprising. Yet, it was hard to believe that he hadn't caught someone's eye long before now.

"Is Mrs. Carver still unwell?" Ben asked, taking his seat across from Emmy and interrupting her wayward thoughts. "She tried to wait as long as she could to give you some time to study."

Dismay filled Emmy's chest. "She didn't have to do that."

"I told her you wouldn't mind, but she insisted."

Emmy shook her head. "She's such a dear, isn't she?"

"I'm very happy she agreed to come and help with the boys." His countenance fell once again and he looked into the flames.

She couldn't hold back her question any longer. "Is everything all right?"

He didn't answer her at first, but eventually looked away from the fireplace and met her gaze. "I visited the boys' grandfather this morning."

Emmy stopped rocking and leaned forward. "And?"

Ben rose and rubbed the back of his neck. "The man is living in deplorable conditions—but worse than that, he had nothing good to say about the boys' father."

"Did you find out where the father is living?"

"He wouldn't tell me."

"What will you do?"

Ben paced over to the window and back to Emmy. "I'm wrestling with that very question. I might have to make a trip to St. Paul and ask around for him there.

I've considered placing some ads in newspapers around the state, but I don't know if it will help."

"What if you don't ever find him? What will happen to the boys then?"

Ben's eyes were filled with uncertainty as he studied Emmy. "I don't know."

"Will you keep them?"

"Mrs. Carver can only stay until after Christmas. I couldn't raise two boys on my own without her."

"Is there someone else who could help?"

Ben sighed and took the poker from the nail next to the fireplace. He readjusted the logs and sparks flew up the chimney. "I don't know of anyone right now." He set the poker back on the nail and faced her again. "But I do know that God brought them here for a purpose and He's not going to leave me guessing forever. Eventually I'll know what to do."

A funny thought came to her and she lowered her eyes, heat filling her cheeks at the thought.

"What?" he asked.

"It's nothing."

"What is it?" he asked again, sitting in his chair.

"It's just a thought I had." She shook her head and waved her hand aside. "It's not worth sharing."

His eyes filled with amusement. "It made your cheeks turn pink."

Her hands flew up to her cheeks as mortification filled her chest.

Ben's laughter was rich and hearty. "I believe you're embarrassed, Miss Emmy."

Emmy wanted to leave the room, afraid he'd get the truth out of her.

"You must tell me now." He came to the edge of

his seat. "I promise there's nothing you could say that would be as embarrassing as you think."

She tried to laugh it off. "I just thought of another way you could keep the boys without finding a housekeeper—but it's just a silly notion."

"Try me."

She did laugh this time. "You won't let it rest, will you?"

He shook his head, a grin on his face. "I'm usually pretty persistent."

"Fine." She might as well get it over with. "I simply thought you could keep the boys if you found a wife."

His smile fell and his face became very serious. "The thought has crossed my mind."

Emmy suddenly felt overly warm sitting by the fire. She and Ben had been friendly from the start, but she always felt a little different in his presence, as if her heart was aware of something her mind could not conceive. The feeling struck her again, leaving her shaky and uncertain of herself.

The silence dragged on and she felt the need to say something, so she started to ramble. "It's not a bad idea—if the boys need a permanent home. They'd be very blessed to have you as a father and they couldn't ask for a better life." More heat filled her cheeks. "I mean, they could do a lot worse."

Ben's smile returned and he finally looked away from her. "I suppose you're right."

"That's not what I meant," she said quickly. "I meant—"

"I know what you meant." He turned his smile back to her, amused at her ramblings, no doubt. "Thank you."

She bit her lip, lest she start prattling on again.

"Have you found everyone you need for the spelling contest?" he asked.

"Yes," she said a bit too quickly, thankful he'd changed the subject, and then went on more calmly. "I have ten gentlemen who have agreed to participate."

"I think it will be good for the community to come together this way."

"I hope so."

He was quiet for a moment. "You're doing a good job, Emmy. The parents are happy, the children are eager to go to school and the school board is pleased."

His words made her cheeks fill with heat once again, but this time she wasn't embarrassed. This time the heat came from the pleasure of his compliment. "Thank you."

"I'm happy we made a mistake—or rather, I'm happy God knew what He was doing when He sent you."

Emmy sat up a bit straighter under his praise, hoping and praying she could continue to find favor with Reverend Lahaye—and the rest of the school board, of course.

Chapter Eight

Emmy smiled at the gathered audience, almost giddy at the number of people who had crowded into the schoolhouse for her first Friday Frolic. Friends and neighbors visited with one another as people continued to come in through the cloakroom door. Ben and Abram Cooper stood near the door, representing the school board and greeting those who were just arriving. Mr. Samuelson and his children had not yet arrived, and she wondered if they would.

Adam Russell walked through the door and paused to speak to Ben, and then he caught Emmy's eye and made his way down the aisle to the front of the room.

"Hello, Miss Wilkes." His smile was dashing and he was one of the best-dressed men in the room. "It's a pleasure to see you again."

"And you, Mr. Russell. Thank you for coming."

"Where would you like me?" he asked. "I've studied all the words on the list and I think I have a fair shot at this spelling contest."

She pointed to the side of the room where the other contestants had already begun to line up. "You may wait over there until we get started."

He nodded and began to walk away, but then he paused and glanced around before addressing her. "Would it be too presumptuous to ask if I may walk you home this evening?"

Emmy glanced toward the door where Ben was shaking the hand of a new arrival. He must have sensed her gaze, because he looked in her direction and smiled. Levi and Zeb sat in the front row, having come to the school earlier with her and Ben to light the lanterns and stoke the fire. They both grinned at her with expectant faces, their little legs swinging beneath the bench.

"I believe I already have several escorts taking me home this evening," she said to Mr. Russell. "Thank you for the offer."

"It is my great misfortune." He took a step back. "Maybe next time I'll get to you first."

She appreciated his manners and agreeable nature, but she also felt bad that she was using Ben and the boys as an excuse to avoid any and every gentleman who made the same request. There had already been several that evening, and each time she gave the same answer.

Emmy pulled her pocket watch out and saw that it was exactly seven o'clock. With a few nerves fluttering in her stomach, she tapped her ruler against her desk to call the room to order.

"Thank you all for coming," she said with a sincere smile.

Everyone found their seats, while others were forced to stand against the walls.

Ben and Abram walked along the side of the room and stood with the other contestants. Still, Mr. Samuelson did not show.

"Tonight I am happy to welcome you to the first Friday Frolic," Emmy said to the audience. "It is my hope to have a social event each Friday night for the remainder of the year, weather permitting, ending with the Christmas pageant on the last Thursday." After that, she didn't know if she'd still be there.

Happy comments were passed from one community member to the next and Emmy was forced to wait until the room quieted once again.

"This first week will be a spelling contest—but not just any spelling contest." She paused and several people in the room met her gaze with a knowing smile. "I have asked ten prominent men from our community to participate and they have generously given of their time and talents."

The audience clapped and the contestants bowed in good-natured fun.

"Each contestant will be given a word to spell and if he has spelled it correctly, he will remain up front. If he doesn't spell it correctly, he will be asked to take a seat. Each round will increase in difficulty until only one contestant remains standing." Emmy took up a piece of paper she had on her desk with the names of each man and then waved them over to the front of the room where she stood. "I'd like to introduce the contestants and then we'll begin."

The men came to the front, though she suspected none but Mr. Russell needed an introduction. Ben stood taller than the other men, his dark hair and eyes drawing her attention. He was one of the handsomest men she'd ever known. When he met her gaze, her cheeks warmed and she was happy he couldn't read her thoughts.

She quickly made the introductions and then moved on to the spelling portion of the evening. Much laughter, teasing and fun ensued. Mr. Fadling was the first to miss a word, followed by Mr. Hubbard and then Mr.

Harper, the owner of an emporium on Main Street. Next went Jude Allen, Dr. Jodan and the attorney, Roald Hall. As each round progressed, the men were forced to sit down one by one. Finally, the last three contestants remaining were Mr. Russell, Abram Cooper, a mill owner and the original founder of Little Falls, and Ben. Emmy stood at the front of the room and faced Abram. "Your word is *ubiquitous*."

"Could you please use that in a sentence?" Abram asked.

"The father's ubiquitous influence was felt by all the family." Her sentence gained several chuckles, but Abram was too deep in thought to notice.

"Ubiquitous," Abram said, his brows furrowed. "*U-b-i-q-u-a-t-o-u-s*. Ubiquitous."

There was a pause and then Emmy said, "I'm sorry, that's incorrect."

The audience applauded his effort, and truth be told, he looked relieved to sit next to Charlotte and be done.

Ben and Mr. Russell looked at Emmy expectantly.

"We have our two final contestants," Emmy said to the audience.

Again, they applauded. Mr. Russell clasped his hands together and shook them over his head, as if he was already the champion. The crowd laughed and cheered him on to victory.

"Mr. Russell." Emmy waited until the room quieted before she continued. "This word is for you. *Bacciferous*."

His brow came up. "Sentence, please?"

"The bush was bacciferous, producing more berries than we could eat."

"Bacciferous. *B-a-c*—" He paused. "*B-a-s-i-f-e-r-o-u-s*. Bacciferous."

Emmy shook her head. "I'm sorry." She looked at Ben. "If you spell this next word correctly, you're the winner. If you don't, Mr. Russell is still in the contest."

Ben stood straight and took a deep breath. "I'm ready."

The room was completely still as she spoke. "Your word is *beneficence*."

"Sentence?"

"Your unswerving beneficence to the community is truly a gift." Emmy smiled at Ben, hoping he knew that she meant what she said.

"Beneficence," Ben said. "*B-e-n-e-f-i-c-e-n-c-e*. Beneficence."

Again, there was a pause.

Emmy couldn't contain her grin. "You're correct!"

The audience clapped and stood to their feet.

"Three cheers for the preacher!" someone shouted from the back of the room.

Ben smiled at those assembled and then shook Mr. Russell's hand.

The room filled with laughter and conversation while Mrs. Carver oversaw setting up the refreshment table. Mr. Russell moved on to speak to the people standing nearby and Emmy used the opportunity to congratulate Ben.

"You did a marvelous job, Ben."

"Thank you. So did you."

"Me?" Emmy pointed at herself. "What did I do?"

"This whole evening was your doing. Well done."

Levi and Zeb ran up to Emmy, their cheeks pink from excitement. "Miss Wilkes, may we have a cookie?" Levi asked. "Mrs. Carver said we needed to ask."

"You may." Emmy ruffled his blond hair. "Tell Mrs. Carver to begin serving whenever she's ready."

The boys shared a grin and ran off to deliver the good news. One of their fellow students, Brett Morgan, stopped Zeb and said something that Emmy couldn't hear. Zeb nodded and turned to Levi, but Levi shook his head, a frown on his face. For a moment, Zeb looked torn between his brother and his friend, but then he took off with Brett. Levi's little mouth fell open as he watched Zeb join Brett and George Cooper as they played jacks in the corner of the room with a few other boys.

"Would you look at that," Ben said. "Zeb found a friend."

Emmy nodded, though her happiness for Zeb was overshadowed by her concern for Levi. "I wish Levi would join in with the others."

"Give him some time."

Emmy had been watching Levi for the past two weeks. Unlike Zeb, who was easy to please and quick to make a friend, Levi was often frustrated and wanted his own way. He hadn't made a single friend in the whole school. When she asked the other children why they didn't include Levi, they often told her he didn't want to play what they wanted, so they didn't ask him anymore. She was watching for ways to encourage the boy, but she had found some children were harder to teach the art of socialization to than others.

"Miss Wilkes." Mr. Archibald, the man who boarded at the Hubbards, was at Emmy's elbow. A hint of alcohol was on his breath and his eyes were glazed with over-indulgence. She hadn't noticed him before now. Had he only just arrived? "Aaron and I wanted to come to the spelling contest. Are we too late?"

The man who had chased her around the table in the Hubbards' front parlor joined Mr. Archibald and was smiling at her with a toothy grin. He looked as if he'd tried to clean up his appearance, but his clothes were wrinkly and his curly hair had slipped down to cover his forehead. "Hello, Miss Wilkes," he drawled in a drunken slur. "Do you remember me? Name's Aaron Chambers."

How could she forget? "Of course I remember you, Mr. Chambers. Thank you both for coming. Please help yourself to a refreshment. There should be some nice, strong coffee, too."

Emmy turned back to speak to Ben, but Mr. Archibald stepped in her way, putting his hand on her arm to stop her.

She looked down at his hand and pulled out of his grasp.

"We didn't come for refreshments," he said, his eyes roaming her up and down. "We came to see you."

"The way I see it, I still deserve a dance," Mr. Chambers said as he swayed. "And one way or the other, I aim to get it."

Ben took a protective step toward Emmy, though she didn't even know if he realized what he did.

"I have no wish to dance with you, Mr. Chambers." Emmy straightened her back and lowered her voice, afraid the others might hear their conversation and report to Mr. Samuelson. "I think it's best if you leave now."

"I won't leave until you tell me when I'll get my dance."

Ben stepped between them and looked right at Mr. Chambers. "Miss Wilkes never promised you anything." His voice was kind but firm. "And a gentleman never demands anything from a lady. Now, you can either walk out of here on your own two feet, or I can get a few friends and we'll carry you out."

Mr. Chambers and Mr. Archibald looked at Ben for a minute, and then Mr. Chambers hit Mr. Archibald on the arm. "Let's leave, Archie. I don't need a sermon."

"What about your dance?" Mr. Archibald asked.

Mr. Chambers looked at Emmy and then at Ben. "It's not worth it."

The men turned away and walked toward the door, tripping over those who stood in their way.

Emmy let out a relived sigh.

"It's the trouble with being single," Ben said, turning to Emmy, his voice serious, yet apologetic. "They think they have the right to take liberties. If you were married, they wouldn't bother."

It was one of the things her parents had been worried about when she planned her trip to Minnesota. Her father was most concerned about her safety—but then he never knew that Ben would be there for her. She didn't know what she would do without him.

Ben stood by the refreshment table, a glass of punch in hand as he watched Emmy interact with her students and their parents. She stood speaking with Mr. and Mrs. Morgan, the owners of Morgan Lumber. Ben had come to know them through the church and in the community. Their daughter, Molly, attended the school with her younger brother, Brett. Two smaller boys were still at home with Mrs. Morgan.

As Emmy spoke with them, he couldn't help but admire her animation and passion. He couldn't hear what she said, but whatever it was, it made the Morgans beam.

"We're about done," Mrs. Carver said, coming up

to Ben. "Would you like me to take the boys home and get them tucked into bed?"

Ben set down his punch glass and nodded. "I'd appreciate that. I'll stay with Emmy to help her close up and we'll meet you back home later."

Mrs. Carver smiled and winked at Ben. "Take your time, dearie."

As the families began to leave, Ben noticed Mr. Russell standing in the opposite corner of the room, his appreciative gaze on Emmy. It was hard not to notice how much time the new banker had spent by her side that evening. For each smile he sent her, she sent him one in return, though Ben wasn't sure if she realized she was flirting. Emmy was too sweet and kind to play the sort of games other women often played. Over the course of two weeks, Ben had found that she was very serious about her promise to Mr. Samuelson. She had not once looked left or right, but continued down the path she had chosen for herself as a schoolteacher. Had her mind been changed by Mr. Russell?

The Morgan family said their goodbyes, and Emmy turned toward her desk, but Mr. Russell stepped into her line of sight. "I was hoping to get a moment to speak to you before I leave," he said.

"I'd be happy to give you a moment." Emmy smiled sweetly.

Mr. Russell looked around the room and his gaze fell on Ben, the only other person now in the schoolhouse.

Ben smiled, letting him know he was still there and didn't have any plans to leave. He liked Mr. Russell well enough, but where Emmy was concerned, he would never take a chance leaving her alone with anyone. He started toward them, anxious to stop the man from making a request of Emmy.

"Maybe I could stop by at another time," Mr. Russell said, his gaze flickering between Emmy and Ben.

Emmy turned and met Ben's gaze with a smile. "I'll only be a moment."

"Take all the time you need." Ben came to stand behind Emmy.

Mr. Russell cleared his throat. "I suppose I'll see the both of you at church on Sunday."

"Wasn't there something you wanted to speak to me about, Mr. Russell?" Emmy asked.

The banker glanced at Ben. "It can wait."

Emmy nodded and reached for a book on her desk. "Thank you, again, for participating this evening. I hope you had fun."

Mr. Russell took her hand and bowed over it. "I had a wonderful time. Good night."

"Good night," Ben said with a satisfied grin.

Mr. Russell walked down the aisle to the door and grabbed his coat and hat off the hook in the cloakroom before stepping out into the dark night.

Emmy secured a couple books in her book strap and turned to Ben. "I'm ready."

He banked the fire in the stove while she blew out all the lanterns. They met in the dark cloakroom, neither speaking as he helped her into her coat. His hands brushed her arms as he slipped the coat over her shoulders.

"Thank you," she whispered.

"You're welcome," he said, equally as quiet.

She put on her bonnet and he put on his cap, and then he took her books and opened the door.

Snow had begun to fall. It came down in large, puffy clumps, sticking to the branches and buildings all around.

Emmy stepped out of the school and Ben followed. When he was out, she closed the door and locked it with her key.

"There," she sighed in contentment. "I would say that was a success."

"More than a success," he agreed. "Everyone had a grand time."

He offered her his arm, tucking her in close to him as they walked down the narrow steps and onto the snow-covered path.

The world was so quiet and still. Lanterns glowed from the homes nearby, sending soft light onto the street. All around, the snow fell, covering the town in a soft blanket.

"How did you come to be the pastor of this town?" Emmy asked, her voice still low.

Ben thought back to the day he'd agreed to stay in Little Falls. "It was three years ago. I had been a circuit preacher for ten years before that. I often stopped to see Abram and his first wife, Susanne, who were the only people here. One day when I stopped, Susanne's sister Charlotte was here and I learned Susanne had died. The next time I stopped, it was Christmas and Abram asked me to stay and be the preacher."

He hesitated to tell her that he had come to stay because he had been attracted to Charlotte. At the time, Charlotte and Abram were not a couple, and Ben had fancied himself in love with her. He'd even asked her to marry him. Though Charlotte had come to care for him, she couldn't marry him, and Ben knew it was because she was already in love with Abram.

"It was the third time I stopped that Abram finally talked me into staying, and I've been here ever since."

Emmy walked close beside him, but her eyes were

roaming the sleepy little town. "What convinced you to finally stay?"

Ben ducked his head, wishing she hadn't asked. "I suppose it doesn't matter now, but I stayed because I was in love with someone who lived here."

Emmy looked up at him, her blue eyes searching his. "What happened?"

He couldn't look at her. "She married my best friend."

"Charlotte?"

He smiled and nodded.

She was silent for a moment, but then she went on gently. "Do you still love her?"

Ben finally looked back at her. "I do, but not in the same way. She will always be special to me, but she has become like a sister."

They walked on, slowly. Ben wasn't in a hurry to get home and Emmy didn't seem to be in a rush, either.

"Where did you grow up?" She looked up quickly. "Is it all right if I ask you so many questions?"

"I don't mind at all—as long as you answer some of mine."

She smiled. "All right."

Ben took a few moments to gather his thoughts, not wanting her pity as he told his story, but feeling the need to be as honest as possible. The snow continued to fall, but there was very little wind, which made the night pleasant in many ways. No one moved about town, making it feel as if it was just the two of them in a snow-covered world.

"My father was a fur trader from Montreal. Originally, he came to Minnesota with the North West Company, but it eventually merged with the Hudson Bay Company. He met my mother who was the daughter of one of his guides. She was a Chippewa Indian, but she had spent most of her life with fur traders and could speak English, French and Scottish Gaelic as well as her native tongue." Ben could hardly recall his mother, but he did remember how beautiful and smart she was. "When I was six, my mother died and my father was so overcome by his grief, he decided to return to Montreal—to his first family."

Emmy inhaled a quick breath and looked up at him. They had stopped walking, though he didn't know how long they stood there. "What happened to you?"

"He couldn't very well take me to Montreal and introduce me to his wife and children, so he left me with missionaries at a place called Pokegama. Mr. and Mrs. Ayers had not been there long when my father left me with them."

"And what became of your father?"

Ben took her arm once again and started walking, his gaze straight ahead. His home was now within sight and the snow had begun to pick up. A gust of cold wind took him by surprise. "I've never seen or heard from him since."

She was quiet for a moment, and then she stopped again.

Ben looked down into her beautiful blue eyes which were now filled with sadness.

"I'm so sorry, Ben. That must have been terrible for you."

He couldn't take his eyes off her. "It wasn't as horrible as it sounds. Mr. and Mrs. Ayers raised me like one of their sons and I had a wonderful education. I learned about our Savior and had more opportunities than most men I know."

"What became of the Ayerses?"

"After an ambush by the Dakota, they fled for their lives and left me with an Indian missionary. I was angry and bitter for a time, feeling abandoned all over again." He smiled, warmth filling his chest, thankful that he could now look back on that time and see it had been part of the journey necessary to bring him to Christ. "But they eventually returned and moved to Belle Prairie to start a mission just north of Little Falls. That's how I came to be in this area to begin with. I still see them all the time."

They crossed the road and drew closer to the parsonage. Ben didn't want their time to end, but he knew he needed to get her inside before the snow started to really blow.

"It reminds me of a passage of scriptures in the Book of Genesis," Emmy said, almost to herself. "When Joseph's brothers went to him in mourning after their father died, and they expected Joseph to be angry at them for all the evil they had done."

Ben nodded, knowing exactly what passage she was referring to. "And Joseph said to them not to worry, that the evil they did to him, God used for Joseph's good."

They stepped onto Ben's front porch and she faced him, putting her free hand on his arm. "Not just for Joseph's good, but to save the lives of many people." She studied him for a moment. "Don't you see? What was meant to harm you is really the thing that God used to bring you to this place so you could minister into the lives of all these people." Her eyes shone with the truth of it. "I think that's beautiful."

He thought *she* was beautiful, but he couldn't tell her what was on his mind and heart. She was out of his reach, and even if she wasn't, what made him think she would love him when there were so many other men worthy of her affection? Men like Adam Russell who could provide her with all the luxuries life had to offer.

"I had a good time tonight, Emmy."

"So did I. Thank you for all your help."

He pushed open the door and watched as she walked into his home—so close, yet unreachable.

Chapter Nine

Ben stood by the window in the front room early the next morning with a mug of coffee in hand. The storm had increased in intensity throughout the night and had not let up when morning arrived. Saturdays were usually reserved for Ben to practice his sermons, but he didn't like to practice inside for others to hear. He often went to the woods or the river, and let his heart fill with the beauty of God's creation, and then he would speak toward the sky, as if God was his only audience. But he wouldn't take the risk and go out in this storm, in case it turned into a blizzard.

Mrs. Carver was in the kitchen, making all sorts of noise as she prepared breakfast. The boys were still asleep, and Emmy had not yet come down.

Though Ben had much to do today, he couldn't deny the pleasure he felt at knowing he would get to spend the whole day with Emmy and the boys. He'd slept very little the night before after walking her home. It hadn't been a restless night. On the contrary, he felt more rested and alive than he had in years. Thoughts of her beautiful smile, her kind words and her gentle presence had filled his mind into the wee hours of the morning.

As he had lain awake, he had thought about the boys, too. What if they never found Malachi Trask? Could Ben make a home for them here? The only way it would be possible is if he had a wife, and one of the only women available was Emmy, though he'd watched her turn down one man after the other. Was it ludicrous to even contemplate her as an option?

He would have to walk carefully. If he overstepped the boundaries she had set in place, she would leave his home, and that was the last thing he wanted.

A commotion on the stairs took Ben's attention off the snow. Levi and Zeb emerged and ran through the front room on their way to the kitchen.

"I get the first flapjack," Zeb cried. "Mrs. Carver promised me."

"The first one there is the winner!" Levi said over his shoulder laughing. "And the winner gets the first flapjack."

"Not fair," Zeb whined, stopping in the front room.

Levi didn't wait for his brother, but pushed open the kitchen door with a bang. "I win!"

Zeb's face turned red and tears streamed down his cheeks. "Not fair," he said again, wiping at his eyes.

Ben set down his coffee mug and crouched in front of Zeb to look him in the eyes. "Did Mrs. Carver promise you the first flapjack?"

Zeb nodded as he continued to wipe his eyes.

"Then you need to dry your tears and go in there and wait patiently for that flapjack. If I know Mrs. Carver, she won't go back on a promise."

"But Levi's the winner and he said he gets it."

Ben smiled and took a clean handkerchief out of his

pocket. He wiped Zeb's cheeks. "Levi's not the boss of Mrs. Carver's kitchen, is he?"

"No."

"Then he doesn't make the rules."

Zeb peaked out from behind his hands and a smile lifted his cheeks.

"Are you better?" Ben asked.

The little boy nodded.

"Then go in there and get your flapjack."

Zeb raced out of the front room, his tears forgotten.

"There he is." Mrs. Carver's voice carried out of the kitchen. "I've been waiting for you to come and get your flapjack. I couldn't serve anyone else until you got the first one."

Ben smiled to himself as he tucked his handkerchief back into his pocket and noticed Emmy standing at the bottom of the stairs watching him.

"Good morning," he said.

She walked into the front room. "You handled that like an expert."

"I'm hardly an expert."

"You could have fooled me." Her gaze wandered to the window and she shook her head. "I'm happy the snow waited until after the spelling contest. No one would take the chance to go out in weather like this."

"Breakfast is ready," Mrs. Carver called out from the kitchen. "Come and get it while it's hot."

They stepped into the kitchen and found Zeb devouring a flapjack smothered in maple syrup as Mrs. Carver served the second one to Levi.

After their meal was over, Mrs. Carver shooed them out of the kitchen while she cleaned.

"What shall we do with ourselves today?" Ben asked the boys as they entered the front room.

"Play games!" Levi said.

"Make popcorn!" Zeb shouted.

Emmy laughed. "We just ate."

"Later," Zeb said with just as much enthusiasm, rubbing his belly. "When we're hungry again."

Ben laughed along with Emmy, but a knock at the front door made the adults pause.

"Who could that be?" Emmy asked with a frown.

"Very few people would brave this snow," Ben added. "They must either be desperate or foolish."

Ben walked to the front door and pulled the latch. The door swung open and a man stood on the porch, his head and body covered in snow. Only his eyes could be seen above his scarf and below his cap. Even his eyebrows and eyelashes were layered with ice.

But it didn't take Ben long to figure out who their caller was, and he surmised he was both desperate *and* foolish—and possibly smitten.

"Hello, Reverend Lahaye. Is Miss Wilkes available?"

"Good morning, Mr. Russell," Ben said, stepping aside. "Won't you come in?"

Mr. Russell crossed the threshold and Ben pushed the door closed against the wind.

"Mr. Russell?" Emmy walked to the front door, concern on her face. "Is everything all right?"

Mr. Russell unwrapped his scarf and revealed his grin. "They don't have storms like this where I'm from. A man could get lost out there."

Ben crossed his arms. "Or freeze to death."

Mr. Russell tore his gaze off Emmy and laughed. "That's exactly what I was thinking on my way here."

Emmy stepped up to him, took his coat and hung it on the hook by the door as Ben just stood there and stared.

"What brings you out in this weather?" Emmy asked. "Is something wrong?"

Mr. Russell took off his cap and smoothed down his dark hair. "Wrong? No, nothing's wrong. I just thought I'd pay a neighborly call."

Emmy looked at Ben with a quizzical expression and Ben just shrugged. If Emmy couldn't deduce why this man would risk his life to come and see her, Ben wouldn't feed her the answers.

"Why don't you come in," Emmy said. "We were just about to play a game."

Zeb and Levi stood in the middle of the front room where they'd left them, their wary glances following the strange man as he walked toward the fireplace, his hands outstretched to the heat. "Hello, boys."

"Hello," they said in unison, though their welcome was not warm.

Ben and Emmy followed Mr. Russell, and Emmy indicated Ben's rocker. "Would you like to have a seat?"

"Thank you." He started to sit, but then he paused. "Would you care to join me?"

Emmy nodded politely and drew up her chair next to the fireplace.

Ben remained standing, his arms crossed. "Zeb and Levi, why don't you go play quietly in your room for a bit while we visit with Mr. Russell."

The boys looked disappointed, but they obeyed. They walked out of the room, casting glances back at the adults. Emmy gave them a promising smile, and they perked up a bit, no doubt trusting that she would eventually play with them.

Mr. Russell looked up at Ben. "Don't let us keep you from whatever you need to do. I'd be happy to entertain Miss Wilkes for the remainder of the morning."

Ben reached down and pulled a heavy chair from the corner of the room, scraping it across the floor, and drew it up to the fireplace, close to Emmy's chair. He took a seat and smiled at Mr. Russell. "That won't be necessary. I have nowhere I'd rather be at the moment."

Mr. Russell sat up straighter in his chair, clearly dissatisfied at Ben's presence, but gentlemanly enough not to make it awkward.

"Would you like something to eat or drink, Mr. Russell?" Emmy asked as she stood. "Coffee to warm you, perhaps?"

Mr. Russell nodded. "I would. And please, call me Adam."

Adam. Ben crossed his arms again.

"I'll be right back." Emmy stepped out of the front room and into the kitchen, closing the door behind her.

Ben leaned back in his chair, watching Adam closely.

Adam looked back at Ben. There was no animosity or threat in his gaze. The man appeared to be decent—though maybe a bit naive and impulsive. If Emmy were to marry, he supposed this man wouldn't be a horrible choice, although no one was worthy enough in Ben's estimation.

Ben was usually a patient man, but for some reason all rationality left him at the thought of this man coming to pay her a romantic call. "What are your intentions toward Miss Wilkes?"

The other man looked at Ben as if he'd lost his mind. "I don't believe that's any of your business, Reverend Lahaye."

"Maybe it's not," he conceded, "but maybe it is. Miss Wilkes is under the protection of my home for the time being and I have an interest in her affairs."

Adam looked toward the kitchen door, which was still closed, and then he leaned forward. "I suppose, as her pastor and a member of the school board, you might be concerned."

As her pastor and one of her bosses? Ben hadn't even been thinking along those lines.

"I assure you I'm an honorable man," Adam said. "I work hard, I make a good income and I try to live my life according to the Biblical principles Jesus taught." He nodded with a bit of satisfaction. "If that's not enough, I don't know what is."

Ben's mood continued to sour with each passing moment. He couldn't think of one good reason this man wasn't right for Emmy, except that he didn't like the idea of it.

"Here we are." Emmy opened the door and entered with a tray filled with a coffeepot, mugs and Mrs. Carver's sugar cookies.

Adam scrambled to get out of his chair and reached over to take the tray for her.

Ben realized that he would be too late to help her with the refreshments, so he quickly stood and repositioned her chair to be in front of the table for her to serve.

"Thank you," she said to both men as she took a seat.

"It's my pleasure," Adam said with a grin. "Anything I can do to make your work a little easier." He moved his chair to be closer to Emmy and gave Ben a friendly nod.

Ben didn't have it in him to return the gesture, so he took a seat, his irritation mounting.

Emmy glanced at Ben with a concerned look, but she didn't say anything.

It would be a long and tedious morning entertaining the banker, and if the snowstorm became worse, they might have to invite him to stay even longer. A thought that made Ben want to growl.

Emmy hadn't known Ben for long, but she sensed he was out of sorts the whole day. Mrs. Carver had sent him a few puzzled looks that suggested she was surprised at his mood, as well.

The long day had finally come to an end and the storm had let up enough for Mr. Russell to make his way home, though he had stayed on through lunch and supper, only leaving when Ben had gone to the hook near the door and brought Adam's outdoor clothing for him. Mr. Russell had wanted to discuss something in private with Emmy, but Ben practically pushed him out the door.

Throughout the day, they had played parlor games with the boys and even made popcorn like Zeb had requested, but there had been an underlying tension that had made everyone a bit uncomfortable.

Mrs. Carver had brought the boys up to bed and Emmy had stayed in the kitchen to put away the popcorn kettle and bank the stove for the night. A single candle gave her enough light to see in the dark room, and heat from the stove offered a bit of warmth, though the wind continued to howl around the eaves.

The house was quiet and Emmy suspected that Ben had also gone to bed. She placed the popcorn kettle on the top shelf with the others and then bent to open the stove door.

Ben's mood left her confused and troubled, though she didn't know why. It was almost as if Ben had been jealous of Adam—but that would be preposterous. Ben had been nothing but a gentleman from the moment they met and had never intimated that his feelings were more than platonic. And though she suspected Adam's feelings ran a bit deeper than friendship, he had also been a gentleman and had not made any advances. She enjoyed the company of both men and had not shown favoritism to one or the other—so why would Ben be jealous, if that's what his mood had been?

A floorboard creaked and Emmy turned to find Ben entering the kitchen.

Her stomach filled with butterflies and her cheeks warmed at his sudden appearance, thankful, once again, that he couldn't read her thoughts. Surely she was making more out of this than she needed to. Some people had bad days, didn't they?

It would be best if she forgot the whole thing and focused on guarding her heart. All she needed to do was remember the torment and agony of losing William five years ago and all romantic notions fled from her mind.

Ben paused at the sight of her and then walked to the cupboard and took out a glass. "I didn't realize you were still awake." His usual warmth toward her had cooled and she found she didn't like it.

"I told Mrs. Carver I'd tidy the kitchen before going up."

He poured water out of the pitcher and into his glass, not looking at her. "You might want to take my buffalo robe and put it over the boys tonight. It will probably get much colder before morning."

She finished banking the fire and closed the door. "I'll do that right away." She straightened and wiped her hands on her apron, nibbling her bottom lip. There was nothing worse than discord, and that's what she felt between them. "Ben—" She paused, unsure of how to set things right again.

He finally turned to look at her. The flame from the candle threw shadows over the striking planes of his face, making her pulse tick a little faster. The look in his eyes was hard to read, but she sensed, again, that something was wrong.

They didn't speak for a moment and the nerves continued to bubble up within her. She needed to ask him what was wrong, but she feared hearing the truth. If he did have feelings for her, she didn't want to know. She loved living with him and Mrs. Carver and the boys, and she hated to think of leaving them. But she couldn't stay if he had romantic ideas. She'd promised herself she would never fall in love again, and what's more, it wouldn't be right to be in the same house with a man who was attracted to her.

"Is something wrong, Emmy?" He took a step toward her, concern now clouding his eyes.

"I—I was going to ask you the same question."

He paused and looked down at the water he'd yet to drink. For a moment, he didn't say anything, and when he looked up she saw the old Ben reappear. "Nothing is wrong."

She wanted to believe him. "Then why the sullen mood today?"

He looked down at his glass again and finally set it on the table. "I'm sorry I've been out of sorts. There's no excuse for it."

"Maybe not, but is there a reason?" The question came of its own accord, as if her heart longed to hear that his feelings did run deeper, while her mind begged her to walk away—nay, run—before he answered.

He studied her for a moment, as if he, too, wanted something he knew he shouldn't want, but then he shook his head and started toward the door. "Good night, Emmy. I'll leave the robe on the hook by the door."

Without another word, he left his glass of water on the table and disappeared into the other room.

Emmy's legs were weak and she took a seat, not sure if she'd have the strength to stand much longer.

Ben's actions were so out of character she didn't know what to think or believe. But his feelings were not what concerned her the most; her feelings scared her even more.

Chapter Ten

The next morning, Ben stood at the front of the church smiling at the few families who had braved the snow to attend. Overnight, the storm had lessened in severity and when he woke, there were only a few flurries, but it would still be difficult for those who lived out of town to get in for the service.

Emmy, Mrs. Carver and the twins sat in the front row. Mrs. Carver had made sure the boys had scrubbed their faces until they shone, and Emmy had combed their hair. Mrs. Carver planned to get fabric for them on Monday and start sewing more outfits for school, church and play. Levi squirmed in his seat and Emmy reached over and gently put her hand on his knee to still him.

"'This is the day which the Lord hath made,'" Ben said to the congregation, quoting Psalm 118:24. "'We will rejoice and be glad in it.'"

His gaze went to Emmy and he found her studying him closely. When their eyes met, she looked down at the Bible lying in her lap. Ben wished things hadn't become so awkward last evening.

Adam Russell sat directly behind Emmy. He had

come in early and monopolized her time while Ben had been busy welcoming his parishioners. Ben supposed that Adam had taken the opportunity to ask if he could call again, but there was no way of knowing unless he asked Emmy, which he couldn't do without making her suspicious of his own feelings.

He directed his thoughts back to his sermon, frustrated that he would let his mind wander while he was in the pulpit. "Let us turn to the Book of Romans, chapter thirteen, verse eight." Ben stood behind his podium and opened his well-loved Bible. The pages were crinkled and the binding was loose, but he couldn't bear to get a new one. It was like an old friend. "'Owe no man any thing,'" Ben read, "'but to love one another: for he that loveth another hath fulfilled the law.'"

The door opened and Ben looked up. An older gentleman walked into the church. Something about his posture struck Ben as familiar, but he pushed the thought aside and glanced back at his Bible—but then he looked up again sharply. The man took off his cap and revealed white, stringy hair. Reginald Trask dipped his head and slipped into the back pew, his face down, as if he was trying to blend in with the others unnoticed.

Emmy watched Ben closely and turned her head to see what he was looking at. The other parishioners also looked up at Ben, questions in their eyes.

Ben shook his head to get his bearings and then he continued reading from the Book of Romans. "'For this, Thou shalt not commit adultery,'" he said. "'Thou shalt not kill, Thou shalt not steal, Thou shalt not bear false witness, Thou shalt not covet; and if there be any other commandment, it is briefly comprehended in this saying, namely, Thou shalt love thy neighbour as thyself.'" He looked down at his notes and tried to recall what he had planned to say. It was unusual for him to lose his train of thought, but seeing Mr. Trask was unnerving. What was he doing in Little Falls? Had he come to take the boys, after all?

Levi swung his legs under the front pew and Zeb played with his fingers. Emmy set her hand on Levi's knee again and his legs stopped swinging, but he looked as bored as Ben remembered being in church as a child. The boys had only been with him for about two weeks, but in that time they had endeared themselves to Ben. The sudden thought of them leaving with Mr. Trask and living in those deplorable conditions made Ben's chest constrict with fear like he'd never known. What would he do if Mr. Trask demanded them?

People began to fidget in their seats and Ben knew he must continue with his sermon before they became more uncomfortable. "The Bible also says in Mark, chapter twelve, verse thirty-one, that the second greatest commandment is to love thy neighbor as thyself. I often think of this verse while I'm about my daily business."

Mr. Trask looked around the church, his gaze skimming the people who had gathered. Was he looking for the boys?

Ben continued, his thoughts scattered. Several people gave him strange looks as he fumbled through his sermon, but it was Emmy who looked the most concerned.

Finally, it was time for the closing prayer. "Let us bow our heads."

Everyone did as he requested, even Mr. Trask.

"Lord—" Ben let out a long breath "—we thank You for Your loving kindness, Your abundant grace and Your perfect will. Help us to accept Your plans and offer love to everyone we meet. Amen."

"Amen," the others echoed.

Ben stepped away from the podium and went to Emmy and Mrs. Carver. He usually walked down the aisle to be at the door to thank everyone for coming, but his first priority was the boys today.

"Mr. Trask has joined us," he said quietly to the ladies. "Why don't you take the boys out the back door and I'll find out what he wants."

Emmy looked over her shoulder, concern on her face. "I was wondering why you were so shaken today. Do you think—?"

"I don't know," Ben answered before she could voice her question. "I'll find out and be home as soon as I can."

"Come, boys," Mrs. Carver said in a merry voice. "Let's see who can get to the parsonage first." She directed them toward the back door, behind the pulpit. They didn't miss the opportunity for a contest and were soon out of the building.

"Would you like me to come with you to talk to him?" Emmy asked.

It would be nice to have Emmy's support as he spoke to Mr. Trask, but then he saw Adam standing near the door, no doubt waiting for Emmy, and he had second thoughts. "Could you go with Mrs. Carver to keep the boys occupied while she prepares lunch?"

Emmy nodded. "I'd be happy to."

He watched her walk out the same door the others had taken a moment ago, and then turned to find Mr. Trask—but he was nowhere to be seen.

Ben's heart rate escalated as he started toward the door. "Pardon me," he said to those in the aisle. "Can I get through?"

His friends and neighbors moved aside, allowing him to pass, though several looked troubled by his behavior. He made it to the door and stepped outside, looking toward the right, where the parsonage sat, but Mr. Trask wasn't there. Ben looked to his left, toward the center of town, and finally saw the older man climbing into a sleigh.

Part of Ben wanted to watch the man pull away and not return, but the other part wanted to reach out to him. Clearly, he'd come a long way for some reason.

"Mr. Trask." Ben jogged toward the sleigh and the other man looked over his shoulder, but he continued to climb into the sleigh.

"Wait," Ben called again.

Mr. Trask sat on the bench and lifted the horse's reins. "It was a mistake to come."

"No." Ben stopped beside the sleigh and put his hand on the box. "Please, don't leave yet. I'd like to talk to you."

The other man shook his head. "I shouldn't have come. I knew it all the way here, but something pulled me. I don't know what I was thinking."

"Please," Ben said. "Come back to the church and let's talk about why you came."

Mr. Trask looked around at the buildings and people and shook his head. "I haven't been in a church since I was a lad. Don't know what I expected, but it wasn't that."

Confusion tilted Ben's brow. "It wasn't what?"

"All warm and cozy-like." He looked at Ben, his gaze somewhere between reverence and disgust. "And those words you spoke, about loving thy neighbor and such—I never heard someone say it as if they truly believed it. Makes me downright uncomfortable."

Ben had barely strung two coherent words together

during his sermon. He didn't think he'd made sense, but apparently, it was what Mr. Trask needed to hear.

Everything in Ben wanted to send Mr. Trask on his way, but he sensed the need to invite him to lunch. It didn't appear as if the man had come to steal the boys away. If he had, wouldn't he be there now? "Would you like to join us in the parsonage? My housekeeper is roasting some beef and she baked a chocolate cake." He paused, but then went on before he changed his mind. "Your grandsons are there now, and they'd be happy to meet you."

Mr. Trask rubbed his whiskers and scrunched his face as if in thought. "I don't know if it's a good idea."

"It must be the reason you came," Ben said. "Don't let fear stop you now."

He sat for a moment, and then he secured the reins to the dashboard and started to climb down. "I'll come, but there's one condition."

"Of course."

"I don't want them to know I'm their grandpa."

Ben frowned. "Why not?"

The old man suddenly looked a lot older. Weariness and heartache wrinkled his face as he met Ben's gaze. "I didn't do right by their pa, and I don't reckon I could do right by them. They'd be better off not knowing who I am in the long run."

"If that's how you want it."

"It is."

"Then I'll honor your request."

Mr. Trask nodded and followed Ben toward the parsonage.

Ben hoped and prayed he had done the right thing by inviting Mr. Trask to join them. Maybe, just maybe, he could help Ben find the boys' father, after all.

* * *

Emmy sat at the small table in the front room with Levi and Zeb, a game of checkers between her and the boys.

"It's your turn, Zeb," Levi said to his brother as he hovered close to Zeb's shoulder. "Move this one over there." He pointed to the checker that he wanted Zeb to move, but Zeb didn't seem to pay him any attention. Instead, Zeb moved a different checker, right into Emmy's path.

For a moment, Emmy vacillated. Should she ignore the checker and move a different one to spare Zeb's disappointment, or should she play the game as it should be played, showing Zeb that he must be more careful where he moved?

"There, Miss Emmy!" Levi pointed at the checker she could use to jump Zeb. "Take that one."

Zeb's mouth fell open into a perfect O and he frowned at Levi. "Don't help her win!"

"I tried to help you," Levi said to his brother, a bit smug, "but you didn't listen."

The front door opened and Ben stepped over the threshold with the man she presumed to be Mr. Trask, saving Emmy from making a decision at the moment.

"Boys, we'll need to finish this game later," she said quietly. "Mr. Ben has brought a guest."

The boys looked disappointed, but neither complained as Emmy stood to greet the men.

She caught Ben's serious gaze and tried to convey her support.

Ben closed the door behind the visitor and indicated the front room. "Why don't you come in."

The man took off his cap and clutched it in his hand, his gaze going from Emmy to the boys.

"Mr. Trask," Ben said, "may I introduce you to Miss Wilkes? She's our schoolteacher and currently boards with us."

Mr. Trask looked back at Emmy, his face filled with uncertainty. "It's a pleasure to meet you, miss."

"And you, Mr. Trask."

Ben looked from Mr. Trask to the twins, his own uncertainty making her heart beat an unsteady rhythm for him.

"Boys, please come here." Ben motioned the boys to come from around the table and stand in front of him. "Mr. Trask, this is Zebulun and Levi."

Mr. Trask inspected them, a bittersweet look filling his eyes. "Hello, boys."

"Hello," they said in unison.

Zeb shied away, but Levi's eyes filled with a question. "We have the same name."

Mr. Trask looked at Ben quickly, but Ben only smiled at Levi. "There are a lot of people with the same last name."

Emmy frowned at the response. Didn't Mr. Trask want the boys to know they were related—or was it Ben that didn't want them to know?

The kitchen door opened and Mrs. Carver stepped out with a dish towel in hand. She looked Mr. Trask over from head to foot, and Emmy could only guess that the stout lady was thinking the man was much too skinny—it was a malady that most people suffered from in her estimation.

"Mr. Trask," Ben said. "This is Mrs. Carver, our housekeeper."

Mr. Trask nodded a greeting. "It's a pleasure to meet you, ma'am." He looked around the room at the boys and then Emmy. "It's a right full house you have here, Parson."

Ben smiled at his makeshift family. "I've been blessed, indeed."

Warmth filled Emmy's chest at Ben's statement. "Won't you come in?" she asked Mr. Trask.

"Lunch is ready to be served," Mrs. Carver interjected. "Let's eat while it's hot."

"This way," Ben said to Mr. Trask.

The group entered the warm kitchen. Mrs. Carver had already laid everything out on the table. A single chair remained empty, so Ben suggested Mr. Trask sit there.

Emmy pulled out the chair beside Ben's, wishing that things hadn't become so awkward between them. She couldn't shake the memory of the previous evening from her mind. It had taken her several minutes to find the strength to rise and go to bed. She had found the robe on the hook, just as Ben had said, but he had gone to bed, his door firmly closed.

Now he glanced at her as they took a seat at the table, and she found herself needing to look away, hoping he wasn't thinking about last evening, as well.

"Let's pray, shall we?" Ben asked.

Mrs. Carver reached out to take Emmy's hand to her right and Mr. Trask's to her left. The older man's eyes grew wide and he stared at her hand for a moment before tentatively taking it. Levi also offered his hand to Mr. Trask, and Mr. Trask was even more hesitant to reach out to the little one, but he finally did. A sense of awe filled his weathered face before he closed his eyes and lowered his head.

Emmy looked at Ben and found him watching her, his own hand hovering, waiting for her to accept it. She slipped her hand into his confident grasp and bowed her head.

"For this meal, and our lives, Lord, we are eternally grateful. Amen."

"Amen," Emmy said, wanting to pull her hand away—but longing to keep it right where it was.

Shame and remorse filled Emmy's chest as she pulled away. Thoughts of William clouded her vision as she went about the task of filling her plate with Mrs. Carver's scrumptious food. Before coming to Little Falls, Emmy had thought of William every day. Now, it had been several days since she had thought of him, and even then, it was only in passing moments. Suddenly, she had a hard time remembering what he looked like.

"Is everything all right?" Ben asked her quietly.

She looked up quickly, her cheeks filling with heat. "I'm fine."

"Eat up, Mr. Trask." Mrs. Carver slopped a spoonful of mashed potatoes on Mr. Trask's plate. "You could stand to put a few layers of insulation on those old bones."

Mr. Trask looked at the lady with surprise lighting his face.

"Don't skimp on the roast beef, either." Mrs. Carver lifted two thick slices off the platter and put them on his plate.

Levi and Zeb watched the stranger as they ate heartily, though neither one looked too curious about their guest.

"It was a pleasure to have you at church today," Ben said to Mr. Trask. "I'm happy you made the trip. It couldn't have been easy with all that snow."

Mr. Trask slowly picked up a fork as he studied the heap of food Mrs. Carver had placed there. "I've been through worse. Um, ma'am," he addressed Mrs. Carver. "I don't want to insult, but I don't think I can eat all this food."

"You can." She nodded. "And you will."

He looked at the food as if he was preparing for battle, diving in with determination.

Emmy longed to inquire why he had come, but she sensed it wasn't the time or the place to ask such things.

Ben and Mr. Trask spoke of mundane affairs as they ate. When the man finished one serving of food, Mrs. Carver gave him another. After a while, he didn't seem to mind, gobbling everything up eagerly.

"You're a mighty fine cook," Mr. Trask said to Mrs. Carver between bites of food. "Don't reckon I've eaten this fine since my ma was alive."

Mrs. Carver's dimpled cheeks filled with color and she dipped her gaze. "That's a real nice compliment, Mr. Trask."

Emmy glanced up at Ben and they shared a smile. It was the first time Mrs. Carver showed any sign of embarrassment since Emmy had met her.

They enjoyed the chocolate cake and then Mrs. Carver rose to bring the coffee to the table.

"May we be excused?" Levi asked Ben. "Zeb and I want to play outside."

"That sounds like a good idea," Ben said. "Make sure you put on all your outside gear, and if it gets too cold, come right in."

"And don't forget your scarves," Emmy added as the boys jumped up from the table and started toward the door.

"We won't," Zeb said with a smile.

Mr. Trask watched the boys leave the room, his gaze stuck on the door long after they had disappeared.

"Well?" Mrs. Carver said as she sat down with a mug of coffee in front of her. "Did you come to take them away from us?"

"Mrs. Carver," Ben said quickly.

"That's all right." Mr. Trask held up his hand to stop Ben. "It's a logical question."

Emmy circled her mug with both hands, gripping the warm, speckled tin harder than she intended.

"I didn't come to take the boys," Mr. Trask said slowly. "I came to tell you where you can find their pa."

Emmy's throat squeezed tight and she looked to Ben. She had half hoped they would never locate Malachi Trask.

"I thought you didn't know where he was." Ben studied Mr. Trask, his gaze focused on the other man.

"I never said I didn't know—I just said it would be best not to know. I still don't think it's a good idea, but I can't shake the feeling that I should tell you." Mr. Trask looked down at his mug of coffee and sighed. "Last I heard, he's living in Owatonna." He looked up and met Ben's gaze. "I doubt he's changed, but I guess everyone deserves the benefit of the doubt."

Emmy swallowed the lump of anxiety in her throat. "Do you think he's married again?"

"I couldn't say, but if I know my son, he's a charmer and he probably talked some sorry woman into marrying him."

Ben leaned back in his chair, his eyes lowered. "If he's married, then he and his new wife could probably manage to take the boys."

Mr. Trask inhaled a breath and then let it out again. "That's what I was thinking."

Ben finally looked up at Emmy and there was sadness within his eyes. No doubt he would miss Levi and Zeb as much as she would.

"I should probably plan to bring the boys to their father as soon as possible—"

"If I was you," Mr. Trask interrupted. "I'd write a letter first. Might come as a shock to him if you just showed up on his doorstep. A letter would give him some time to process the information and prepare for the boys."

Ben nodded. "That's sound advice."

"And," Mr. Trask continued, "he might have moved on. It wouldn't be good for the boys to risk going all that way in weather like we're having, especially if he's no longer in Owatonna."

"Where is Owatonna?" Emmy asked. "Is it close?"

"It's down by the Iowa border," Ben supplied. "At least a hundred and fifty miles, or so."

Mr. Trask took a long drink of his coffee. When he set down his mug, he looked at Mrs. Carver. "That's good coffee, ma'am."

Mrs. Carver's eyes shone as she stood and retrieved the coffeepot to fill his mug again.

"I'll send a letter out immediately," Ben said with resignation. "And then we'll wait to see what he'd like to do."

Emmy took a sip of her coffee, but it didn't set well in her stomach. They had received some answers, but more questions had surfaced. If Malachi was remarried, would he and his wife want the boys? And, if they did, how could Emmy say goodbye?

Chapter Eleven

The last week of November had arrived, bringing with it more snow and more excitement for the coming Christmas season. Emmy closed the schoolhouse and called out to Levi and Zeb that it was time to go home. Every morning, Ben walked them to school and helped her bring in enough wood for the day, but in the afternoon, she walked the boys home. Ben had volunteered to fetch them after school, but she insisted it wasn't necessary. With the twins by her side, and her stance clear about gentlemen callers, most of the men left her alone.

Zeb laughed and ran as Levi tried to get him with a snowball. It sailed over Zeb's head and hit Emmy's knee.

Levi stood straight, his eyes growing wide. "I'm sorry, Miss Emmy."

She secured her books under her arm and smiled. "I'm fine, but it's time to go."

The boys ran to her side, trudging through several inches of newly fallen snow. The local citizens claimed they had never seen a winter so early, or so fierce. There had been at least one snowstorm each week, some lasting for several days at a time. Today, the air was colder than usual, pinching Emmy's exposed skin on her cheeks and nose. She had only been outside for a few minutes, and already her fingers and toes were hurting from the cold.

A man appeared on the other side of the street, walking toward Emmy and the boys. It didn't take her long to recognize Adam. He waved and sprinted across the street to meet up with her.

"Hello," he said. "I was hoping to catch you before you left the school."

"I dismissed the children early, on account of the cold. The temperature has dropped steadily all day and I didn't want to wait another hour before sending them home."

"May I walk with you?" he asked.

"Of course."

Levi and Zeb ran ahead and Emmy didn't stop them. The sooner they arrived home, the happier she would be. They had been outside longer than her, and though they had been running around, it wasn't safe for them to be exposed to the cold for much longer.

Adam patted his upper arms with his mitted hands. "I've never experienced anything like this weather in my life," he said. "I came from South Carolina."

"I remember," she said with a smile. It seemed every time she saw him, he reminded her that he hadn't been in Minnesota long and that he wasn't fond of the weather.

The church was another block away, but Emmy saw Ben step outside the building all bundled up in his knitted cap and mittens. He waved at the boys as they rushed past and then turned his attention to Emmy and Adam.

Adam sighed. “I was hoping for a few moments alone with you.”

“Would you care to come into the parsonage?”

“I'd rather have more privacy than the parsonage can afford.”

Ben came down the steps and started toward them.

Adam scowled. It was the first time she saw him act ungentlemanly. “He seems dead set on preventing me from talking to you.”

Emmy lifted her eyebrows. “Who? Ben?”

“Yes.” There was a hint of irritation in Adam's voice. “Does he consider himself your beau?”

“Ben?” Emmy stopped. “Of course not.”

“Then why won't he let me speak to you alone?”

“I don't think he minds if you speak to me.”

“Oh, no?” Adam indicated Ben's advance. “There he is again.”

Emmy glanced at Ben, warmth filling her cheeks despite the bitter cold. Was Ben preventing Adam from speaking to her? And, if so, was it because Mr. Samuelson had forbid her to entertain callers? Or was there another reason?

“Hello, Emmy,” Ben said. “Adam.”

“Well,” Adam said with resignation, “if I can't have a moment alone with you, Miss Wilkes, I'll have to ask you what I came to ask you with Reverend Lahaye present.”

Ben straightened, his shoulders growing taut.

“What did you need to ask me?” Emmy ignored Ben's behavior and the accusation Adam had just made.

“The Allens have just announced a Christmas Eve ball that will be held at the Northern Hotel.”

Ben took a step forward, but Adam continued. “Will

you allow me the pleasure of escorting you to the ball, Miss Wilkes?"

A ball? Emmy hadn't been to a ball since William died. She had loved to dance at one time, but now she couldn't stomach all the attention lavished on her at balls. It didn't feel right to be in another man's arms, or to play all the flirting games so many men and women played. If she attended a ball, there would be more of the same trouble she'd had at the Hubbards' home.

The cold made her thoughts feel sluggish and her lips go numb. She needed to get inside and warm herself by the fire, but she couldn't go until she gave Adam an answer.

Both men watched her, waiting for her to say something.

"I'm sorry, but I won't be attending the ball."

Adam's disappointment was swift and Ben's relief was palpable.

"Is there anything I can do to change your mind?" Adam asked hopefully, turning himself as if to exclude Ben from the conversation.

"Emmy, we should get inside." Ben was taller than Adam and he looked at her from over Adam's head.

She turned her full attention on Adam, hating to disappoint him. "There is nothing you could do to change my mind." She smiled, though her lips felt like stones. "I don't attend balls anymore. Thank you for the invitation, but I must get inside."

Adam straightened and gave her a curt nod. "Good day, Miss Wilkes." He turned and strode toward the bank.

"Here." Ben reached for Emmy's books. "We need to get inside." He offered his arm and she accepted his help over the snowbanks.

They entered the parsonage and Emmy quickly took off her mittens to blow warm air onto her frozen hands while Ben closed the door. He placed a rag rug against the bottom to prevent the draft from seeping past the threshold.

Emmy's hands were red and completely numb. She rubbed them together and continued to blow air onto them, but it didn't seem to help.

Ben set her books down on the table next to the lantern and took off his own mittens. He reached out and took her hands into his, rubbing them gently.

Emmy's breath stilled as they stood face-to-face.

He didn't say anything as he continued to rub her hands, though she sensed he was very aware of her—just as she was of him. His shoulders were so broad and well built, she felt safe and protected standing so close to him. He smelled of soap and wind and books.

She didn't pull away, though everything in her warned her not to let him get so close. Slowly, life returned to her hands, and her fingers began to tingle—but the feeling in her fingertips was nothing compared to the feeling coursing through every nerve in her body. Her senses were on fire.

"Is that better?" he asked quietly, his voice deeper than usual.

"Yes," she said, just as quietly. "Thank you."

His hands stilled over hers, and she looked up into his beautiful eyes. Longing kindled in the depth of his gaze, frightening her because it mirrored her own heart.

She stepped away quickly, pulling her hands from his grasp.

He took a step toward her, an apology in his eyes. "Emmy—"

"Mr. Ben!" Levi raced out of the kitchen, his eyes

bright. "Mrs. Carver said we can make taffy, if you don't mind wasting sugar."

Ben didn't take his eyes off Emmy, but he nodded. "That's fine."

"Yes!" Levi spun on his heels and ran back toward the kitchen. "Mr. Ben said yes!"

Emmy swallowed and took a step around Ben to go upstairs. She needed some space to collect her thoughts and still the erratic beating of her traitorous heart.

"Emmy." Ben reached out and put his hand on her arm to stop her.

She did stop, but she couldn't look at him. "It's fine," she said, though her trembling voice betrayed her wayward emotions. "I'm going upstairs to change so I can help Mrs. Carver."

"It's not fine." He dipped his head to get her to look at him. "I'm sorry I made you uncomfortable. I didn't intend—"

"Really." She tried to laugh it off as if nothing had passed between them. "I'm fine." She stepped away from him and moved into the sanctuary of the stairway. She forced her feet to climb the steps and cross the hall to her bedroom, but as soon as she entered her room, she closed the door and leaned against it, breathing hard.

What was happening to her and her resolve to protect her heart? She had told herself that she would never be vulnerable again to love. It wasn't worth all the pain. Losing William was the most difficult experience in her life. The weeks and months after his death were darker and harder than she had ever imagined possible. She couldn't live through another heartache like that. It would surely destroy her.

Yet—she couldn't deny that she longed to fall in love again, to experience the beauty and joy of joining her heart to another. The thought of being close to Ben, of looking into his eyes and feeling his touch, sent a thrill of excitement through her. She loved to hear his laughter and watch him with the twins. She enjoyed his appreciation for Mrs. Carver's food and the way he lit up when he preached. He was kind, good, handsome and selfless. A woman would be blind not to fall for his charms—yet, she wasn't foolish enough to believe it would last forever. Life was temporary. Death was permanent. The fleeting days of love were not worth the lifetime of pain after.

She wrapped her arms around her middle and closed her eyes, nibbling her bottom lip and willing herself not to cry. She had to force herself to deny the feelings growing inside. It was her only hope of survival.

Ben ran his hands over his face, frustrated at his actions. He had no right to take such liberties with Emmy. He had overstepped his bounds and he feared it would change everything between them.

He walked into the front room and stood by the fireplace. Mrs. Carver had kept it roaring all day, but it barely touched the cold air seeping into the house.

Emmy's footsteps echoed above and Ben glanced at the ceiling.

He had watched her with the other men. She was guarded and cautious. He had loved that she felt comfortable around him and had a place to relax in his home. If she suspected his true feelings, she would be just as rigid and wary with him. What must she think of him now, holding her hands longer than necessary, about to tell her things she didn't want to hear?

He wanted to go upstairs and apologize again—but what would it matter? His actions spoke for themselves.

At first, he had simply intended to warm her hands, but then the feel of her soft skin and the floral scent of her perfume had made him lose all common sense and he had wanted to pull her close and revel in her presence.

If Levi hadn't interrupted, there's no telling what foolish thing he would have said or done.

"Reverend." Mrs. Carver stepped out of the kitchen. "I could use some help with the taffy pulling when it comes time. Is Emmy close at hand? The boys don't want to begin without her."

Ben nodded, though he didn't want her to suspect something was wrong. "She's upstairs changing. I'm sure she'll be down soon."

Mrs. Carver studied him for a moment. Very little went unnoticed by her, and no doubt she sensed something was amiss, but thankfully she didn't pry. "I'll get everything ready as we wait."

She went back into the kitchen and Ben stayed by the fire. With the bitter cold, there was little he could do outside. He could go back to the church and prepare his sermon, but he didn't think he could concentrate, even if he tried. That left him in the house, with Emmy. The only place he could go to stay out of her way was his bedroom, but there was very little heat in there.

He picked up a copy of *Uncle Tom's Cabin*, by Harriet Beecher Stowe and took a seat near the fireplace. He had read the story many times, but he needed something to keep his hands busy.

After a few minutes, Emmy's footsteps crossed the room overhead and fell on the stairs.

Ben's stomach clenched at the idea of facing her again. No matter what, he needed to act as if nothing had happened. He wanted her to trust him and his intentions again. The last thing he wanted was for her to look at him the way she looked at other men.

She stopped at the bottom of the steps, but he didn't look up.

Should he acknowledge her? Should he ignore her?

She started across the front room and he couldn't help but look up at her. She glanced in his direction and he forced himself to smile.

"The boys don't want to start until you are there to help them." He closed his book. "Mrs. Carver asked for me to help pull the taffy when it's ready."

Emmy stopped on her way to the kitchen and nodded. "I'll let you know when the time comes."

It was all she said before leaving him alone with his book.

He shook his head at his foolishness and stared into the flames. Emmy would never open her heart to him. He had known it from the start, yet he continued to do things that threatened the boundaries she had established.

It was vital that he keep his distance from her. It was the only way to keep her close.

Chapter Twelve

The following evening was Friday, so Emmy sent the boys home after school and stayed to prepare for the Friday Frolic. They would have a singing party and she had asked one gentleman to bring his fiddle, one to bring his mouth organ and another to bring a fife.

Her stomach growled as she set out some sheet music she had brought from home and stoked the fire in the stove. She could have gone to the parsonage with the boys for supper, but things had become so unsettled between her and Ben, she preferred to keep her distance.

She went to her desk and pulled out the cold potato Mrs. Carver had sent to school with her that morning. It had been hot as she carried it to school, but it had lost all its heat throughout the day. It was intended to be her lunch, but she had planned to stay on through supper, so she had skipped her afternoon meal. Now she brought it to the stove and placed it in the coals at the front to warm it.

As she stood near the stove, waiting for her supper, she yawned. She had tossed and turned the night before, hoping she hadn't kept Mrs. Carver awake, recalling what had happened between her and Ben. Part of her wanted to be angry at him—but she couldn't find a reason. In all truth, she was angrier at herself. Ben was a gentleman. If he had feelings for her, he had chosen not to say a word. He respected her wishes and for that, she was grateful. Could she fault him for holding her hands a bit longer than necessary? After all, she had allowed it.

The door creaked open and Emmy's breath caught. Had Ben come to find out why she had not returned home with the boys? Excitement made her heart pound a bit too hard as she turned to face him.

"May I come in?" Adam poked his head around the cloakroom door. "I know I'm early, but I saw the light was on and thought you might need some help getting ready."

Emmy's disappointment was stronger than she would have liked, but she hid it behind a smile. "Come in out of the cold."

She moved away from the stove and met him at the door. It wasn't proper to be alone with him, but she couldn't send him back outside without warming himself first.

He stepped into the schoolhouse, his handsome grin in place. "When will this cold let up? I've about had as much as I can handle."

"And it's only the last week of November." She closed the door behind him. "We might have to endure it until March."

The look of pure horror on his face was enough to make Emmy giggle.

His face smoothed and a smile lifted his lips. "I think I could bear almost anything if I could hear that laughter more often."

Heat warmed her cheeks at the comment and she tried to ignore the amorous look he gave her.

"I'll let you warm up, but then I must ask you to leave and come back later."

He kept his distance as they walked to the stove, and he stood on the opposite side as he stretched his hands out to the heat. His gaze was on her as she gingerly reached into the stove and turned her potato.

"Your supper?" he inquired.

"Yes. I thought it best to stay here and prepare for tonight."

Adam looked around the schoolhouse. "What's there to prepare?"

Emmy let her gaze circle the room, but she couldn't think of anything she needed to do. Abram would bring the sawhorses and planks for the refreshment table when he and Charlotte came, and Mrs. Carver would bring the cookies. Elizabeth Allen had promised to bring a large pot of hot coffee from the Northern Hotel.

"How is the bank?" she asked Adam, trying to avoid answering the question.

He smiled, his gaze filled with a knowing look. "I thought Reverend Lahaye would be here."

"Oh?" Emmy lifted her eyebrows, but avoided looking at him, lest he discern the hitch in her emotions at the mention of Ben.

"I'm happy he's not."

Emmy took a quick breath. "Maybe it's time for you to be on your way. If one of the board members found you here…" She let the comment trail away, hoping he'd get her meaning and be a gentleman.

"I'll go," he said. "But not before I ask you one more time if you'll allow me to escort you to the Christmas Eve ball."

She shook her head. "My answer has not changed. I don't plan to attend."

He nodded and let out a sigh. "I thought you'd say that."

Emmy felt it only right to be honest with him. "I appreciate your friendship, Mr. Russell—"

"Adam."

"Adam." She smiled. "But you must know that I am committed to my job and I have no intentions to enter into a romantic relationship." Her cheeks warmed at being so frank, but she couldn't have him pursuing her any longer. "I appreciate your friendship, but that's all I will allow."

He studied her with his green eyes, gentleness softening his features. "Thank you for your honesty."

She wanted to sigh in relief that he understood, instead, she moved toward the door and he followed. When she stopped to open it, he put out his hand and placed it on her arm.

"I understand you completely," he said. "But I would still very much like to pursue our friendship."

"So would I."

"I'll be back later, Miss Emmy." He reached for the doorknob and let himself out of the school.

Emmy closed the door and leaned against it, thankful their conversation had gone so much better than she had feared.

The door started to open again, and Emmy jumped back, her heart sinking into her stomach. Ben?

Mr. Samuelson stood outside the schoolhouse, his eyes narrowed on her even before he said hello.

"Miss Wilkes?"

"Mr. Samuelson." She swallowed hard. "Won't you come in?" She stepped aside and allowed him to pass into the school. His five children followed him inside and Emmy didn't miss the smirks Annabeth and Margareta sent in her direction.

She closed the door and faced him, trying to mask the fear snaking up her legs. Had he seen Adam leave?

Mr. Samuelson looked around the schoolhouse and then back at her. "I see you're alone."

"Yes." She didn't dare move. "I decided to stay after school to prepare for tonight's social."

"I suppose it was easier to be alone with Mr. Russell here, rather than at the parsonage."

She shook her head, forcing herself to smile. "He saw the light on and thought he'd stop by to help me, but I quickly sent him on his way."

Mr. Samuelson did not return her smile, and neither did his children—all of whom were students of hers.

"Would you care to warm yourselves by the stove?" she asked. "I could take your wraps if you intend to stay until the frolic begins."

"I decided to come see for myself what all the fuss is about these frolics, or whatever you call such nonsense. I can see now I made the right decision in coming early."

"Are people making a fuss about the Friday Frolics?" she tried to make her tone as light and innocent as possible—though why she would feel guilty over Adam's visit was beyond her. She hadn't invited him to come.

"Don't change the subject, Miss Wilkes."

Emmy closed her mouth.

"You were warned, several times, about entertaining gentlemen callers—here or anywhere else."

She did not contradict him, knowing it would not go well.

"Well?" he asked. "What do you have to say for yourself?"

Emmy looked at the children who eyed her with unveiled disdain.

"Must we discuss this in front of my students?" she asked through tight lips.

"I don't see why not. I use every opportunity to teach my children morality and decency. This will be a good example of the type of wanton behavior my daughters will learn to avoid."

"Wanton?" Emmy's mouth fell open, her anger mounting. "Mr. Russell stopped by in a gentlemanly attempt to help. I sent him on his way. There is nothing wanton about my behavior and I resent your accusation."

The door opened and Mrs. Carver entered with Ben and the boys close behind. Ben carried an empty platter in one hand, and a sack in the other—no doubt full of cookies.

"My lands," Mrs. Carver said as she stomped her feet. "The wind is liable to freeze a campfire."

Ben closed the door behind their little group, but paused when he caught sight of Mr. Samuelson. His concerned gaze went to Emmy's face and she didn't try to mask her frustration or anger at the superintendent.

"What's going on?" Ben asked.

Mrs. Carver also glanced at Emmy, but she turned the boys away and brought them to the hooks where she helped them take off their coats and scarves, talking in hushed tones, no doubt to distract them from the adult conversation.

"I caught Miss Wilkes with yet *another* man." Mr. Samuelson crossed his arms, a self-righteous look on his face. "Her wanton behavior is grounds for termination."

"Wanton?" Ben frowned, glancing at the Samuelson children who looked on eagerly. "Isn't that a harsh accusation?"

The door opened again, and Adam walked into the schoolhouse. "I saw the others started to arrive—" He paused as he took in the heated looks of those assembled.

"Mr. Russell," Mr. Samuelson said. "Just the man I wanted to see."

Emmy suppressed a groan, but knew she must not show any signs of impropriety.

"Mr. Russell?" Ben looked at the other man, his frown deepening.

"I saw this man leaving the schoolhouse moments before I arrived," Mr. Samuelson accused. "He was alone here with Miss Wilkes, for who knows how long."

"Just a few minutes," Emmy said.

Ben studied Emmy for a moment, and then he sighed and set the tray and sack of cookies on a nearby bench. He addressed Mr. Samuelson. "Dennis. Your mistrust in Miss Wilkes is unfounded. She has not once acted inappropriately and it is a dishonor to her reputation to make such wild accusations."

Adam looked from one person to the next, his bewilderment evident. Finally, he looked at Emmy and realization seemed to dawn. "They think...?" He didn't finish and Emmy couldn't bear to look him in the eyes.

Her cheeks warmed and she wanted to crawl under her desk to get away from the stares Mr. Samuelson and his children sent in her direction.

"The others will soon arrive," Ben said to Mr. Samuelson. "We will put this behind us and have a good time this evening. Miss Wilkes has put a lot of effort into these social events and we will not wreck it with such nonsense." His voice was firm as he continued. "I will personally vouch for Miss Wilkes's reputation, and if you have anything else you'd like to discuss about this situation, you can take it to me."

There was such finality in his voice, no one said another word.

The door opened once again and the Coopers crossed the threshold with their five children in tow. The cloakroom was filled to capacity.

Emmy forced a smile on her face and greeted the young family as Mrs. Carver and Ben led the Samuelsons into the classroom.

Emmy's stomach growled again and she recalled her potato, which was surely burned by now, but it was the least of her worries. If she wasn't careful, she'd be out of a job, and then what would she do? Return to Massachusetts? To what, her parents? Their disappointment in her decision to come west had ruined any chance she might have at reconciling a healthy relationship. The only other thing that would greet her if she returned were her painful memories of losing William too soon.

No. She would lift her chin and pray Mr. Samuelson would listen to Ben.

The last of the singers departed the schoolhouse and Ben crouched down to bank the fire in the stove as Emmy blew out the lanterns. They had followed the same pattern for the past few Friday Frolics, taking their time getting home.

He wondered what they would possibly find to talk about tonight.

They had not shared more than a few necessary words between them since he had warmed her hands the day before. All throughout the singing, their gazes had met, and each time it felt like Ben had been punched in the gut. He believed her when she said nothing happened with her and Adam, yet he couldn't stop wondering if there was something going on between them. She hadn't turned Adam away like she had all the other men who had made their intentions toward her known, so what did that mean? Was she entertaining the possibility of a romantic relationship with the banker?

Ben tried not to let his thoughts go any farther than that. Three years ago, when he had fallen in love with Charlotte, he had watched her pine after Abram, though she hadn't realized that's what she was doing at first. The same thing happened two years later with Elizabeth and Jude. Was it the same with Emmy? Was she falling in love with Adam and still in denial?

Ben was a fool to let himself have feelings for another woman who was out of reach.

Emmy moved about the schoolhouse silently, but she stopped before extinguishing the last lantern. "Are you ready?" she asked softly.

Ben closed the door of the stove and it squeaked in protest. "I am."

She cupped her hand behind the lantern's chimney and blew out the light.

The schoolhouse became dark and Ben walked up the aisle toward the cloakroom where their coats were waiting.

He reached for her coat and held it out for her.

"Thank you," she said as she slipped her arms inside and then took a step away from him to button it.

They worked in silence as they put on their scarves, mittens and caps.

Emmy opened the door and stepped out into the starry darkness. Ben followed, surprised to find the temperature had risen since they went inside. His breath still billowed out in a cloud, but the air no longer bit at his skin.

He heard her sigh of wonder as she paused on the top step, her gaze lifted to the sky.

Ben also looked up, his breath hitching at the glorious sight above them.

Millions of stars sparkled overhead, their brilliance giving glory to their Creator. Tiny pinpricks of light, winking at them as if they held a secret they wouldn't share.

"Why does the sky look so much brighter in the winter when I'm less likely to sit outside and enjoy it?" she mused.

"I suppose it's one of the great injustices of the ages," he teased.

She took her key out of her reticule and inserted it into the lock. With a quick twist, she secured the door, and then put the key back into her bag. "Shall we?" she asked as she stepped down the stairs, not waiting for his assistance.

They walked in silence over the icy boardwalks and snow-covered streets.

"I've been meaning to show you something," he said tentatively. "Maybe it will make up for all the blunders I've made this week."

"Ben." She stopped and looked up at him.

He lifted his hand and shook his head. "Let's leave it all behind us. I want to take you somewhere special."

She studied him for a moment and then finally nodded. "All right."

Stepping off the boardwalk, he offered his arm to her. "It's this way."

There were people out this evening, some coming and going from the Northern Hotel, others on their way to the saloon, no doubt. Since the vigilance committee had routed out the desperadoes from town the year before, there had been relative peace in Little Falls. Ben was still cautious, but he wasn't as concerned about their safety as he would have been a year ago.

"Where are you taking me?" Emmy asked, her hand secure around his arm as they walked west on Broadway.

"It's a surprise."

She didn't ask any more questions as they made their way toward the Mississippi.

Though it was cold, the water still flowed in the center of the river. Ice ran along the edges and would soon cover the expanse completely. The river wasn't very wide there. If the sound of the rushing water wasn't so loud, he could probably scream across and be heard on the opposite bank.

Ben directed her to take a left onto Wood Street and they descended a slope. The stars offered enough light for them to see their way as he brought her to the waterfalls that gave the town its name.

Under the stars, the river took on a dreamlike state. The water rushed over the rock outcropping, crashing down in a tumultuous dance, tossing and turning on its journey south.

"It's beautiful," she said on a feather-like breath, the roar of the waterfalls almost drowning the sound.

"The Chippewa Indians called this place KaKaBikans, which means 'the little squarely cutoff rock,'" Ben said, his voice lowered, almost in reverence for this place his ancestors had respected and honored for so many generations. "It is one of only four waterfalls on the Mississippi, and the largest source of power north of St. Anthony Falls near St. Paul."

A sawmill and gristmill were now crowding the banks of the river, and a log boom and millpond hindered its original beauty, but it was still a sight to behold.

"Thank you for bringing me here," Emmy said to Ben.

Ben looked down at her, loving how the starlight reflected in her eyes. He took a step back, forcing himself to put space between them. "Are you ready to go home?"

She shivered, but shook her head. "Not yet."

He wanted to put his arm around her, to offer warmth, but he refrained. The cold meant little to him as he stood so close to her. Nothing seemed to bother him when Emmy was near—nothing, but Adam Russell.

The reminder of their earlier trouble returned to Ben.

"I'll speak to Mr. Samuelson tomorrow," Ben said. "It's not right that he is slandering your name."

Emmy closed her eyes briefly. "It's unfortunate that he arrived when he did—both times. It's almost as if he's watching and waiting to catch me doing something wrong."

"What *was* Adam doing there?"

"He stopped by to see if I needed help. I invited him in to warm his hands before sending him on his way."

"That's all that happened?"

Emmy turned to face Ben, an injured look on her face. "Do you doubt my integrity, as well?"

"Of course not," he said quickly. "I just need to make sure I know exactly what occurred when I speak to Dennis."

Her shoulders relaxed and she nodded in understanding.

The soft breeze played with the curls around her face as she shivered again.

"I should get you back home," he said begrudgingly. "But, before we go—" He paused, unsure how to tell her what he wanted to say. "I'd like to start over."

"Start over?" She looked up at him, confusion wedged into her brow.

"The past couple of days have been awkward, and we'd both be lying if we denied it."

She lowered her gaze. "People don't speak of such things, Ben."

"Why not?" He shook his head, not wanting anything between them left unspoken. "Life is too short for pretenses, isn't that what I told you when you first came to town?" His voice teased. "You agreed with me then."

Her lips turned up in a charming smile. "I suppose I did agree with you."

"Does that mean you're willing to start fresh and put everything behind us?"

She played with her mitted hands, still not meeting his gaze. "I don't know if we can start over."

Regret stabbed at his insides. "Why not?"

"I told you that I am devoted to my teaching and nothing else."

"And?"

She finally looked up at him. "I've never told you why."

"So tell me now." He put his hand on her arm, hoping he wouldn't scare her away, but allow her to trust him. "I value your friendship and I want to do everything in my power to help you find happiness."

Her gaze caressed his face and she offered him a sweet smile.

Another breath of wind blew against them, and she wrapped her arms around her waist.

He took his hand away from her arm, giving her space to tell her story.

"I was engaged five years ago to a man named William Harrison," she said. "We had known each other for years and our love had grown slowly, but deeply."

The realization that she had given her heart to another man hurt him in ways it shouldn't, yet he held no claim on her now, or in the past.

"We had such plans." She shook her head, a smile on her lips, but tears in her voice. "We were going to go west. First to St. Louis and then on to California. I was teaching to earn money, and he was working even harder at the blacksmith where he was an apprentice. As soon as he was ready to strike out on his own, we would get married. My hope chest was bursting with all the things I would need to start a home." She paused and looked back at Ben. "We set our wedding date and I had two days left to teach school before we would be married and start west. I was in the middle of an arithmetic lesson when the door banged open and my father stood on the threshold. William had been shoeing a horse and it had kicked him in the head. He was asking for me, so my father had come—but by the time I got to him, he was gone."

She looked away, nibbling on her lip as a tear slipped from her eye. "I didn't get to say goodbye, and in one day all my dreams had died."

Ben wanted to pull her close and offer comfort, but would she let him? He put his arms around her to protect her from the memories that brought her such pain. She shivered in his embrace, but didn't pull away. Instead, she leaned into him and he rubbed his hands up and down her back to warm her.

"I fell into a dark hole inside," she said against his

chest. "And it took years for me to climb out. There were days I didn't think I would survive the devastation, but slowly, with God's help, I did survive." She pulled back to look at him, though she didn't pull away completely. "And I promised myself I would never fall in love again, Ben. It's a promise I aim to keep because I'm afraid that if I was forced to endure the same kind of pain, I would sink back into that hole and never climb out again."

They looked at one another for a few heartbeats. "I'm sorry, Emmy."

She wiped at her cheeks. "I'm sorry, too, Ben. I care about you, very much, but I think it's time I start looking for another place to live."

Her words were both surprising and exactly what he had suspected she'd say. "I wish it could be different."

"So do I."

Without another word, he led her away from the river, past Abram and Charlotte's home, and up the old wagon road toward the parsonage where he would soon be alone once again.

Chapter Thirteen

On Monday morning, Emmy sat behind her desk and quietly observed each of her students as they worked. She had given them some free time to catch up on their lessons, or work quietly in groups of two or three, if they needed help. It gave the older children the opportunity to help the younger children and freed Emmy up for some one-on-one time with those who needed a little extra attention.

Today, however, no one needed her, which she was thankful for. She had asked Mr. Samuelson to meet with her during the children's recess time, and she could hardly think straight beyond what she needed to say to him. The memory of standing with Ben at the waterfall, knowing she was too weak to say no forever, prompted her to make a decision she didn't want to make.

She was leaving the parsonage, and she needed Mr. Samuelson's help finding somewhere else to live.

Her gaze wandered to the front row where Levi and Zeb sat. She would miss eating meals with them and playing games in the evenings, tucking them into bed at night and hearing their prayers, and then waking up to the sound of them whispering in their bedroom in the mornings. Most of all, she'd miss their sweet laughter.

Emmy swallowed back a rush of emotions she didn't expect and bit her bottom lip to prevent herself from exhibiting her pain in front of her student.

Sunshine poured in through the side windows, shining bright on the five first-year students sitting in the front row next to Levi and Zeb. The twins sat side by side in the middle, with Brett Morgan next to Zeb and little Maggie Ritters on the other side of Levi.

As Levi worked alone on his sums, Brett was helping Zeb. Brett and Zeb's friendship had grown over the past few weeks, and Emmy had been happy to see Zeb reaching out to other classmates.

Levi, on the other hand, had not made a single friend. He was very intelligent and caught on to his lessons quickly. He had moved ahead of Zeb at a steady pace and didn't struggle like Zeb to understand.

Emmy sighed as she put her chin in her hand and watched Levi scowl at Zeb and Brett out of the corner of his eye. It was evident that he was jealous of Zeb's friendships, and Emmy suspected that Levi wanted to reach out to the other children, too, he just didn't know how.

"Levi." Maggie tugged on the sleeve of the new shirt Mrs. Carver had sewn for him, her brown ringlets bouncing with the effort. "Would you like to play tag during recess?"

Levi's frown deepened and he shook his head. "I don't like tag."

"What about hide-and-seek?"

He shook his head again, not bothering to look at her. "No."

Maggie's mouth turned down. "What do you like to play?"

"Nothing with you."

The pain on Maggie's face almost broke Emmy's heart—yet she knew Levi hadn't meant to be hurtful. His own pain was making him unhappy.

Emmy straightened in her seat. "Levi, would you please come to my desk?"

Levi looked up quickly, his green eyes going round at being summoned by the teacher. He stood and set his slate on the seat, and then he turned and walked to Emmy slowly.

Empathy and compassion for him and Zeb had always filled her heart. She couldn't imagine what it would be like to lose a mother and then be dropped off at a stranger's house by an aunt who didn't want you. She was proud of all that Ben was doing for the boys, but she long suspected they also needed the soft touch of feminine love, so she had showered it upon them as best as she could, while keeping their relationship at arm's length because she was first and foremost their teacher.

Levi blinked at Emmy, his almond-shaped eyes filled with uncertainty at what she planned to say or do.

Emmy wanted to pull him into her arms and comfort him, yet she knew he also needed some discipline. She had him come close and spoke quietly, so only he could hear.

"I heard what you just said to Maggie."

His facial expression did not change as he watched Emmy.

"Was that kind?" she asked.

"No, Miss Wilkes."

"Then why did you say it?"

"'Cause I don't like playing with girls."

"If you don't want to play, simply say 'no, thank you.'" She tried to make her voice sound as kind as possible. "You wouldn't like someone to tell you what you just told Maggie, would you?"

Tears gathered in Levi's eyes and he tried so hard to blink them away. "They do."

"People say they don't want to play with you?"

He nodded and sniffed hard. "Nobody likes me."

"That's not true." Yet, she hadn't noticed anyone reach out to Levi until today when Maggie asked him to play.

"It is true. They say they don't like me. I don't have any friends."

Emmy sighed and noticed Mr. Samuelson walking toward the school. It must be time to dismiss the children for recess, but she didn't want Levi to feel as if she was dismissing him and his problem. She looked him in the eyes. "Levi, do you know how to make friends?"

He wiped at his nose and shook his head.

"If you want to make a friend, you must be a friend. Do the things you think a friend would do. Ask people questions, find out what they like, let them go first." These were all things she had noticed Levi struggled with. "But, above all, be kind and treat others well."

He nodded, his eyes solemn.

"You are a good, loving and fun little boy." She smiled and all the love she had for him welled up within her and brought tears to her eyes. "You will make a wonderful friend. I just know it."

Levi took a step toward her and put his arms around her neck. "I like how you treat me," he whispered into her ear.

She didn't make it a habit to show affection to her students during school hours, since it was her job to be the disciplinarian—but she couldn't stop herself from wrapping her arms around this little boy. "And I like how you treat me, too."

The door opened and Emmy pulled away from Levi. "Now," she said with a smile in her voice, "go sit and wait to be excused for recess."

"Yes, Miss Wilkes." He turned and walked back to his desk with a skip in his step.

Emmy stood and rapped her ruler against her desk. "Everyone is dismissed for recess. I'll call you inside in fifteen minutes."

The children stood and filed into the cloakroom in a double row. They went to the hooks and put on their outer gear while Mr. Samuelson made his way to the front of the classroom where Emmy stood waiting.

"Miss Wilkes," he said with a curt nod.

"Mr. Samuelson, won't you have a seat?" She motioned to a chair she had pulled from the corner of the room and set next to her desk.

He removed his cap and waited for her to take her seat before he took his.

Emmy clasped her hands on the desktop and waited until the last child had gone outside before addressing the superintendent.

"Thank you for coming." She didn't want to reveal her tumultuous emotions, so she tried to control her voice. "I have a request I'd like to present to you."

"Before you continue, I'd like you to know that Reverend Lahaye came to me on your behalf."

Emmy knew Ben had gone to speak to Mr. Samuelson on Saturday, but she and Ben had barely spoken since then, so she didn't know how it had gone.

"He spoke on your behalf concerning the incident with Mr. Russell and I'll tell you what I told him." Mr.

Samuelson's mustache twitched as he spoke to her. "I will overlook this incident, just as I did the first one, but I am warning you that I will not overlook it again. The next time I catch you alone with a man, you will be immediately terminated."

She hadn't intended to speak to him about this incident, but she couldn't resist. "Both times the men came uninvited. How am I to stop that from happening again?"

He put up his hands, his pompous attitude grating on her nerves. "It's been my experience that men do not approach a woman unless they've been lured. I'd advise you to stop enticing them, and then you won't have to worry about the repercussions."

"Entice? Lured?" Her mouth fell open and she began to stand. "Mr. Samuel—"

"Was there something you wanted to discuss with me?"

It took all her willpower not to slap the arrogance off his face. Of all the callous, ill-mannered men she'd ever met, this one was the worst. Instead, she took a deep breath and lowered herself back into her chair, remembering that he was, first and foremost, her boss. "I am in need of different living arrangements, but I have no desire to return to the Hubbards' boardinghouse. Do you know of somewhere I could live?"

Mr. Samuelson stared at her for several heartbeats, his calculating eyes watching her closely. "Has something happened that I need to be aware of?"

"No." She straightened her back. "I just need somewhere else to live. Mrs. Carver will be leaving after Christmas, so I thought I should begin my search now." It was partially true—and he didn't need to know her other reasons.

"I never thought it was a good idea to have you at the parsonage, anyway." Mr. Samuelson leaned back in his chair and crossed his arms. "I'd prefer you stay with a family, where the temptation to dally isn't as strong."

"Dally?" Did the man think of nothing else?

"I know of one family that has a room they rent out, but I don't know if it's available. I will check and get back to you."

Emmy stood, wanting this meeting to be over with. "Thank you. Now, if you'll excuse me, I have work to do."

The superintendent rose and looked Emmy over from head to foot. "You are a pretty little thing, aren't you?"

Her eyes grew wide as she met his gaze. "Please leave, Mr. Samuelson. You have not only insulted me, you've now made me very uncomfortable." She walked toward the door and opened it wide, her hands trembling from this encounter. "Good day, Mr. Samuelson."

He put his cap on and strode down the aisle, his unpleasant chuckle lingering long after he walked out the door.

With a quick flick of her wrist, she slammed the door behind him. The meeting had been distasteful from beginning to end, and though she was happy it was over, she already dreaded the next time she'd have to see him.

The sunshine warmed Ben's shoulders as he pulled his surprise for the boys and Emmy through the fluffy snow. He waved at Mr. Fadling in the grocer's store window and said hello as he passed Martha Dupree who worked at the Northern Hotel. With the weather so warm, and the sky so clear, dozens of people were moving about town, running errands and enjoying the reprieve from winter's icy grasp.

Up ahead, the schoolhouse stood white and fresh, the coat of paint he and Abram had applied last fall still gleaming under the sun. The windows sparkled and the snow in the school yard was packed tight from the children's feet.

Right on time, the door flew open and the children rushed out, their laughter and excitement making Ben pick up his pace.

Emmy and the boys always stayed after for a few minutes to close the school and get things ready for the following day. After that, they usually went home to do their afternoon chores, which Ben had already done for them.

Today he had a different plan. One he hoped would patch things with him and Emmy, and give the boys a happy memory they could take with them no matter where they ended up.

Ben stopped next to the school and left his surprise outside. He climbed the steps and opened the door. Emmy was at the front of the room, sitting at her desk, and the boys were standing on either side of her. All three had their heads bent together as they looked at a piece of paper on Emmy's desk. She lifted a pencil and made a couple marks. "What do you think of this?"

Levi shook his head. "No, it should be bigger."

"But it can't be much bigger, or it won't fit," Emmy told him. "How about if we do this?" She made a few more marks, and then she looked up at Levi. "Do you like that?"

Zeb noticed Ben first, his eyes growing wide. "Mr. Ben!"

Emmy and Levi snapped their heads up, and Emmy quickly flipped the paper upside down.

"What are you three up to?" he asked.

"It's a surprise," Levi said quickly.

"For Christmas!" Zeb added.

"Boys." Emmy put her finger to her lips. "Shh. We don't want to give him any hints."

They were doing something for him for Christmas? He hadn't even contemplated such a thing. Every year, for the past four years, he'd spent Christmas as a guest of the Coopers.

Would he and Emmy and the boys be together for Christmas? Or would everything change in the next three weeks?

"We've been talking about it for a while," Emmy explained to Ben, her cheeks turning pink. "It's nothing too fancy." She slipped the paper off the desk and into a drawer. "What brings you to school?"

He wanted to tease them and draw out a few more hints, but he suspected the boys weren't good at keeping secrets, so he wouldn't ruin Emmy's fun by asking. Instead, he smiled at them. "I have a surprise waiting outside."

"A surprise?" Levi asked, his eyes getting brighter.

"Yes. Put on your outdoor gear and wait inside until Miss Emmy is ready."

The boys didn't wait for a second invitation. They raced down the aisle and into the cloakroom where they quickly put on their coat, hat, mittens and scarves.

Ben gave his full attention to the pretty teacher. "That is, if you'd like to come with us."

She suddenly looked very busy shuffling papers and books around on her desk. "I don't know if I should."

"Why not?" He asked, disappointment replacing his joy.

"I assigned each child their part for the Christmas pageant today, but I don't have the speaking parts written down yet. I promised the children I would bring them tomorrow so we can start practicing."

"How many speaking parts are there?"

"The narrator, Joseph, the three wise men and the shepherd."

"I'll help you tonight," he promised, "after the boys go to bed." He grinned. "Who better to help than the pastor?"

She smiled and her blue eyes sparkled from the sunshine coming in the windows. "What kind of a surprise is waiting?"

"If you won't tell me what your surprise is, I won't tell you mine."

For a moment, he thought she'd refuse again—but then she rose from her desk chair. "All right, Reverend Lahaye, but don't forget your promise to help me later."

"I don't see how I could." The idea of spending time alone with Emmy was something he'd look forward to all day.

They met the boys in the cloakroom and found them hopping from one foot to the other with impatience.

"What's the surprise, Mr. Ben?" Zeb asked. "Is it a pony?"

"A pony?" Ben lifted his eyebrows as he reached for Emmy's coat and helped her into it. "If you're hoping for a pony, my surprise will pale in comparison."

Emmy buttoned up her thick coat and put on the stylish cap she had knitted over the past couple of weeks. It tied under her chin, much like a bonnet. "It will be wonderful, whatever it is," she laughed.

Levi was so excited, he jumped high in the air and came down on Zeb's foot.

"Ow!" Zeb cried.

"Levi," Ben warned. "You need to be careful."

"I want to hurry," Levi said.

"You still need to be careful."

"Sorry, Zeb," he said quickly.

"I'm almost ready." Emmy wrapped a scarf around her neck and then pulled on her matching mittens. "There," she said. "Let's go."

Ben opened the door and the boys rushed out. Emmy followed, stepping past Ben with a half smile tossed in his direction.

He closed the door and watched as Levi and Zeb raced down the steps.

"It's a sled!" Levi exclaimed.

"With steel runners and everything," Zeb added as he knelt in the snow to examine the sled that Ben had borrowed from Abram's boys. "I've never been sledding."

"Never?" Ben asked.

Levi shook his head.

"I've never been sledding, either." Emmy walked down the steps and admired the sled along with the boys. Her cheeks filled with color and her eyes lit up with delight. "Are you taking the boys sledding?"

"I'm taking all of you," Ben said. "There's a hill perfect for it, just to the south of town. It's such a nice day, I thought we could spend a couple hours playing outside."

The boys cheered and Emmy smiled.

"Here." He held out his hand. "I'll lock up the school and then we'll be on our way."

Emmy gave him the key and he locked the door, and then he handed it back to her and took up the rope on the sled. "Hop on board," he said to the boys. "I'll pull you to the sledding hill."

Levi started to climb onto the front of the sled, but

then he stopped and glanced at Emmy, a sheepish look on his face. "I'll let Zeb ride up front."

Zeb clapped his hands and found his spot, and then Levi climbed on behind him.

"That was very nice," Emmy said to Levi. "Exactly what a friend would do."

Ben wasn't quite sure what their exchange was all about, but he trusted Emmy had everything under control. "We're off," Ben said to the boys, tugging the sled into motion. "Hold on tight!"

The boys clutched the sides of the sled and Ben put the rope over his shoulder, leading the way. Emmy walked beside him, the hem of her gown brushing the top layer of snow, leaving a wide trail behind her.

They walked in silence for the first part of the way. Though the boys laughed with delight, Ben sensed something was on Emmy's mind. As they passed the parsonage, he decided to ask her. "Something wrong?"

She glanced up at him, almost as if she'd lost track of where she was, and who she was with. "It's nothing."

"You're being awfully silent for it to be nothing."

"It's Mr. Samuelson—but I'd rather not discuss it."

"Did he say something unkind to you again?"

She looked up at Ben, appreciation on her face, but she shook her head. "You've done enough. It will be okay."

He wouldn't press the matter if she didn't want to talk about it, though he wished she would let him do more.

"Shall we sing some Christmas songs?" Emmy asked the boys.

They cheered in agreement and she led them in some of Ben's favorites. "I Saw Three Ships," "God Rest You Merry, Gentlemen" and "Joy to the World."

"Have you heard 'One Horse Open Sleigh'?" she asked Ben.

He shook his head.

"It was very popular back east last year when it was first published," she explained. "The chorus goes like this.

Jingle bells, jingle bells,
Jingle all the way;
Oh! what joy it is to ride
In a one horse open sleigh."

She sang it several times for Ben and the boys, and they caught on quickly.

"Now," she said, "I'll sing the verse and you three can sing the chorus, all right?"

"We're ready," Ben said.

She grinned and sang.

"Dashing thro' the snow
In a one horse open sleigh,
O'er the hills we go,
Laughing all the way;
Bells on bobtail ring,
Making spirits bright,
Oh what sport to ride and sing
A sleighing song tonight!"

She pointed at the boys and they sang.

"Jingle bells, jingle bells,
Jingle all the way;
Oh! what joy it is to ride
In a one horse open sleigh."

Emmy continued, her voice and face animated.

"A day or two ago
I thought I'd take a ride
And soon Miss Fannie Bright
Was seated by my side,
The horse was lean and lank
Misfortune seemed his lot
He got into a drifted bank
And we, we got up sot."

The boys giggled as Emmy and Ben sang the chorus. Emmy grinned, and continued.

"A day or two ago,
The story I must tell
I went out on the snow,
And on my back I fell;
A gent was riding by
In a one horse open sleigh,
He laughed as there I sprawling lie,
But quickly drove away."

Levi giggled so hard, he almost fell off the sled, but they managed to sing the chorus again, this time with great gusto.

"One more," Emmy said out of breath, her cheeks filled with color.

"Now the ground is white
Go it while you're young,
Take the girls tonight
and sing this sleighing song;
Just get a bobtailed bay

Two forty is his speed
Hitch him to an open sleigh
And crack! You'll take the lead."

Emmy joined them in singing the chorus one last time. By then, they were all laughing and singing loud enough for people to stop and take notice.

The sun was warmer than Ben had first thought, and with the exertion of pulling the boys, he could have easily removed his jacket and still been comfortable. With the added heat, the snow had become sticky—perfect for building a snowman.

Out of breath from singing, Ben finally stopped and pointed to the hill. "There it is, boys."

Levi and Zeb rolled off the sled and stood to take a look.

The top was level with the main road, but it sloped down to a flat bottom that was level with the river, just off in the distance. It wasn't too steep, but it wasn't too gentle, either. About two hundred feet of gradual hillside—perfect for sledding.

"I'm first!" Levi called.

"No, I'm first!" Zeb said.

"Ladies first." Ben grinned at the boys. "Miss Emmy will be the first to try out the sled."

Emmy's eyes grew round. "I wouldn't know how to steer it or stop it. I'd crash for sure. You or the boys can take it down and I'll just watch."

"Nonsense," Ben said. "I don't want you to just watch."

"You take her down," Levi said to Ben. "You can show her how to steer."

Ben looked at Emmy. "Would you like me to go down with you the first time?"

Emmy looked from Ben, to the sled, to the hill. "I don't need to sled today."

"Please, Miss Emmy," Zeb begged.

"You have to," Levi added.

After a moment, she finally sighed. "All right. Show me how it's done, Mr. Ben."

Ben winked at the boys and then he positioned the sled where he wanted it to go. It was long and narrow, perfect for more than one person.

"Where do I sit?" Emmy asked.

"In the front. I'll sit behind you."

He held the sled for her and she took a seat in the front, tucking her wide skirts all around her.

Levi scrunched up his face. "Why do girls wear so much stuff?"

"It's called modesty," Emmy said to Levi. "And fashion—though who determines fashion is beyond me. These wide skirts are not very sensible."

"I think you look pretty," Zeb said, his cheeks turning pink from more than just cold.

Ben wanted to agree, but he kept his thoughts to himself.

After Emmy secured all the material, Ben took the spot behind her. "I'll need to reach around you and hold the rope," he said close to her ear. "Is that all right?"

A slight nod was all she offered, so he reached around her and took the rope in his mitted hands. "Okay, boys." He looked up at their smiling faces. "Give us a push."

"Wait!" Emmy said. "Don't I need some instructions first?"

Zeb and Levi didn't wait, but pushed against Ben's back, putting the sled into motion.

"Just hold on tight," Ben told her as they crested the top of the hill.

Before the words were out of his mouth, the sled picked up speed and started swishing down the hill.

Emmy squealed and grabbed Ben's arms, her grip stronger than he would have expected. The force of the momentum pushed her back, causing her to lean into his arms. She continued to squeal and Ben smiled, tightening his hold on her. Faster and faster they went, the wind rushing past them, and the landscape flashing by. Snow blew into his face, melting against his skin.

Before they even reached the bottom, Emmy's squeals turned into delightful laughter, her hold on his arms loosened, though she didn't let go completely. When they finally came to a stop at the bottom of the hill, she still leaned against him, breathing hard, her laughter slowly subsiding as she wiped snow off her face.

"That," she said, sitting up straight, "was incredible."

Ben stood and waved at the boys, who jumped for joy at the top of the hill, waiting impatiently for their turn. He offered his hand to help Emmy stand, loving the way her face glowed. "I'm happy you liked it."

She took his hand and tried to stand, but her foot caught on the material of her gown, and she started to trip. Ben tried to save her, but they both ended up falling into a drift of snow.

She giggled and he laughed as he stared up at the bright blue sky.

When he turned to look at her, he found that she was smiling at him.

"Thank you," she said. "I won't soon forget this."

"That's what I'd hoped."

It felt good to be laughing with her again.

Chapter Fourteen

Emmy sat at the table in the front room, a lantern offering enough light for her to write. The fireplace crackled behind her and another snowstorm had moved in, piling snow outside the window. Frost etched the edges of the glass and painted beautiful winter scenes with feathery white ice.

Levi and Zeb sat on the rug in front of the fireplace looking through a picture book Emmy had pulled from her trunk. It was filled with paintings from Africa. Lions, elephants, straw huts and dark-skinned people were but some of the mysteries they'd never seen before.

Ben's home was so cozy and much more inviting than her own home had been growing up. This house was exactly what she had pictured when she and William had dreamed of coming west. It wasn't grand, by any means, but it was elegant in its simplicity. There wasn't an unnecessary room or superfluous piece of furniture, and everything was well cared for and dearly loved. Even the piles of books were stacked with care, having been read and reread several times—nothing wasted.

Emmy paused in her musing, realizing that it was

the first time she'd thought of William and not had a pang of grief hit her or dampen her mood.

Mrs. Carver opened the kitchen door and entered the front room wiping the back of her hand across her forehead. "I'm about through," she said with a sigh. "My throats been hurting something awful today."

Emmy rose from the chair. "Are you running a fever?"

Ben exited the kitchen, two coffee mugs in hand. He set them down on the table where Emmy had been working. "I told her to go to bed an hour ago, but she insisted on finishing her work."

Zeb left his picture book and walked up to Mrs. Carver, taking her hand in his small one. "Would you like me to help you up the stairs?"

She patted his head. "That won't be necessary, dearie, but thank you for the offer."

"I'll see that the boys are put to bed," Ben told her. "You should take yourself upstairs and get some rest. If you don't feel better in the morning, stay in bed and don't try to get up. If you think you need to see Dr. Jodan, I'd be happy to fetch him."

Mrs. Carver waved his concern aside. "No need to go to all that fuss. I'll be right as rain in the morning." She hugged Zeb and then motioned Levi over. "Hug my tired bones and be good for Reverend Lahaye."

Levi hugged the housekeeper and then she waddled to the stairs and disappeared.

"I hope she feels better in the morning," Emmy said. "I've heard several people have been sick this week and Dr. Jodan is having a hard time trying to keep up."

"I'll pray for her tonight," Zeb said. "God will heal her."

"God didn't heal Mama," Levi countered, though

there was no censure in his voice—just a matter-of-fact statement.

It was the first time Emmy had heard either boy talk about their mother. "What was her name?"

Levi scrunched up his face in thought, but then he shook his head. "I don't know."

"It was Clara," Ben supplied.

The twins looked at Ben.

"Clara?" Zeb asked.

"And your pa's name is Malachi." Ben looked down at the boys, watching their reactions.

"Did our pa die, too?" Levi asked.

Ben sat on his rocking chair and motioned the boys to come over. He pulled them up on his lap, first Levi and then Zeb. "Your pa didn't die. I'm trying to find him, so he can take care of you once again."

Levi's eyebrows pulled together in a frown. "Don't you want us, Mr. Ben?"

From the look on Ben's face, Emmy could tell the question hit him hard.

"Of course I want you," he said gently. "But you don't belong to me. I'm only taking care of you until we can find your pa."

Zeb snuggled into Ben's embrace and put his head against Ben's shoulder. "I like living here, Mr. Ben. Can you be our pa?"

Levi didn't snuggle in, but he looked up at Ben with such hope and adoration, Emmy's throat grew tight.

Ben must have felt the same way, because he took a few moments before answering the boy. "I wish I could be your pa, but I don't have a wife and it wouldn't be right to raise you without a mother."

"Can't Miss Emmy be our ma?" Zeb asked, peeking out at Emmy from where he was safely ensconced in Ben's arms.

Ben looked up at Emmy, affection in his eyes. "Miss Emmy is a teacher, and besides, it wouldn't be right to keep you away from your pa."

Levi sighed and then he, too, leaned into Ben's embrace. He rested his cheek on Ben's chest and looked at his twin brother. "I don't think anyone wants us, Zebby."

Tears sprang up in Emmy's eyes and she moved across the floor to kneel in front of the boys. "We want you," she said in a trembling voice. "We love you. But we can't keep you, because your pa will want you."

Ben looked down at Emmy, his own eyes glistening with unshed tears. He repositioned Levi so he could look into his face. "I know exactly how you feel, Levi. I didn't think I was wanted when I was a boy, either. My pa left me with strangers, too. But you know what I learned?"

Both Levi and Zeb sat up straighter.

"What?" Levi asked.

"I learned that no matter what, God wanted me, and that was more important than anything else." He smiled at Levi and then at Zeb. "I want both of you to know that God loves you and He wants you desperately. All you need to do is ask His son Jesus to live in your heart forever, and He will. You'll never be alone again."

Zeb and Levi shared a wide-eyed look, and then Zeb tapped Ben's arm. "Mr. Ben?"

"Yes, Zeb?"

"I want Jesus to live in my heart forever." He took Levi's hand and said, "Levi wants Him, too. Don't you, Levi?"

Levi nodded, his face solemn.

"Then let's close our eyes and each of you can ask Jesus to live in your hearts."

Levi looked at Emmy. "Will you pray with us, too, Miss Emmy?"

"I'd love to pray with you."

"Then close your eyes," Levi said in a whisper. "'Cause I'm gonna ask Him now."

Emmy's chest felt tight with joy as she closed her eyes, a smile on her lips.

"Dear Jesus," Levi started. "I don't want to be alone ever again. Will you live in my heart forever?"

Silence filled the room for a heartbeat and then Levi whispered, "Did He say yes, Mr. Ben?"

"Jesus always says yes when we ask Him to live in our hearts."

"Good. Now it's Zeb's turn."

Zeb took a deep breath and then he forged ahead. "I want you, too, Jesus, just like Levi." He paused and then said, "Amen."

"Amen," Emmy and Ben echoed in unison.

She opened her eyes and met Ben's happy gaze.

"Miss Emmy's crying," Levi said. "Are you sad?"

"No." She wiped the tears from her cheeks and then stood to pick up Levi. "I'm happier than I've ever been."

Levi wrapped himself around her and gave her a tight hug. "I love you, Miss Emmy."

"I love you, Levi." She held him for a moment longer and then set him down and picked up Zeb. "I love you, too, Zebby."

He giggled as he hugged her back.

Ben stood and wiped at his face, too, though he hid his emotion better than Emmy did. "Tomorrow we can tell Mrs. Carver the good news, but for now, it's time to tuck you into bed. Miss Emmy and I have some work to do tonight."

Emmy sighed as she set Zeb down. "I suppose Mr. Ben is right."

They followed the boys up the stairs and into their bedroom. Ben had grabbed the lantern from near the front door, so they had light to help the boys get ready for bed.

With one more quick kiss for each boy, Emmy tucked them into their bed and then she and Ben said good-night and left their room.

The hallway was drafty as Emmy closed their bed-room door.

"I've told countless people about the love of God," Ben said in a hushed whisper as they stood in the hall. "But never, in my whole life, have I felt such a rush of joy as I did tonight listening to those boys ask the Lord into their lives." He shook his head. "I don't think I'll ever forget that moment."

"Maybe," Emmy said just as quietly, "the reason God sent them here was for this very reason. Even if that's the only reason, it's more than—"

"More than enough," he finished for her, his voice gentle.

She smiled, happy for the twins, happy for Ben and happy she had been there to witness such a tender moment.

"Thank you, Emmy." He reached out and touched her cheek for a heartbeat and then lowered his hand.

"For what?" she asked.

"For loving those two little boys."

"It's been my pleasure."

His face became pensive under the soft glow of the lantern.

"What?" she asked.

"I just wish I had heard from their father by now." His voice was so low, she had to lean in to hear him. "I need to make some decision before Mrs. Carver leaves in three short weeks."

"What will you do?"

"I'm thinking about going to Owatonna to see if I can find him."

"I hate to think of you traveling in weather like this. What if a blizzard comes up?"

He smiled, and the look of affection returned. "I'm honored that you would worry about my safety, but you need to remember that I was a circuit preacher for ten years. I'm familiar with traveling in all types of weather."

She didn't care how much experience he had on the open trail, she'd still worry about him until he returned safely. The thought of losing Ben made her stomach clench in an old, dreadful way, just like it did when she had worried for William—and look what happened to him.

Emmy's breathing became shallow and panic threatened to invade as she suddenly realized that despite her best efforts, she had allowed Ben into a corner of her heart that she had tried to keep closed. What would she do if he broke past her barriers and overtook it all?

"Shall we go downstairs and get to work on the pageant?" she asked, needing some distance from this man who had snuck past her defenses.

She didn't wait for his answer, but walked around him and started down the narrow stairs.

The sooner Mr. Samuelson found her another place to live, the better. It was getting harder and harder to keep her heart safe from Benjamin Lahaye.

* * *

Ben didn't want to wait a moment longer than necessary to leave for Owatonna. The next afternoon, when Emmy and the boys were still at school, he packed his old saddlebags for the trip.

Mrs. Carver was still feeling ill, but she insisted on getting out of bed and going about her regular chores. The smell of fresh-baked bread wafted into his bedroom and his stomach growled. She was making him more food than was necessary for his trip, but he wouldn't complain. It was better than the hardtack he used to carry with him when he rode his circuit. Then, he had been forced to depend on the kindness of friends and strangers for most of his meals. He smiled at the memory, missing the old days—yet, he wouldn't trade his time with Emmy and the boys for anything in the world.

Though he didn't plan to leave until early the next morning, he wanted to have everything ready to go tonight so he could spend the evening enjoying his temporary family.

He had just slipped his small Bible into one of the bags when he heard a knock at the front door.

"I'll get that," he called to Mrs. Carver.

"I'm already on my way, dearie."

Ben was thankful for Mrs. Carver, wishing she could stay on permanently, but knowing he wouldn't need her after he located the boys' father.

The front door squeaked open.

"May I help you?" Mrs. Carver asked.

"Is this the home of Benjamin Lahaye?" The man's deep voice had a French accent.

"This is Reverend Lahaye's home. May I ask who's calling?"

Ben already knew he was needed, so he stepped out of his room and closed the door behind him.

"My name is Phillippe Lahaye. I'm Benjamin's father."

Ben held his bedroom doorknob, his heart beating like a wild drum. His father?

Slowly, he let go of the doorknob and turned around. Mrs. Carver stepped back, allowing Ben to look at his father for the first time in over twenty-five years.

"Benjamin?" Phillippe Lahaye was a mountain of a man. He filled the door frame, and the very room, with a presence unlike any other. His gray beard was thick and long, reaching down to his chest. His clothes were made of buckskin leather and he wore a large buffalo robe, much like the one Ben owned. The man before him didn't resemble the memory Ben had of his father—yet, he didn't doubt this *was* his father, simply older.

Ben was at a loss for words. He had imagined this scene a thousand times, yet he never believed it would actually happen—and without warning.

"Will you invite the man in?" Mrs. Carver asked. "Or should we continue to heat the great outdoors, dearie?"

It took a moment for Ben to find his voice, but he nodded. "Come in."

Phillippe entered Ben's house with a tentative step, looking around the humble room with a keen gaze.

"Shall I take your robe?" Mrs. Carver asked as she shut the door. "Would you like something to eat? Perhaps to drink?"

"We're fine," Ben said to his housekeeper. "If you could give us some privacy, that's all we need right now."

She nodded and then left the front room, closing the

kitchen door behind her—though he suspected she was still listening intently.

Phillippe didn't move as he looked Ben over, a combination of awe and disbelief in his dark brown eyes. "I can hardly reconcile this man standing before me. Last time I saw you—"

"Do you remember the last time you saw me?" The question came out harsher than Ben had anticipated—yet he didn't want to take it back. Decades of pain, abandonment and rejection returned to Ben in one instant and he was overwhelmed with the weight of his emotions. "I was six years old. Do you remember? I do, like it was yesterday."

Sadness, deep and fierce, filled his father's eyes. "There hasn't been a day, from that one to this one, that I haven't thought about you and your mother."

There was so much Ben wanted to say—yet, he couldn't think of a single thing that would make anything better. Every word that wanted to come to his tongue was laced with bitterness and anger. They would get nowhere if he uttered what was on his heart. The enormity of it frightened him. "What do you want? Why are you here after all these years?"

"I've come for several reasons." He looked toward the fireplace, which was blazing with heat, and Ben knew he should invite him to have a seat, warm himself by the fire and offer him some nourishment. No doubt he had been traveling for a long time and would need somewhere to stay—but none of these things mattered to Ben right now. All he could think about was the pain this man had caused him.

Ben crossed his arms and planted his feet, unwilling to give him even the slightest comfort.

"I hear you're a man of God." Phillippe nodded his approval. "That's good, son, real good."

His father's statement made Ben feel deflated. He was a man of God, and God probably wasn't too pleased with Ben at the moment. He loosened his stance and indicated the fireplace. "Would you like to warm yourself by the fire? I will take your robe and have Mrs. Carver bring you something to eat and drink."

"I'd like that." He took off his buffalo robe and Ben set it on the hook by the door.

A few minutes later, Ben and Phillippe sat near the fire, a plate of Mrs. Carver's stew on their laps, and mugs of her steaming coffee on the hearth before them.

Ben wasn't hungry, but Phillippe ate heartily. Time had been kind to him, Ben realized as he watched him. He was still a healthy-looking man, even handsome, Ben supposed.

"I came all the way from Montreal," Phillippe said to Ben. "I left a month ago and was surprised by the early winter."

"We all were."

Phillippe mopped up the stew with a thick slice of fresh bread. "I haven't eaten like this since I left home."

"Is your wife a good cook?" Ben heard the sarcasm in his voice and immediately wished to recall the words—or, at least, the tone.

"Juliette?" He scoffed. "She hasn't cooked a day in her life. I have a cook, Jean Claude, but he doesn't make stew like this."

"I'll be sure to pass on your compliment to Mrs. Carver." His tone was dry, flat.

Phillippe set aside his dish and took up his coffee mug. He turned to look at Ben. "I suppose I should tell you why I've come."

"I wish you would."

Phillippe cleared his throat and let out a sigh. "I had three daughters and a son in Montreal with Juliette. After I left you at Pokegama, I planned to leave the fur trading business behind. I had already made my fortune and I had no desire to return to all the memories here."

Ben couldn't look this man in the face as he recounted his life. Phillipe had left heartache in his wake, but Ben didn't think his father would ever truly understand how his actions had affected him. Ben set down his stew, knowing he could never stomach it.

"I didn't return to trapping, but I did stay in the fur trade. I became an outfitter and made yet another fortune."

While his father had gained wealth, Ben had received charity from the Ayers and other missionaries who had taken pity on him. Was his father trying to rub salt in his wounded soul?

Phillippe looked down at his coffee mug, grief in the lines of his face. "My son, Sébastien, was to inherit my business and all my wealth, but he died, very recently, and I find I am without an heir."

Ben finally met his gaze. "Why are you telling me this?"

Phillipe leaned forward. "I need you, Benjamin. You are my only hope to keep the Lahaye legacy alive. I need heirs—as many as I can get."

"Heirs?"

"Sons, grandsons," he said with a robust voice. "Strapping young men to carry on the business."

"I don't have any sons."

"But surely you will." Phillippe set down his coffee mug and turned his pleading gaze to Ben. "If you return to Montreal with me, you will have the pick of young ladies to choose from. You will marry into one of the best families in Montreal and you will be rich beyond your wildest dreams. Everything you've ever wanted or needed will be at your fingertips. All you need to do is say yes."

Confusion and anger melded inside Ben's head, making him feel as if he was being pummeled by dozens of fists. He stood, his heart beating hard and his lungs wanting to burst with the need for fresh air. "Do you know what you did to me? Do you understand the pain of growing up, unwanted and abandoned? Knowing I was the illegitimate child of a man bent on fortune and dishonest gain? You saddled me with baggage I wasn't meant to carry, yet I overcame everything. And now—now you want me to give up the life I've created and go to Montreal to live the life you created?" He shook his head, his jaw tight. "I won't deign to even give you an answer."

"Benjamin." Phillippe stood. "You must at least consider—"

Ben strode toward the front door, needing to get out of the confinement of his home. "Do not ask me again."

He opened the door, walked out onto his porch, and slammed the door shut behind him.

Taking a huge gulp of air, he bent forward and placed his hands on his knees, too overcome to do anything but breathe.

Chapter Fifteen

The weather was warmer than it had been since Emmy's arrival, causing the snow to melt and her mood to brighten. She held the twins' hands as they walked home from school, singing "One Horse Open Sleigh" and laughing at the silly song.

Over the last couple of weeks, Emmy had met several people from town. She smiled and acknowledged many of them as they walked past the grocer's, the Northern Hotel, the livery stable and various other establishments.

As they went by the bank, Adam Russell came to the window and waved at Emmy. She smiled back, thankful that he wasn't angry at her refusal to attend the ball with him. He had kept his distance since asking, which she appreciated, but she didn't want to lose his friendship altogether.

"There's Mr. Ben." Zeb pointed at the parsonage up ahead.

Emmy's smile widened at the thought of seeing Ben—but something didn't seem right. Ben was bent at the waist, his hands on his thighs as if he was in some sort of distress.

The boys ran ahead of Emmy and she hurried through the slush and mud puddles, her gaze on Ben.

When he saw the boys, he straightened and tousled their hair as they ran by him and into the house, no doubt hoping Mrs. Carver had baked them some fresh cookies.

Ben met Emmy's concerned gaze, but instead of a smile, his face was lined with grief.

She rushed the last few yards. "What's wrong? Is it Mrs. Carver? One of the parishioners?"

Ben shook his head and stepped off the porch. "I'm sorry, Emmy, but I need some space."

He started around the parsonage, but Emmy trailed behind, needing to know what was troubling him.

Ben followed a path between the parsonage and the church and opened the door to his barn.

Emmy raced to keep up with him and entered the barn, not willing to let him be alone. "Ben, you're scaring me. What's wrong?"

He led Ginger out of her stall and then picked up a pitchfork. "It's my father."

"Your father?" Emmy walked across the small barn and stood outside the stall. "Did something happen to him?"

Ben mucked out the stall, thrusting the pitchfork with surprising force. "He's here. In the house."

Emmy's eyes grew wide. "Your father is here?"

He pitched the soiled hay into a wheelbarrow. "Yes."

"Why?"

Ben stopped and leaned against the handle of the pitchfork, breathing hard. "In short? He wants me to return with him to Montreal and become his heir."

"His heir?" Emmy frowned as dozens of thoughts

cascaded through her mind, though only one question was worth asking. "Will you go?"

He paused as he began to work at the hay again, tilting his head at her like she'd just said something preposterous. "Of course I won't go."

Relief made Emmy weak. He wouldn't leave.

"I don't know what to do with him." Thrust, pitch, thrust, pitch.

"What do you mean?"

"Part of me wants to send him away immediately, the other part wants me to invite him to stay—yet, what do I expect? Reconciliation?" Fear weighed down his countenance and he stopped and looked at Emmy, again. "I'm afraid I can't forgive him. All these years, I thought I had, but when he showed up, and I had to look him in the face, I realized I'm still very angry."

"Of course you're angry." Emmy stepped around the stall and placed her hand on his arm. "There's nothing wrong with being angry, Ben. The Bible says that there were times when Jesus was angry—but He never sinned in his anger. That's what you must remember. Work through your anger, but as you do, show your father the love of God."

He was silent, but she detected a subtle nod.

She wanted to comfort him and offer her strength, yet, she was afraid if she did, she might not want to leave his embrace.

"I never thought I'd see him again," he said quietly, lifting a pile of fresh hay from the corner to spread it in Ginger's stall. "I feel like I've relived the past twenty-five years in a single hour."

"Maybe, with time, you'll find a way to forgive him."

"How much time?"

"As long as he's willing to give you."

He finished with Ginger's stall and led the horse back into place. Petting her, he shook his head. "So it's up to him all over again? I'm supposed to let him stay as long as he wants, hoping he can somehow make things up to me? Why can't I send him away and be in control of the situation for once in my life?"

"Is that really what you want?" Emmy asked. "Does it matter who's in control? You're both adults now. Both of you can come and go as you please. You're no longer a child at his mercy."

Ben took a limp carrot from a bin along the wall and gave it to Ginger, his gaze on the horse, his voice low. "Why do I feel like the child he abandoned all over again?"

Probably the same reason she relived William's death every time she felt threatened by someone getting too close. "It's fear." She joined Ben to pet Ginger's coat and sighed. "There are people and situations that make us feel helpless, and when we find ourselves facing them again, we're afraid history will repeat itself, but this time we won't survive if it does."

Ben looked over at Emmy, his brown-eyed gaze filled with empathy. "I'm sorry for what you endured when William died."

Tears pricked the back of her eyes and she bit her lip to keep it from trembling. She would not cry. She had cried enough tears to last a lifetime. Instead, she forced herself to speak past the emotions. "And I'm sorry that your father hurt you."

She didn't know if he opened his arms to her, or if she invited him, but she found herself in his powerful embrace, her face pressed against his chest, inhaling his scent as the tears trailed down her cheeks. She could hear the steady beat of his heart and feel him take a breath in and then let it out again. It felt good and right to be in Ben's arms, to share her burdens and to shoulder his.

He placed his cheek against the top of her head, his arms firmly wrapped around her. She sensed he needed her strength just as much as she longed for his, yet she didn't feel as if he was asking for more.

Right now, it would be enough that they had friendship. It had to be enough.

Emmy stepped away and wiped at her cheeks, a nervous smile on her lips. "I should return to the house before the boys come looking for us."

Ben watched her, his expression hard to read. "Would you like to meet my father?"

"I would."

He walked around her and held the door open. "I can't ask him to stay right now. I still plan to travel to Owatonna tomorrow to look for the boys' father."

"What will you tell him?"

"That I made plans before he arrived, and I can't change those plans because he decided to show up after twenty-five years. If he wants to stay at the hotel and wait for my return, he's welcome to, but I'm still going."

She couldn't blame Ben for sticking with his plans. They needed to locate Malachi Trask before Mrs. Carver's departure, and the sooner the better.

They entered through the kitchen door and found the boys at the table, milk and cookies in front of them, as Mrs. Carver bustled about the room, banging pots and pans together.

"There will be a guest for supper tonight," Ben said as Emmy passed into the kitchen ahead of him.

"I'm well aware of our guest, dearie. He's in the front room twiddling his thumbs as we speak." She lifted her eyebrows and tilted her head toward the door. "Are you going to entertain him, or should I put him to work making biscuits?"

"We'll go." Ben closed the back door and crossed the kitchen, waiting for Emmy to follow.

He pushed open the door, allowing her to enter the room first.

Mr. Lahaye sat on Ben's rocker, his elbows on his knees, as he stared into the fire. He turned his head when he heard them and immediately stood.

She could see where Ben got his height and broad shoulders. She could even see some of Ben's handsome features in this stranger, though Ben's high cheekbones and darker skin was probably from his mother.

Ben closed the kitchen door and stood beside Emmy. He appeared as if he was gathering his strength before he addressed his father.

"May I present Miss Wilkes?" Ben asked his father. "She is our local schoolteacher and a boarder in my home."

Mr. Lahaye stepped forward and Emmy extended her gloved hand, but he didn't shake it, instead, he lifted it to his lips and placed a kiss on top. "*C'est un plaisir de vous rencontrer, mademoiselle.* It is a pleasure to meet you, miss." His charm was unforced and she suspected she would have liked him, had she not known who he was or what he had done to Ben.

"The pleasure is mine, Monsieur Lahaye." She curtsied as she had been taught by her mother.

Mr. Lahaye looked between Ben and Emmy, a question in his gaze. Did he suspect they were a couple? If he did, was that why she could see disappointment in his eyes?

* * *

The next morning, Ben woke up hours before anyone else would rise. He had sent his father to the Northern Hotel the night before and said his goodbyes to Emmy and the boys before they went to bed. He didn't know how long it would be until he returned from Owatonna, but he hoped it would only be a few days. His time was running short with his temporary family, and he didn't want to waste a single day with them.

Mrs. Carver had packed his food and he had placed all his things by the kitchen door so he could leave the house without waking anyone.

He lifted his saddlebags to go outside, but a creak in the floorboards stopped him. He looked up and found Emmy standing at the door, her hair around her shoulders, a modest robe cinched tight at her waist. It took everything for Ben not to stare.

"Did I wake you?" he asked as he set his bags on the floor.

"I couldn't sleep."

"That makes two of us, then."

"Is that why you're getting such an early start?"

Ben let his gaze feast on her beautiful blond hair. It was thick and curly, and it extended past her waist. For a fleeting moment, he wondered how it would feel to run his hands through the silky strands—but he stopped his wayward thoughts before he got too carried away. "The sooner I get there the sooner I can come back."

She took a tentative step into the kitchen, but stopped in the middle of the room, keeping a respectable distance between them. "Godspeed, Ben. I will pray for you every chance I get."

He wanted to pull her into his arms again, to inhale the sweet fragrance she wore. Never, in all the years he had been a circuit rider, had he wanted to stay more than he did in this moment. "Thank you."

"Will you be safe?"

"I'll try."

"Do you have enough provisions?"

He glanced at the bulging saddlebags. "More than enough."

Emmy surveyed his things. "I suppose there's nothing left to say, except goodbye."

He held her gaze for a moment, the bright moon illuminating her features. "Goodbye, Em." With a nod of farewell, he lifted his saddlebags and opened the back door.

"Wait!"

Ben turned and watched as she raced across the kitchen to throw her arms around him. He inhaled a sharp breath and dropped his saddlebags, and wrapped his arms around her slender waist. She melded perfectly into his body and felt like she belonged there. He held her tight, not wanting to ever let her go. No one had ever cared this much about his comings and goings in the past, and the knowledge that she cared was enough to make him clear his throat, lest his emotions get the better of him.

She pulled away and took several steps back, her hands on her cheeks. "I'm sorry," she whispered. "I just want you to come back safe."

"Don't apologize." He wanted to follow her retreat and take her into his arms again—but he refrained. Instead, he simply said, "Thank you."

He sensed she was embarrassed by her hasty actions, so he picked up his bags and slipped out the back door before either one of them said something they would regret.

A man stood by the barn, nonchalantly leaning against the siding, a saddled horse tethered to a tree nearby. The darkness of the predawn hour made it hard to see his features, though Ben knew exactly who he was.

"What are you doing here?" Ben asked as he walked past his father and into the barn where Ginger greeted him with a whinny.

"I thought you might like some company." Phillipe followed him into the barn. "It makes more sense than me sitting here with nothing to do."

Ben filled Ginger's feed bag and began to brush her down, the full moon offering enough light to see by. "I don't need company."

Phillippe leaned against Ginger's stall and chewed on a clean piece of straw. "Then I'll ride along to be an extra gun in case there's trouble."

With one last swipe, Ben finished brushing his horse and then he took the saddle blanket off the rack and placed it on Ginger's back. "The trails have been clear for the past year, and I haven't heard of any trouble. I don't need an extra gun."

"Maybe I just want some time with my son."

Everything within Ben recoiled at being called this man's son. The warmth he felt from Emmy's farewell was quickly replaced by the frost from this encounter. "I don't want you to come."

Ben lifted the saddle from its stand and placed it on Ginger's back. He set the stirrup over the top and let down the straps, and then he fastened them together, pulling them tight.

Phillippe tossed the hay aside and joined Ben, securing the saddlebags behind the saddle. "We have a lot to discuss, Benjamin. I'd like if you'd give me the honor of accompanying you on your journey."

"We don't have anything to discuss. I'm not going to Montreal with you."

"Montreal is not the only thing we need to talk about."

Ben took the bridle off the peg and placed it over Ginger's head, securing it in her mouth. "There's nothing else to talk about."

Phillippe rested his large hand on Ben's shoulder. "I disagree."

Ben stiffened under his father's touch. More than anything, he wanted peace. The Bible admonished him to seek peace and pursue it. Peace was a Fruit of the Spirit and something Christ spoke of so often in the Bible, Ben couldn't deny it was important. How would he have peace with his father if he didn't give him a chance? With a resigned sigh, Ben nodded. "Fine."

Phillippe didn't say anything, but Ben sensed his relief by the way his shoulders loosened and the new purpose behind helping Ben prepare to leave.

After untying Ginger, Ben backed her out of her stall and out the wide doors of the barn. The moon was low on the horizon and the first blush of dawn was visible in the eastern sky, making the stars fade.

Phillipe mounted his gelding and pulled on the reins to turn it around to face Ben.

"I plan to ride as hard and as fast as Ginger will allow," Ben said to Phillipe, pulling himself into the saddle. "I want to make good time so I can return as soon as possible."

"To the teacher?" The question was filled with curiosity and a hint of disapproval. But why would his father disapprove of Emmy? He hardly knew her.

"To all of them."

"Is the mademoiselle special to you?"

Ben frowned at the question. "Does it matter?"

"I have hopes for you to marry well."

Anger burned inside Ben's gut, but he held his frustration in check, remembering his need for peace. "If Emmy would have me, I could do no better, even if I combed every last continent."

"*Oui*, but she is not well connected. I have a list of debutantes for you to choose from, if you'd only say the word. The young lady may be everything you hope for in a wife, and more, but if she does not further your career, what good is she?"

"What do you recommend?" Ben faced his father, his anger boiling to the surface. "To do as you have done? Marry for advancement, but misuse an unworthy woman for pleasure?" Visions of his beautiful mother surfaced and Ben ached with her memory. "My mother loved you—but she meant nothing to you, did she?"

With panther-like reflexes, Phillippe grabbed Ben's lapel, his jaw tight. "There, you are wrong, *mon fils*. I loved your mother with all that I was. When she died, I thought I would die with her."

Ben's shoulders tightened and he breathed hard through his nostrils. "Then why did you leave her son all alone in the world?"

Phillipe let go of Ben as quickly as he'd grabbed him. "I was young and stupid."

"Maybe you were, but if you had it to do all over again, would you have made a different decision?"

Resignation bent Phillipe's broad shoulders and he turned away from Ben's penetrating gaze. "*Non*. I would do it again. I had no other choice."

Ben sat for a moment and absorbed what his father

had said. All his life, the only thing that had given Ben any sort of hope was that his father had regretted his actions. He'd always believed that given a second chance, Phillippe would have taken Ben with him. The childhood delusion was now shattered, and in its place Ben felt nothing.

He spurred Ginger into motion, directing her down the alley and onto the old wagon road that ran from the Coopers' home to Main Street.

Neither one said another word as they picked up speed and headed south toward Owatonna and a future that looked as bleak as Ben's past.

Chapter Sixteen

"Are you ready, boys?" Emmy stood from her desk at the front of the schoolroom and addressed Levi and Zeb, who sat on the front row looking through a picture atlas Emmy kept at the school. She had already dismissed all the other children earlier and prepared her things for the next day.

Zeb was the first to stand, his wide smile revealing a missing tooth that he had lost the day Ben had left. "Can we take the book home with us?"

"May we take the book home?" Emmy corrected, and then said, "No, you may not. I need that book for a lesson I'm teaching tomorrow."

Levi sighed and closed the book. He stood and handed it to her. "I like books, Miss Emmy."

"Good." She smiled at the little boy. "Books make leaders out of men. The more books you read, the more you'll know." She set the book on the edge of her desk.

"Is Mr. Ben coming back today?" Zeb asked with a lisp.

The mention of Ben brought back the memories of the embrace they'd shared in the barn, and then in the kitchen just yesterday. Something had overcome her when he was about to leave, and she had thrown herself into his arms. Heat had filled her cheeks and she was thankful for the dark room, or he might have seen the effect he had on her. Shame and fear had prevented her from going back to sleep, and she had lain awake long after he'd left, worried that if she didn't leave his home soon, she would not be able to keep from falling in love.

"Miss Emmy?" Zeb tugged on her hand. "There's a man walking this way."

Emmy looked toward the window and saw Mr. Samuelson on his way to the school. Anxiety filled her stomach as she watched his approach.

"Sit here," Emmy said to the boys as she pointed to the front row and reached for the book on her desk. "You may continue to look through the picture book until he leaves."

She was thankful the boys were still with her. The thought of being alone with Mr. Samuelson made her scalp crawl.

Emmy took a seat at her desk and readjusted the books and papers she had been working with earlier. She had already arranged everything, but she needed to do something with her hands as she waited for the door to open.

A creak at the back of the room made all three of them look up.

Mr. Samuelson removed the hat from his head and walked down the aisle toward her desk with determined steps.

Emmy rose and gave a slight curtsy. "Mr. Samuelson. To what do I owe this visit?"

"I don't have much time today, Miss Wilkes, but I wanted to let you know I've found alternative accommodations for you."

Her heart sped at hearing the news. It's what she had wanted, wasn't it? Then why did she feel grief and sadness at the thought?

"The Janner family lives just north of town on the Belle Prairie road about a mile from here," he said, his voice all business today. "They have one small room they rent out to boarders and it's just become available."

Emmy nodded, as she looked at the boys. She hadn't told them she was planning to move, and by the look on their faces, they didn't like the idea one bit.

"How long do I have to decide?" she asked.

"Mrs. Janner likes to keep the room full, so she sent word that you must move in today, or she'll give it to someone else."

"Today?" Emmy lifted her eyebrows, her response louder than she intended. "But I have other plans for today." She and Mrs. Carver had cut the fabric for the angel costumes Levi and Zeb would wear during the pageant and had planned to spend the evening sewing them.

"Mrs. Janner insists you make the move today, or you'll need to look for a different place to live." He leaned forward, his lips pursed with purpose. "I would recommend you take this opportunity, Miss Wilkes. There's no telling when another room will open. Mrs. Janner's home is clean and respectable—which is more than I can say for several other places I've investigated on your behalf."

Emmy clasped her hands together on her desk as she thought about her options. She had so few, it didn't take her long to come to a decision. She couldn't stay with Ben any longer and she didn't know of another home where she would have space and privacy to study. "I'll make the necessary plans to move today."

"Good." Mr. Samuelson stood and Emmy used the opportunity to glance at the boys.

They were looking at one another the way they had the first day she'd met them, as if their world was crashing down around them and they were all alone. Levi reached for Zeb's hand.

"I will let Mrs. Janner know you'll arrive before supper." Mr. Samuelson put his hat on. "That should give you a couple hours to pack the necessary items you'll need for a few days and then you can have someone help you move your other things after that. Do you know where the Janner family lives?"

She was familiar with them. They attended church and their two youngest children attended school, though they were the oldest students Emmy taught.

"They're just a mile north on the road out front," Mr. Samuelson said. "A white picket fence around their yard. You can't miss them."

"I think I know which house you mean."

"I'll leave you to your work." He left without another word and Emmy was both relieved to see him go and anxious that she would have to face the boys now.

"Come," she said to them. "We need to get you home."

They rose from their bench, their hands firmly clasped together, and walked to the cloakroom without saying a word. As they put on their coats, Emmy studied their faces, wishing things could be different.

She locked the door behind them and then walked them home through the melting snow.

When they reached the parsonage steps, Emmy couldn't handle the silence any longer.

"I'm sorry, boys, but this move is for the best."

"Why?" Levi asked. "Did Mr. Ben make you angry?"

Emmy bent to be eye level with the boys. "No. Mr. Ben is kind and thoughtful. He would never intentionally hurt me."

"Did I do something wrong?" Levi asked, his eyes wide with fear.

Emmy's chest tightened with sadness as she pulled him into her arms. "Of course not. We've always known that this living arrangement was temporary—I just didn't realize I would be leaving so soon."

Levi pulled away and frowned, his anger covering his sadness. "I don't want you to leave."

"You'll still see me every day at school." Emmy adjusted his cap. "And I'll come to visit as often as I'm able."

She straightened and put a smile on her face, even though she'd rather cry. "Chin up, boys. We'll get through this and be stronger on the other side."

Emmy pushed open the front door and looked at the dear home. She would miss the smell of Mrs. Carver's fresh-baked cookies after school, and the sound of the boys' laughter as they played on the rug. She would miss the greeting Ben gave when he came home for supper in the evenings, and his thoughtful way of making time for her to study.

"Miss Wilkes?" Adam appeared on the street behind her, a smile on his handsome face.

"You go on inside," Emmy told the boys. "I'll be just a minute."

Adam waited for Emmy to close the door and then he took a step toward her. "I heard Reverend Lahaye is out of town for a few days."

"He is." Emmy nodded.

The banker took another step toward her. "I was hoping to call this evening, if I may."

"I'm sorry." Emmy glanced toward the parsonage where she had a lot of work to do if she was going to make it out to the Janners' by supper. She would pack a small bag, one that wouldn't be too cumbersome to carry on the mile-long trek. "I have plans this evening."

"Oh?" He waited patiently for her to explain.

What did it matter if he knew? Eventually everyone would hear.

"I am moving to the Janner residence this evening. I plan to pack a few things and go as soon as possible."

He took another eager step forward. "I'd be honored to help. I can hitch up my wagon and take your trunks."

"I wouldn't want to be a bother."

"No bother at all." He grinned. "I'd like to help."

It would be nice to have all her things with her right away—and it would prevent the awkward situation with Ben when she'd need to return for them later.

She nodded. "I'll have my things ready in an hour. Will that be convenient for you?"

"I could have my wagon here even sooner."

"An hour will be just fine. Thank you."

"I'll be back shortly." He waved and walked toward the north, but Emmy didn't watch him go. She had far too much to do.

She entered the house just as Mrs. Carver left the kitchen, a dish towel in hand. "What's this about you moving?"

"The boys told you?"

"They said you're going tonight."

"In an hour, I'm afraid."

"Land's sakes, dearie. When did all this happen and where are you going?"

Emmy didn't have time to explain everything in great detail, but she did tell her that Mr. Samuelson had been looking for a place and one had been found with the Janner family. "I need to move in today or Mrs. Janner will give the room to someone else. Mr. Russell has agreed to take me there in an hour."

The older woman's eyebrows rose. "After what happened the night of the last frolic, you'd be seen with Mr. Russell?"

"He's just being neighborly, and besides, we'll be in plain sight the whole time. He's just taking me to the Janners' place, nothing more."

Mrs. Carver shook her head, a sigh on her lips. "I don't like any of this—not a bit."

"I don't, either, but it's for the best. You'll be leaving soon and if Ben is successful, the boys will go, too. I had to find somewhere to live sooner or later."

"I just wish it was later." Mrs. Carver's voice was filled with sorrow. "I had so looked forward to spending Christmas together. I can't even make you one last meal."

"I'll visit," Emmy promised, and added on second thought, "If I'm invited."

"Ack, dearie!" Mrs. Carver pulled Emmy into her thick embrace. "I'll see that you're invited back as soon as Mr. Ben is home."

Emmy swallowed hard as she returned the hug. She hated to think of how Ben would feel when he discovered she had left without warning. He'd been through so much with his father, and she couldn't imagine what he might face in Owatonna.

Yet—he couldn't be surprised by the turn of events. They both knew she needed to leave.

It didn't make it any easier, though.

It had been two days since Ben had left Little Falls. He and Phillippe had barely spoken, and Ben wanted to keep it that way. No matter what was said, it seemed to come out hurtful.

Clouds hung thick over the expanse of snow-covered prairie and Ben was forced to pull his collar up to protect his neck from the blast of cold air that swept over the hill where he and Phillippe traversed. They had arrived in the small town of Owatonna the night before and started asking for Malachi Trask. No one had ever heard of the man before, and Ben had started to suspect that Reginald had given him faulty information.

That morning, when Ben had left his hotel room and gone down to the dining room for breakfast, he had asked the waitress if she'd ever heard of Malachi. She had looked at him with suspicious eyes and asked where he'd heard that name. When Ben explained, and told her about the boys, the woman had finally shared that Malachi had changed his name and he was living west of town.

Now, as a storm threatened the northwestern sky, Ben and Phillippe rode toward the farm where they believed Malachi lived under the name of Oscar Webb. Why he had changed his name, Ben didn't know, but he had a few ideas. More than likely he was avoiding the law.

"Is that it?" Phillipe pointed to a sod house tucked between two rolling hills. A rickety corral encircled two scrawny cows, and a sod barn sat nearby. A thick blanket of snow topped the house and barn, and Ben imagined it kept them well-insulated from the frigid winter air. Smoke puffed out of a metal stovepipe sticking through the house roof.

As they drew closer to the home, Ben took in the wax-covered windows and the wood door, with cracks wide enough for critters to get through. Not a tree was in sight—nothing but endless rolling prairie for miles and miles.

They brought their horses to a stop and Ben climbed out of his saddle, watching the house, looking for someone to greet them. Anxiety churned in his gut as he thought about losing Zeb and Levi. The boys had become like family to him and he hated to think of them leaving—yet somehow, he also knew he was doing the right thing.

Phillippe also dismounted and he came to Ben and took the reins. "You go ahead, I'll stay with the horses."

Ben nodded and traipsed through the snow to the front door. Footprints crisscrossed the yard around the house, but the wind whipped up the snow, making it hard to tell how fresh they were. He knocked and waited.

A shadow at the window told him someone was inside, though he couldn't make out the figure. He stood in his warm buffalo robe, but even then, it was still cold.

The door creaked open and a haggard-looking woman glared out at Ben through a slight crack. "What do you want?"

"Is this the home of Malachi Trask or Oscar Webb?"

"Who are you?" Her teeth were crossed in the front and her wiry hair stood out in disarray. Deep wrinkles lined her once pretty face, though he didn't think she was more than twenty-five or twenty-six. The prairie had a way of doing that to people, aging them before their time, but he sensed there was more to this woman's plight than the prairie wind. She looked disillusioned.

"My name is Reverend Ben Lahaye," he answered. "I am here on behalf of Mr. Trask's twin boys, Levi and Zebulun."

The lady's eyes narrowed. "I don't know no Mr.

Trask." A little hand appeared at the door and it creaked open wider to reveal a girl of about three years old standing there in nothing but her underwear. With the door open, Ben could now see the woman held a feverish child of about a year, and she was well along in another pregnancy. The home was disheveled. Clumps of dirt were breaking away from the walls and ceiling, and moth-eaten rugs covered the earthen floor.

Ben wondered what else she didn't know—and he hated to be the one to tell her. "Is Mr. Webb at home?"

"He hasn't been here in days," she said with a scowl. "Went into town drinking, so I don't 'spect I'll see him until he's spent all our money on booze."

The little girl blinked up at Ben with the same almond-shaped green eyes as Levi, and his heart went out to her. No one deserved to live this way. He had a mind to turn around and head back the way he'd come, protecting Levi and Zeb from the reality of this life, but he didn't think God had brought him all the way here just to leave now. "Do you know where I might find him?"

She snorted. "Nowhere a preacher-man would want to go."

"I need to speak to him immediately," Ben explained. "If you'd be so kind as to tell me, I will take my leave."

The woman's eyelids drooped as she looked at Ben with disdain. "Why are you here? If you came to get money for some church or something, you're wastin' your time. Oscar ain't got two pennies to rub together, and if he does, he spends it on drink."

"I'm not here to get money." Ben glanced at his father who stood a respectable distance away, his eyes on the rolling prairie. Ben looked back at the lady. "I'm here because I believe the two boys in my home are Mal—

Oscar's children and they need a home. I thought it best to tell their father."

The baby in her arms fussed and she bounced, her threadbare dress sweeping the dusty floor with each movement. "How do you know them kids is his?" He suspected her look of disinterest veiled a deeper fear. "Was it a prostitute that made the claim?"

Ben shook his head, his fears about Malachi Trask becoming more and more disconcerting with each statement. It wasn't his place to tell this woman about her husband's past, was it? Yet, he couldn't leave her thinking the worst. "The boys were born to his wife, Clara—"

"He has another wife?" Her voice was first surprised and then resigned. "I should have known."

"She died, three years ago, and her sister took them in. Recently, her sister brought them to me."

"Three years ago?" She snorted again. "Three years ago I already had this baby with Oscar," she nodded at the little girl. "He never told me he had a wife and kids someplace else."

Ben rubbed the back of his neck. "Could you please tell me where I might find him?"

"What does it matter?" she asked, more to herself than to Ben. "He's probably at the saloon in Owatonna. Seems to spend more time there than he does here."

Ben nodded. "Thank you."

She started to close the door with no further comment, but Ben held up his hand to stop her. "I have a few things I'd like to leave with you, if I may."

"What kind of things?" Her eyes were narrowed again.

"Here." Ben walked to the horse and dug into his saddlebags for the food Mrs. Carver had sent with him.

If he grew hungry, he could stop along the way home and find food at a restaurant or hotel. Ben handed her the cookies, bread, fried chicken and other tidbits Mrs. Carver had packed.

The woman stared at his offerings as if he had presented her with a bomb. "I can't take that."

"Why not?" he asked. "I have more than enough."

Big green eyes blinked up at him as the little girl gazed upon the food.

"Take it." He held it out to her. "For the children, if nothing else."

She finally took the food and closed the door without another word.

Ben didn't need a thank-you—just knowing the children would have a bit of food to fill their tummies for a couple of days was all the thanks he needed.

They mounted their horses and headed back toward town. Ben's prayers started to change from asking God to help him find Malachi, to asking for Malachi to give Ben the right to adopt Zeb and Levi.

Before, Ben had been convinced he wasn't a good fit for the boys—but then he realized that they were a good fit for him. Yes, he would have a lot of obstacles to overcome if he wanted to keep them, but it would be worth any price he would have to pay. If he could prevent their separation, he would do whatever it would take.

They rode back toward Owatonna, the wind nipping at them the whole way.

Finally, they arrived and located the only saloon in town. It was a two-story building with a wide front porch. The windows upstairs were shuttered tight.

Ben dismounted, but Phillipe remained on his horse.

"Are you coming inside?" Ben asked.

Phillipe looked over the establishment and shook his

head. "I gave up drinking twenty-five years ago and I make it a habit not to put myself in a position to be tempted. I'll wait here." He paused and studied Ben's face. "Unless you need me."

Ben shook his head and walked up the steps to the saloon door. The place was open for business, though there were only three customers inside. The bartender stood behind a long counter, a piece of paper in one hand, a pencil in the other, taking inventory of the bottles behind the bar. Someone sat in the corner of the room at the piano, a lively tune echoing off the ivory keys, the other two men played poker.

"Can I help you?" the bartender asked when he saw Ben.

"I'm looking for Oscar Webb."

The barkeep nodded toward the corner of the room at the piano player.

"That's Mr. Webb?"

"The one and only."

Ben walked across the room, feeling the gazes of the other two men on him.

"Mr. Webb?"

Oscar—Malachi—looked up at Ben, a ready smile in place. "That's me."

Ben had anticipated an older-looking man with dingy hair, rotted teeth and threadbare clothes. This man wasn't anything like Ben had expected. He had a youthful look about him, though the years had caused creases to wrinkle his forehead and the corners of his eyes. Ben supposed he was handsome, and from the quick smile, he suspected the man could easily charm anyone. His gaze was clear and cheerful, with no haze of alcohol lingering.

Malachi stopped playing the piano, a frown of concern marring his brow. “Why the long face, mister? Someone die?”

“Is there somewhere we could talk in private?” Ben asked.

The boys’ father glanced around the bar. “This is as private as it gets. What’s on your mind? You look too serious for a man who just stepped into the bar—or is that why you came? You need to drink away your sorrows?” He chuckled as he watched Ben with curiosity.

If he wanted to talk here, then here is where they would talk. “I have come on behalf of your sons, Levi and Zebulun Trask.”

The good-humored smile fell from his face. “What was that?”

“Your sons.”

“You know where my boys are?”

Ben nodded. “They’ve been with me for a couple months now. Their aunt dropped them off.”

“Bertha. I should have known.” He shook his head. “Did she tell you where to find me?”

“Your father told me where you might be living.”

“My father?” Malachi’s frown deepened. “How do you know my father? More importantly, who are you?”

“I’m Reverend Ben Lahaye. Clara’s sister dropped the boys off at the parsonage on her way through Little Falls. All she told me was the boys’ names. I’ve had to deduce the rest on my own.”

Malachi’s shoulders drooped and his hands hung loose between his knees. A deep melancholy seemed to slip over his head and rest like a heavy garment around him. “I’ve wondered where those boys went.” He stared at a spot on the floor, the tenor of his voice changing at an alarming rate. “I suppose you’ve heard all about me.”

"I've heard enough." Ben wouldn't sugarcoat what he'd heard.

"Why are you here?" Malachi looked up at Ben, defeat in his gaze. "Do you want something from me?"

This was the hardest part of his journey. The moment he'd been dreading for months. "I came to see if you'd like your sons back."

Again, Malachi stared at the floor, lost in his thoughts. "I'm not proud of who I am, Reverend Lahaye." He leaned forward and put his elbows on his knees, clasping his hands together. "I didn't deserve Clara and when she left me, I didn't follow her, because I knew she could do better. Instead, I continued to drink and I took up with Katrina." He looked down at his limp hands. "Something's broken inside and I don't know how to fix it, Reverend. Sometimes I'm soaring with the birds, other times, I'm groveling with the pigs." He was quiet for a long time. "When I heard Clara died, I did right by Katrina and the children and I married her—but that seems to be the only decent thing I've done for her." Desperation filled his gaze. "I want to be a better man, truly, I do. But when the melancholy sets in, I can't seem to crawl out of it for days. The only thing that relieves the darkness is playing this piano." He motioned to the instrument. "I come in here and spend my money on liquor, sitting at this wooden box for days until my mood lifts, then I go home to Katrina."

Ben took a seat across from Malachi. He'd met other men like him before. They swung between a pendulum of intense joy and penetrating sadness. Alcohol seemed to make it worse, but it also seemed to be the only thing that made it better. He'd seen men come out of it, too. Men who had been desperate enough to change their lives. Start over. Cling to Christ. Malachi wasn't beyond saving.

"Your life is not my business," Ben said as kindly as he could, "but Zeb and Levi are."

"Zeb and Levi." Malachi smiled and looked at Ben. "I knew Clara had twin boys, but I didn't know what she named them."

"They're Biblical names," Ben said.

"Strong names." He hung his head again. "I'm sorry you were dragged into my pitiful life. You didn't ask for any of this, and here you are, trying to make sense of me because you care about those boys." The smile he gave Ben was genuine, if ashamed. "I can see it in your eyes. You're like Clara. Good and honest and caring."

"I just want what's best for Zeb and Levi."

"So do I, ironically."

"I don't find it ironic."

Malachi straightened. "I'm ready to make a change, Reverend Lahaye. I know I can do it this time." He squared his shoulders and looked Ben in the eye. "I'm going to do right by my sons."

Ben's chest tightened. "What do you plan to do?"

"I plan to go to Little Falls and get my boys, make a real family once and for all. Might come as a shock to Katrina, but she's a strong woman. She can take on two more young'uns, and it'll be good to have more help on the farm."

Disappointment rammed against Ben and took his breath away. Though he'd done what he thought was best, he couldn't shake the feeling that he'd just sentenced Levi and Zeb to a life of pain, bitterness and drudgery.

Chapter Seventeen

The snowstorm that overtook Ben and Phillippe on their way home from Owatonna was nothing like the tempest raging inside Ben's heart. A week and a half after he left Little Falls, he finally arrived back home, weary, frustrated and heart sore.

Everything in town was buried under a fresh layer of snow as they plodded through the street to the barn behind the parsonage. The storm was common for December, but they had been living with winter for two solid months and it was starting to wear on his mood.

"I'll rub Ginger down," Phillippe said to Ben when they dismounted in the barn. "You go on inside and see those boys."

Ben was too tired to argue. In about two weeks, Malachi Trask would come for the boys. Ben had tried to convince him otherwise, telling Malachi that he would keep the boys, and that they would be happy and safe with him—but Malachi had become adamant that it was time he made something of his life. When he said he'd come immediately for them, Ben had at least convinced him to wait until Christmas Eve, so they could participate in the pageant at school the day before. Malachi had hesitantly agreed.

The sky overhead was a brilliant blue and the sunshine was dazzling as it reflected off the snow. It was hard to believe that just yesterday Ben and Phillippe had been holed up in a run-down hotel in St. Cloud, waiting to be free of the storm.

"Hello," Ben called as he entered the kitchen through the back door. It was Saturday morning, which meant everyone should be home—so why was it so quiet?

"Hello, dearie," Mrs. Carver answered as she walked into the kitchen from the front room, a dust rag in hand. Concern lined her face and the dear old lady looked as if she had aged overnight. "What news do you bring?"

"Are the boys here?"

"They're playing with the Cooper boys today. Mrs. Cooper came up here earlier and asked if they could go to her house. I didn't think you'd mind."

"No, I don't." Ben took out a chair and rested his fatigued muscles. There was a small measure of relief knowing he could discuss the boys' future with Emmy and Mrs. Carver without the boys hearing. "Is Emmy studying upstairs?"

"Emmy?"

Ben looked up at her. "Yes, Emmy."

His housekeeper walked to the stove and lifted a lid, then set it down absentmindedly, mumbling something under her breath.

"Mrs. Carver?" Ben stood, hating the dread he felt in the pit of his stomach. "Where's Emmy?"

"Oh, dearie." She turned and wrung her hands. "She moved to the Janners' house two days after you left. She's been there a week now."

"Moved?" Ben had never raised his voice inside

his home before, but it ricocheted off the walls of the kitchen now. He didn't intend to be so loud, but the shock of hearing that Emmy moved was too much on top of everything else. "Why did she move?"

Mrs. Carver swallowed. "Mr. Samuelson found her a place and she had to move that day or she'd lose the opportunity. Mr. Russell was kind enough to take her out in his wagon—"

"Mr. Russell?" Again, his voice was much louder than he intended, and Mrs. Carver flinched.

He paced across the floor, his hand massaging the back of his neck.

"I'm sorry," Mrs. Carver said.

Ben shook his head. "No, I'm sorry. None of this is your fault."

"People talk," Mrs. Carver said slowly, "and they're saying that Mr. Russell has gone out to visit Emmy several times since she moved..."

Ben sat back in his chair and put his elbows on the table, his face in his hands. Adam Russell had been waiting for an opportune time, and he'd found it. But what about Emmy? Did she welcome Mr. Russell's attention? When Ben had fallen in love with Charlotte, he'd hoped and prayed she would love him in return, but Abram had been a stronger contender. Was Adam the same? Did it even pay to go after Emmy and tell her how he felt about her?

"Go, dearie," Mrs. Carver said. "Go and tell her you love her."

"I don't love her." He couldn't. The risk was far too great.

"You do, and she needs to know."

"Why, so she can reject me?" He knew he sounded pathetic, because he felt pathetic.

"Just go. Tell her the truth and then let the matter go into God's hands. Pray for His will, and then pray for His grace, no matter the outcome."

It was something he preached all the time. Seeking God's will and then walking it out in His grace. Shouldn't he do what he told others to do?

He took off his buffalo robe and went to his bedroom to change. If he was going to see Emmy, he was going with the intention to court, and a courting man always looked his best.

Twenty minutes later, after Phillippe had brushed Ginger down and given her something to eat, Ben hooked her up to his sleigh and pulled out of the barn. He wanted her to have more rest, but his need to see Emmy made him push the horse. "I'm sorry, girl," he said. "But I need a little more from you today."

It didn't take long to get to the Janners' place. Ben had been there before on church business. The oldest Janner daughters had been married the previous summer, one right after the other. The two youngest Janner children, boys, were students at the school, though they were a little older than most boys who attended. They were good people, but they held on to a strict set of ideals and were the only people in the congregation who Ben tried not to look at when he preached. Their stern faces usually made him squirm.

The harness jingled as he pulled into the Janners' property. A two-story house stood off in a neat yard, the white clapboard gleaming under the sunshine. A large barn was surrounded by dormant fields that produced some of the best wheat in the state.

Ben exited the sleigh and tied Ginger's lead rope to a hitching post out front. He didn't plan to stay long, only long enough to ask Emmy to go riding. He needed to tell her about his trip, and he didn't want an audience.

He walked up the path and knocked on the front door. It opened quickly, and he suspected that someone had seen his approach. Mrs. Janner stood on the other side of the door and ran a hand over her hair to smooth it back. She was a tall, skinny woman with a sharp nose and pale blue eyes. "Reverend Lahaye. To what do I owe this pleasant surprise?"

"Is Miss Wilkes available?"

"Why, yes, she's in her room." She lifted her eyebrows, as if in judgment. "My, but she gets her share of gentleman callers, doesn't she?"

He chose to ignore her statement, his chest tightening at the idea of Adam Russell visiting her. "May I speak to her?"

"Of course. Won't you come in and wait in the parlor?"

Ben entered the home, but when she offered to take his hat and coat, he kindly refused. "This won't take long," he explained.

She raised her eyebrows again and didn't say anything as she disappeared.

He sat on the sofa, but finding the need to pace, he rose and walked across Mrs. Janner's parlor, looking at the curiosities on one of her shelves.

"Ben?" Emmy entered the parlor, Mrs. Janner nowhere to be seen.

The sight of her melted away all the angst and pain he'd felt since speaking with Malachi. He longed to go to her and pull her into his arms. There was nothing else in this world that he needed more at this very moment.

"Hello, Em."

Her gaze was wary as she studied him. "What are you doing here?"

"I came to tell you about my trip to Owatonna."

She nibbled on her bottom lip, her eyes filling with uneasiness. "I can tell it didn't go well."

How could she tell? Just by looking at him? Did she know him so well?

"Can we go for a drive?" he asked. "I have my sleigh waiting out front."

Again, she nibbled on her lip. "I don't know, Ben."

"Emmy. I need to talk to you."

She nodded slowly. "All right. I'll get my things."

He waited for a few minutes before she returned all bundled up.

With a quick word to Mrs. Janner about where she was going, Emmy preceded Ben out of the house and toward the sleigh.

He helped her inside and tucked the buffalo robe around her skirts, and then he lifted the reins and away they went over the soft snow.

Emmy hadn't expected to see Ben that afternoon, especially in his Sunday best clothing. She suspected that if he had made it home from Owatonna, she would see him the next day at church. When Mrs. Janner told her she had a visitor, she had thought Adam had returned, but when she saw it was Ben, her heart had sped up and pleasure had coiled through her stomach.

But the look on his face had made the pleasure disappear. She knew things had not gone well in Owatonna and she wanted nothing more than to comfort him—yet, she couldn't trust herself where he was concerned.

As they sped across the open prairie, a high bluff to their right and the frozen ribbon of the Mississippi to their left, the wind numbed her cheeks and nose, but felt surprisingly refreshing.

"What happened in Owatonna?" She needed to know, to prepare her mind and heart for what was to come.

He shook his head, his disappointment weighing down his shoulders. "Malachi Trask lives under the name Oscar Webb. He has a wife and two children, one on the way. They live in a sod house on the open prairie—and he's not well." He continued to tell her about finding Malachi in a saloon and the trouble he had with his moods swinging from one extreme to the other. "He needs help, but I don't know how to help him. I know he can be well again, but I don't know if he will."

Emmy sensed that Ben's unhappiness was from the outcome of the visit as well as the state of Malachi's health. Ben's heart was so good and so pure, she knew he wanted what was best for all of them. He understood the suffering of people far better than Emmy ever could, and he always gave people the benefit of the doubt, believing in them and the power of God's love to bring healing. It was something she had come to admire about him.

There were several things he told Emmy about his trip. He spoke about the worries and concerns he had for the boys' future and for the safety and well-being of the new Mrs. Trask and her children. He told Emmy the little girl had eyes just like Levi's and she had clearly left an impression on him. Emmy could tell he needed to unburden his heart with someone who loved the boys as much as he did.

"He's coming to get them on Christmas Eve," Ben said at last. "I asked if they could stay for the pageant, and thankfully he agreed."

Christmas Eve? How could she say goodbye to them in two weeks? Tears stung the back of her eyes and she had to wipe one away before it fell down her cheek. "This will be a hard Christmas."

Ben pulled back on the reins, forcing Ginger to come to a stop. The sunshine was bright and Emmy had to squint to look at Ben. He was watching her, his brown eyes soft and full of both joy and sorrow. "Will you come and spend the day before Christmas Eve with us? We will have a Christmas party for the boys after the pageant. We can give them their gifts, play all our favorite games and have Mrs. Carver's mashed potatoes one last time."

The thought of being back with Ben and the boys filled Emmy with joy. It had been hard to get used to the Janner family. They were a cold, distant group, more work than play. In the evenings, they sat in their parlor, silently, as each did their own thing. Mr. Janner read the newspaper, Mrs. Janner knitted and the Janner boys read. There was no companionship to be had, so Emmy spent most of her time alone in her room. When she had first come to Little Falls, that's all she had wanted—but after spending time in Ben's home, she craved the warmth and affection of a family.

"I will be there."

They sat close in the open sleigh and Emmy felt warmer just knowing he was near. He looked at her now, his handsome features in full light. She could gaze upon him for hours and still not tire of admiring his form. He was all things masculine, yet his gentle countenance and tender care made him the most desirable man she'd ever met. The feelings stirring within her made her self-doubt all the promises she'd made to herself about guarding her heart.

"Emmy," he whispered her name as he looked deep into her eyes.

She couldn't have moved, even if she had tried. She felt rooted and frozen in place—yet, despite the cold, she didn't feel the chill. Warmth coursed through her from head to foot and she felt herself leaning toward him, wanting to draw more heat from his nearness.

He slipped off his mitten and gently lifted his hand to place on her cheek.

She closed her eyes, loving the feel of his warm skin against her cool face. Tilting her cheek toward his hand, she nestled into his touch, not caring about anyone or anything in this lovely moment.

His lips rested upon hers in the next heartbeat and she pressed into his kiss. She wanted this kiss, needed it when all else felt lost and out of control.

Ben's other hand came up and rested on her opposite cheek. She lifted her fingers and touched his arm, half wanting to pull away—half wanting to tug him closer. His kiss was soft and it took her breath away. It filled her with the most delightful feeling she'd ever known—even more so than William's kisses.

William.

Searing agony sliced through Emmy's haze and she pulled back from Ben, confused and ashamed that she had let him kiss her—and invited him to prolong. Her heart was in turmoil as she looked into his dear face. She had fallen in love with Ben Lahaye—deeply and truly—yet her greatest fear was being realized.

Panic welled up and her breathing became shallow. The thought of losing Ben was terrifying to her, and she had not even made the ultimate promise to love and cherish him for life. She had simply fallen in love. But it was impossible. She couldn't love him. Couldn't risk the real possibility that he would be pulled from her in an instant, just as William had been.

He lifted his hand again, but she pulled back. "I can't, Ben."

"Em." He took her hand. "I—"

"Please don't say another word," she begged. "No matter what you say, I won't return the sentiment. I won't make any promises. I refuse to take a risk again." She spoke the words as if she believed them, and she hoped she was convincing, because even as she said what must be said, she didn't think she had the strength to follow through. If he would but kiss her one more time, or tell her the words her heart longed to hear, she would be lost to him forever.

She must keep him quiet.

He finally spoke, his voice low, not meeting her gaze. "Is it because of Adam?"

Adam? She frowned. Why would he think it was because of Adam?

"Do you love him?" he asked.

Love Adam? She looked at Ben and found him staring ahead.

"I'm fond of Adam," she admitted.

He gave a quick nod and then lifted the reins, prompting Ginger to start up again.

As they drove, she wanted to beg him to understand. She didn't want Ben to think she cared for Adam, but it seemed easier that way. If he suspected her true feelings, he might push her and she didn't know how long she could refrain. They drove back to the Janners' place in complete silence.

The cold overtook her toes, and then her feet, and then her legs. Eventually, her torso was frozen and then it spread to her fingers and up to her scalp. She was cold and numb all over, but the air had nothing to do with the chill she endured sitting next to Ben, moments after rejecting the most precious thing he had to offer—his heart.

He stopped in front of the Janners' and Emmy wanted to groan when she saw Adam's sleigh. No doubt he had come to pay another call and was waiting for her return.

Ben saw it, too. She could tell by the way his shoulders stiffened and he lifted his chin.

After he helped her from the sleigh and walked her to the door, he stepped back and nodded. He didn't seem angry or even frustrated, but the look of rejection on his face was worse than if he had railed at her.

"Goodbye, Emmy."

She wished she could give him her heart. "Ben, you deserve so much more than—"

"Please don't." He shook his head.

Shame and embarrassment overtook her and she nodded. "Goodbye."

He walked back to the sleigh and picked up the reins without looking back.

And in that moment, Emmy felt as dark as she did when she learned William had died.

Chapter Eighteen

When Ben pulled the sleigh into the barn, he realized he had seen nothing and no one all the way home from the Janners' place. Nothing had ever felt like Emmy's rejection. Not Charlotte's, not Elizabeth's and not even his father's. He'd been a fool to fall in love with her, when he knew all along that she'd fall for someone else, just like Charlotte and Elizabeth had.

Yet, this time it was different. When Charlotte rejected Ben, he knew she would be better off with Abram. When Elizabeth turned Ben down, he knew Jude was right for her. But now? In the depths of Ben's being, he knew Adam Russell was not right for Emmy. He couldn't put a finger on why, though. Russell could provide Emmy with a nice life, a good home and a proper name. He was a Christian, he was kind and he seemed utterly devoted to her. But Emmy needed more.

"There you are." Phillippe entered the barn and began to unharness Ginger. His movements were smooth and practiced as he spoke to the horse.

Ben hadn't moved from his spot in the sleigh. If he was tired before, now he was bone-weary. He didn't think he had the strength to walk into the house.

Phillippe worked silently, letting Ben wallow in his misery.

After a few minutes, Phillippe spoke. "You never asked me why I left you."

Ben frowned and looked at his father. "What?"

"You made assumptions, but you never asked."

It was the last thing Ben wanted to talk about today. He pulled himself out of the sleigh and grabbed the currycomb, just wanting to be done with Ginger and inside the house, away from his father.

Yet, as they worked, Ben couldn't deny the curiosity that picked at his conscience. Was there a reason his father left that he wasn't aware of? His mother had died, his father was embarrassed and ashamed of having an illegitimate Indian son, and it had been easier to let someone else deal with Ben. Right?

He stopped brushing Ginger and looked at his father. "Why did you leave me?"

Phillippe hung the harness on the peg and turned to face Ben, the years suddenly catching up to him as his shoulders slouched. "I loved you very much." He stopped and swallowed several times before continuing. "When I brought you to the mission, I was heartbroken. Not only for the loss of your mother, but knowing I had to make the hardest sacrifice of my life and leave you, too."

"Sacrifice?" The word tasted of bitterness and bile. "How was abandoning your child a sacrifice? You were probably happy to be rid of me and the reminder of your transgressions."

The words penetrated his father's countenance and he seemed to lose all strength as he slowly sat on a clean pile of hay, his head hanging low.

Ben stood frozen in place, his heart beating hard

and his pulse ticking in his wrists. The large man before him had been reduced to a pile of brokenness and sorrow. Compassion welled up in Ben's heart and he walked across the barn and sat beside his father, overcome by the depth of pain he felt.

Ben finally saw his father as he truly was. A man who had carried his sins with him like a sack of rocks, weighing down every moment, whether good or bad, with the knowledge of his mistakes.

He reached out and placed his arm around Phillipe's shoulders, trying to comfort one of God's children who was suffering. It's what he would have done with anyone else in the world—so why was it so hard to do with his own father?

"I knew I was doing the right thing," Phillippe managed to say through the emotion. "Even though it was the hard thing. I had to leave you in the interior and return to Montreal knowing I had betrayed you and your mother. Every day since then, when the guilt and shame threaten to overwhelm me, I've reminded myself it was for your own good."

Ben stared at him with incredulity. "How could being abandoned be for my own good?"

Phillipe finally looked at him. "If I would have brought you to Montreal, you would have been shunned and ridiculed your whole life. My wife is a cold, heartless woman. Our marriage had been arranged and we never loved each other. She didn't care because she had status and wealth and all the things her cold heart desired." He paused and took a steadying breath. "That's why it was so easy to fall in love with your mother. She was good and brave and all the things Juliette is not."

Ben pulled his arm away from his father, needing a little space to absorb the things he was saying.

"I left you with missionaries because I wanted you to be brought up properly, with no stigmas. I wanted you among others like you, where you would be sure of yourself. If I had brought you to Montreal, you would have floundered and been mistreated." He looked at Ben with vulnerability and honesty. "I wanted to do the selfish thing and take you with me. I wanted to have you close and be reminded of your mother every time I looked at you. But I knew it wouldn't be for your good. I was stuck, Benjamin. Either way, I knew you'd be angry and bitter at me."

Ginger whinnied and stomped her foot, drawing Ben's attention to his horse. He'd never once thought about how hard his father's decision must have been.

Just thinking about Levi and Zeb, who were not even his, and how hard it had been to go after Malachi, even when he knew what the outcome might be, made Ben understand his father in ways he never had. Ben had sacrificed his happiness to do what he thought was best for the boys.

Conversely, hadn't Ben asked Malachi to do what his father had done? Sacrifice the right to raise his boys and give them to someone who could offer them a better life?

For the first time since his arrival, Ben looked at Phillippe with respect and admiration. Yes, he'd made poor choices and he'd hurt a lot of people, but Ben could now see that those choices had hurt his father far more.

"Je suis désolé, Père." I'm sorry, Father.

Phillippe turned to Ben, surprise on his timeworn face. "I'm the one who should apologize, my son. You did not ask to be born the way you were born, and you did not ask to be left at a mission. Those decisions were mine, and mine alone. *I'm* sorry, Benjamin."

Ben reached out and embraced his father, a fierce desire to get to know this man overtaking him. They had lost twenty-five years already.

Phillippe hugged Ben back, his hold tighter than Ben had expected.

"Is it too late?" Ben asked as he pulled away.

"Too late for what?" Phillipe asked, running his sleeve over his wet cheeks.

"To be friends?"

His father's smile was large and bright. "It is never too late for a father and son to be friends." His smile lingered on Ben's face and he looked hopeful. "You have done well, my boy. I am proud of you, and your mother would be proud, too."

Ben sat up a bit straighter and felt a rush of energy at the praise.

"I know you have a life here, but—" Phillipe paused as he studied Ben. "I would be honored if you would return to Montreal with me and have the life I could not give you before."

When the invitation had come the last time, Ben had been angry and hurt. This time, with the thought of the boys leaving and Emmy rejecting him, he suddenly realized he had nothing left to keep him in Little Falls. He would miss his friends and the people he'd come to shepherd at the church, but they could all get along without him.

"Would Juliette mind?" Ben asked.

"Juliette?" His father laughed, though it wasn't filled with humor. "She is safely ensconced in a world of parties, ball gowns and status. As long as that is not threatened, she won't make a fuss."

"And the others?" Ben asked, thinking of the society in Montreal.

"There are so many men like you in Montreal now, no one will think twice about you or me or something that happened over thirty years ago."

"What about you?" Ben asked, looking at his father as a man in need of salvation, and not as the man who gave him life. "Have you made peace with God over what happened?"

Phillipe clasped Ben on the back. "That's where I thought you and I could start. Tell me about this God of yours and I will listen, Révérend Lahaye."

The thought of sharing the Gospel with his father, and having him receive the light of Christ's salvation, made all the heartache of the past twenty-five years suddenly dim.

But then he thought of Emmy and the boys, and the brief joy disappeared. If he had a choice, he would stay in Little Falls to make Emmy his wife and the boys his sons—but he couldn't have those things.

He rarely made a decision without a great deal of time and prayer, but he didn't foresee anything changing his mind this time. He would take this opportunity to make a new life with his father, one he felt God had provided to help him forget the brief and wonderful days with his makeshift family.

If only it would be so easy to forget.

"I will go," Ben said at last, resignation in his voice. "I will return with you to Montreal."

"C'est merveilleux!" Phillipe's face lit up with joy and he stood. "When shall we leave?"

"Christmas Day, after my last church service." Ben also stood, wiping the dirt and hay from his backside.

"Christmas Day?" His father frowned. "Why then?"

Because it would be the day after the twins left, and there would be no other reason to stay.

* * *

Emmy stood behind the curtain a few older students had helped her string across the front of the schoolroom for their Christmas pageant. The children scurried to find their places, all chaos and distraction. Thankfully she had put on enough pageants to know that as soon as the audience quieted and the play began, the children would remember their parts and do well. And, if they didn't, their parents would still be proud and clap as loud as they could.

Levi and Zeb stood in the angel costumes Mrs. Carver had sewn for them, their bright faces glowing with expectation as they spoke to their friends in hushed whispers. She'd said hello to Mrs. Carver when they arrived, and had watched for Ben, though he hadn't come with them.

Emmy had only seen him twice since their ill-fated kiss, and that had been at church. He had been cordial and as kind as ever, though there had been distance between them. Adam had asked to take her home from church last Sunday and she had agreed, though she noticed Ben's attention on them as they left.

Zeb giggled and put his hands up to his mouth, while Levi let out a laugh that filled the space where the children were waiting.

"Shh," Emmy warned, though she couldn't stop from smiling. Her students were excited, and she was, too. She just wished she could hold on to this moment for a bit longer, knowing Levi and Zeb would be leaving the next day. From what Mrs. Carver said, Ben had decided not to tell the boys their father was coming. He wanted them to enjoy their last days in Little Falls with nothing hindering their joy.

She looked out a crack of the curtain, scanning the

full room for a glimpse of the man her heart longed to see. The schoolhouse was packed from front to back. There wasn't a seat left to be had, or a spot left to stand in.

Her breath stilled when she finally found him. Ben stood along the wall with Mrs. Carver seated next to him and his father standing beside him. Ben smiled at something his housekeeper said, though she could sense a heaviness about his countenance that made her want to go to him and carry his burdens away.

He couldn't see her, which offered her the luxury of taking in her fill of him. She had missed him dearly and had hoped for a glimpse of him every day, but the boys had come and gone from school like all the other children—alone. When she ran her errands in town, she had hoped she might run into him, but she hadn't had the pleasure. He was more handsome than ever before and the flutter in her stomach more pronounced. She closed her eyes, willing her feelings for him to disappear.

"Miss Wilkes." Greta Merchant spoke quietly beside Emmy. She was dressed as Mary and held little Louise Cooper, asleep and as peaceful as Emmy imagined the Christ child had been. "It's almost seven."

Peeking at her watch, Emmy realized they only had two minutes before the play would begin. "Children," she whispered in a voice loud enough for them to hear. "Find your places. We will begin shortly."

Once everyone was situated, Emmy took a deep breath, smiled at her students and then stepped out from behind the curtain, her heart pounding at the idea of speaking in front of such a large crowd—though the only one she was truly conscious of was Ben.

The room quieted and Emmy clasped her hands together, meeting the gazes of several people she knew.

Adam sat in the front row, his besotted smile for her alone. She nodded acknowledgment and tried not to let her gaze go to the side of the room where she knew Ben was standing, but she couldn't stop herself. She met his eyes and offered a brief smile, her insides warming at the intense look in his eyes.

She glanced away quickly.

"Good evening and merry Christmas," Emmy managed to say to the audience.

"Merry Christmas," several people responded.

"On behalf of the students, I'd like to welcome you to the Christmas pageant."

Applause broke out and Emmy could hear some of the children giggling behind the curtain.

"Tonight, we will celebrate Christmas with a pageant and then some carols. The children have been practicing for weeks and they are eager to share their joy for the holiday season with you. Please sit back, relax and enjoy the program." She smiled and took the seat that had been reserved for her up front where she could prompt the children, if necessary—and it happened to be next to Adam.

The pageant began, with Mary and Joseph journeying to Bethlehem for the census. Emmy sat back in pleasant surprise as the children performed the play with very few mistakes and little prompting.

When the Christ child was born and the angels stepped out to proclaim the King's birth, Levi and Zeb stood among them, their voices joining in glorifying Jesus's birth. Both boys beamed at Emmy, Zeb's toothless smile especially wide.

Baby Louise woke up, her eyes huge as she blinked. She began to cry and the angels stopped singing. Charlotte had to go forward to take her from Greta's arms.

With no baby Jesus, the students looked at one another, unsure how to proceed, but then Levi stepped forward, his voice high and clear, and picked up the song where the angels had left off.

Soon, the other children joined in, and the pageant continued as if the baby was still in Mary's arms.

Levi looked at Emmy and grinned, his eyes shining. Emmy placed her hand over her heart, feeling as if it was expanding inside. She smiled back, hoping her eyes conveyed her appreciation and love.

When the pageant came to an end, the room erupted in applause. The children clasped hands and took a bow. Emmy stood and joined her students, receiving more applause from those gathered.

After the applause quieted, she nodded at the children and Maggie Ritters, the smallest child in the class, stepped forward and began to sing "Silent Night." Her sweet voice filled the room, causing many eyes to tear up.

Emmy motioned for the other children and the audience to join in the second verse.

Outside, the world was dark and the stars were sparkling. Inside, the room swelled with the beautiful melody of Emmy's favorite Christmas carol. Her eyes met Ben's again, and this time he offered the slightest smile. Warmth filled her cheeks and joy filled her heart.

They sang two more songs, and then Emmy called the evening to a close, wishing everyone a merry Christmas and a happy break from school.

Parents gathered their children, and Mrs. Carver came to collect the boys. "You're coming for our Christmas celebration, aren't you, dearie?" she asked Emmy.

For two weeks she had thought about the invitation Ben had extended to spend this evening with him and the boys, but that had been before the kiss. "I'm not sure. Is Ben expecting me?"

"I am," he said from behind her.

She turned and found him standing a few feet away.

"The boys and I cut down a tree and decorated it for our celebration," he said. "We'd all be disappointed if you didn't join us."

"I came in with the Janners," she explained. "I won't have a way home..."

"I'll drive you." His face was stoic and hard to read as he looked at her.

What would they say alone in the sleigh, under the stars? Would it be awkward? Healing? She didn't care. She just wanted to be with him and the boys one more time. "Thank you."

"Come, boys," Mrs. Carver said to Levi and Zeb. "Let's run home and light the candles on the tree before Miss Emmy comes."

The boys jumped and cheered, and Zeb gave Emmy's legs an impromptu hug.

"I'll go with you," Ben's father said to Mrs. Carver. "If I may be of any help."

"We'd be happy for it." Mrs. Carver nodded at Mr. Lahaye.

Adam approached Emmy, his face shining as he reached for her hands. "That was marvelous, Emmy."

She allowed him to give her hands a squeeze and then she pulled away. "Thank you, Adam."

Ben started to take down the curtain, though he appeared to be ignoring her and Adam. It would be impossible not to hear them—but it looked like he was trying.

"Do you need help setting the classroom to rights?" Adam asked as he eyed Ben.

"I don't think so. Reverend Lahaye has stayed to

help." Though he hadn't asked if she needed help. He'd just gone to work doing whatever needed to be done.

Adam nodded and gave his full attention to Emmy. "Have you changed your mind about the Christmas Eve ball? If you have, I'd be honored to escort you."

"I plan to stay home and write some letters to my family back east." She smiled, hoping he wouldn't take it to heart. "I hope you have a very merry Christmas."

Adam looked from her to Ben and back. "May I come to call on Christmas Day?"

Emmy nibbled her bottom lip, unsure if she should continue to give her permission when she had no intentions to pursue a romantic relationship with Adam. Yet she hated to be alone on Christmas with the Janners. "If you'd like."

His smile was hopeful. "I look forward to the day."

He took his leave, along with many other families.

Emmy spoke to several parents who waited in line to visit with her.

Ben finished taking down the curtain and then he moved Emmy's desk back to the front of the room.

Mr. Samuelson approached and Emmy braced herself.

"That was a pleasant pageant," he said, his mustache twitching. "But I'm disappointed that my Annabeth wasn't Mary."

"It was a hard decision to make," Emmy said. "This is Greta's last year in school, but Annabeth has a couple years left. Perhaps she can be Mary next year."

He narrowed his eyes, studying her as if she was on display in a store window.

"I haven't made a decision about you, Miss Wilkes." He stroked his mustache. "I suppose we've come to the end of the term, and you'll be wondering if you still have a job."

She had wondered that very thing, but she thought she wouldn't address the issue, hoping it would resolve on its own.

Ben approached and Mr. Samuelson looked his way. "Good," the superintendent said. "I had wanted another board member here when I discussed my concerns with Miss Wilkes."

Ben crossed his arms, watching Mr. Samuelson closely. "What concerns do you have now?"

"It's come to my attention that Miss Wilkes has been entertaining Mr. Russell at the Janners' home. I just saw her speaking to him now."

Emmy swallowed, wishing anyone but Ben was standing there.

"Do you deny these claims?" Mr. Samuelson asked Emmy.

She shook her head. "I do not deny them."

"So, you're guilty, then?"

"Guilty of what?"

"You said you would not marry or even entertain a gentleman caller."

"Mr. Russell is just a friend, nothing more."

Ben didn't look at Emmy as she spoke.

"I can promise you I will be single and ready to continue teaching after the first of the year," Emmy said to the superintendent. "I would very much appreciate retaining my job."

The older gentleman stared at her as he stroked his mustache. Finally, he looked at Ben. "What do you think, Reverend Lahaye?"

"I think Miss Wilkes has been an outstanding teacher and we would be blessed to have her stay on."

His simple statement made Emmy feel as if she was floating. Even though he was upset at the turn of events in their relationship, he was still kind and gracious.

"You will remain on probation." Mr. Samuelson pointed at her. "Any hint of impropriety and you'll be replaced."

She wanted to sigh. Would they play this game for the next several years, until he knew she was serious about her desire to stay single?

"Goodbye, Miss Wilkes," Mr. Samuelson said. "I hope you have a merry Christmas."

It was the kindest thing he'd ever said to her, and it left her speechless.

Everyone drifted out of the schoolhouse, leaving Emmy and Ben alone like so many other times—yet, this time was much different. The air between them was thick with awkwardness. She didn't know what to say or how to behave.

She blew out the lanterns and didn't bother to bank the stove, since she wouldn't return for several weeks. The bleak and dreary winter break spread before her with yawning boredom. How would she endure day after day with the Janners and no school to fill her time?

She shook the thoughts away. Instead of dwell on her troubles, she would look forward to the next few hours with Ben and the boys.

Ben held her coat for her and she slipped into it, and then she locked the doors behind her.

They started toward the parsonage, the air crisp and thin. The snow crunched under their feet and the tree branches were laden with snow.

"It's going to be strange to go back to the school without Zeb and Levi sitting in the front row." Her voice caught and she had to bite her lip to stop it from trembling.

"I can't even think of it," Ben said quietly, shoving his hands into his pockets. "I keep pretending like it's not happening."

She took a deep, cold breath and let it out in a billowing fog. "Let's not think about tomorrow. Instead, let's make tonight the best it can be. No sadness allowed."

He looked at her and nodded. "No sadness allowed."

They could make-believe for one night, couldn't they?

Chapter Nineteen

Mrs. Carver's merry laughter brought a smile to Emmy's face as she sat near the Christmas tree and watched the dear old lady open a gift from Levi and Zeb. The potato masher was shiny and new, and she waved it at the boys with a chuckle. "My daughter is looking forward to my mashed potatoes again. I just had a letter from her yesterday and she said it's the only food she can think about as her time is drawing near to have that grandchild of mine."

Zeb snuggled in next to Mrs. Carver and looked up at her. "Can I be one of your grandchildren?"

The sweet old woman drew him as close as she could and nuzzled her head against his. "You always will be, my Zebby boy."

Emmy looked across the room where Ben was sitting with his father. Her gaze caught his and she was afraid she might start to cry at the look of sadness in his brown eyes.

Phillippe must have sensed the shift in everyone's mood, because he stepped forward and handed his gift to Mrs. Carver. "Madame Carver," he said with a bow as he presented the wrapped box to her. "For all your fine meals and your hospitality."

Mrs. Carver's cheeks blossomed with color as she accepted the box. "You didn't need to bother."

"It is not every day that a man can eat so well. I only wish I could give you more." The large man took his seat beside Ben again, and Emmy couldn't help but notice that something had changed between father and son. She'd even heard Ben call him père several times that evening, and if she wasn't mistaken that meant *father* in French.

She longed to ask Ben what had happened, but she didn't think it was any of her business. After tomorrow, when the boys left, she would no longer have a tie to Ben and it was better that way.

Emmy studied Levi's and Zeb's little faces, listened to the cadence of their speech and watched their mannerisms as they laughed and played, trying to memorize everything about them. She would need these memories to hold on to when she missed them the most.

It was something she hadn't had the luxury of doing when William died. The last time she'd been with him, she hadn't known it was the last time. They had been so busy making plans to head west, she had been distracted most of the time, and when they had said their final goodbye, she had hardly glanced in his direction as he left her parents' home.

She wouldn't let that happen with her and the boys.

Mrs. Carver unwrapped the box and took off the lid. She pulled out a beautiful straw bonnet with a wide pink ribbon and a sprig of pink flowers near the left ear. It was a simple bonnet, yet very elegant, and if Emmy was correct, it was the one in the milliner's window that had cost far too much for her to consider owning.

"Monsieur Lahaye!" Mrs. Carver's eyes grew wide and she shook her head. "I cannot accept this gift."

"And why not?" he asked with a frown.

"It's too extravagant for a widow."

Mr. Lahaye slapped his thigh and began to laugh. "If you keep cooking the way you do, I imagine that bonnet will become a courting bonnet soon."

Her color deepened and she placed the hat back in its box, though she didn't insist on returning it to him.

Everyone had already given the boys their gifts, clothes from Mrs. Carver, books from Emmy, boots and hats from Mr. Lahaye and warm coats from Ben. The gifts were practical, but Emmy knew they would go a long way in helping the boys stay comfortable and educated once they returned home with their father.

Mrs. Carver had received her gifts, and there had been a few things for Mr. Lahaye.

"Now it's Miss Emmy's turn!" Levi jumped to his feet and went to the tree where he lifted a small box and brought it to her as if he was carrying a platter of fine crystal. "I asked if I could be the one to give it to you."

She took the small box and smiled at him. "Thank you."

"Open it!" Zeb cried from his place near Mrs. Carver, his impatience making everyone laugh.

The box fit comfortably in her hand as she untied the white string and let the paper fall away. With deliberate care, she lifted off the lid and her breath caught when she looked at the beautiful gold locket. A tree had been intricately engraved into the face of the piece of jewelry, its leaves unfurling in a whimsical pattern.

"It's from all of us!" Levi said. "Mr. Ben picked it out, but we—"

"Hush, Levi," Mrs. Carver said. "Let her open it and see for herself."

Tears filled Emmy's eyes and her lips trembled as she lifted the delicate chain from the box, watching the locket spin when it was free. She set down the box and then took hold of the locket.

"See the latch," Levi said, crowding her to point at it. "Touch the latch and—"

Ben stepped over and lifted the boy into his arms, tossing him into the air with a smile. "Let her open it and see for herself."

Levi laughed, and the others followed, but Emmy was too focused on the locket to join in.

She touched the latch and the two halves parted. On one side was a picture of Levi and the other was a picture of Zeb—perfect likenesses.

"We sat for a pho-to-graph-er." Levi concentrated on each syllable, but then he smiled and wiggled out of Ben's arm. "So you can look at us whenever you want."

Emmy fingered the images as tears streaked down her cheeks. Now she wouldn't have to rely on memory alone. She would always have these pictures to cherish.

"Don't you like it, Miss Emmy?" Zeb asked, coming to stand beside her.

She wiped away her tears and offered a wobbly smile to the little boy. "It's the best gift anyone has ever given me."

Levi raced across the room and threw himself into her arms, and then Zeb hugged her, too, and she held both boys. "Thank you," she whispered to them.

When they pulled away, she looked at Ben. He was watching her with his own joyful sorrow. She smiled at him, too. "Thank you for this lovely gift. I will cherish it forever."

He nodded, but didn't say anything, and she imagined he was just as emotional as her. He turned and poked at the logs in the fireplace, taking several deep breaths.

"And you, too," she said to Mr. Lahaye and then Mrs. Carver. "Thank you."

"It was our pleasure, dearie." Mrs. Carver's sweet smile warmed Emmy's heart.

Ben turned back to the group. "I hate to be the one to break up this party, but it's gotten very late and the boys should be in bed."

"We haven't given you your present yet." Levi ran to Mr. Lahaye's side and whispered into his ear.

Mr. Lahaye nodded and went to the hook by the front door. Levi and Zeb also went to the hook and Mrs. Carver joined them to help them get on their outside clothing.

"What's all this?" Ben asked.

"They're getting your present," Emmy said.

"Where?"

"I had it delivered to the barn this evening—at least, I hope Mr. Caldwell delivered it."

"The furniture maker?" Ben asked.

Emmy smiled, wiping at her cheeks with her handkerchief. "I'm not giving you any more hints."

The boys pulled Mr. Lahaye into the kitchen and out the back door, while Mrs. Carver slipped into the kitchen herself, closing the door behind her.

It left Emmy and Ben alone in the front room.

He stood with his hands in his pockets, while Emmy fingered the locket.

"Would you like me to put it on you?" he asked quietly.

She nodded and handed it to him when he approached.

For a few seconds, he fumbled with the clasp on the chain. "I don't know why they make these things so small."

"They're meant for a lady's fingers," she supplied.

"There." He looked up a bit triumphant. "I have it."

She turned and waited as he reached around her and placed the chain around her neck. It rested gently on her chest and she looked down to admire it. "It's beautiful, Ben."

He secured it in place and she turned back to show him.

"I thought you'd like it." He looked at the fine piece of jewelry, and then met her gaze. "I picked a tree, because it reminded me of the work you're doing with all the students. You're giving them roots in education, and later, the fruit of that education will feed families for generations to come."

Tears threatened again as she bit her bottom lip to stop it from trembling.

A moment later, Mrs. Carver opened the kitchen door and held it for Mr. Lahaye and the boys as they traipsed in with Ben's gift.

His eyes grew wide as he looked over the bookshelf.

"It's for all your books," Levi pronounced. "Miss Emmy helped us design it and then she gave the design to the builder."

"Is that what you were working on the day I took you sledding?" Ben asked.

The boys nodded vigorously.

"You can get all your books off the floor now," Zeb said.

"It's perfect." Ben ran his hands over the smooth walnut. "It's the most beautiful shelf I've ever seen."

He picked up Zeb and then Levi, giving them both a hug. "Thank you."

"Shouldn't Miss Emmy get a hug, too?" Levi asked.

Ben set the boys down and looked at Emmy. "Thank you for this gift."

"It'll fit perfect over here," she said quickly, walking across the room to where his books were piled on the floor.

"And I bought a few books for you to add to your collection," Mrs. Carver said, taking her gift from under the tree and handing it to Ben.

His hands were full now, and Emmy hoped he wouldn't try to hug her in front of all these people. Not that she didn't want to be hugged—but she didn't want anyone to see what his hug might do to her.

"All right, boys." Mrs. Carver clapped her hands. "All good things must come to an end, as my pappy used to say."

The boys groaned.

Mr. Lahaye stretched his arms. "I'm ready to go to sleep myself. Been a long day."

"Say good-night," Mrs. Carver said to the boys.

Zeb and Levi hugged Emmy and Ben, and shook Mr. Lahaye's hand before Mrs. Carver rushed them up the stairs. She peeked her head around the stairway door. "There are warm bricks in the oven for your feet, dearies. Take your time and enjoy a nice sleigh ride."

Mr. Lahaye said good-night and went into Ben's room where he'd been sleeping on a pallet since their return from Owatonna.

"Are you ready?" Ben asked.

She nodded, though she hated to see this evening end. When she thought of missing the boys, her hand went up to the locket and it offered a bit of comfort.

He helped her with her outdoor clothing and she went into the kitchen to wrap the bricks in towels. Ben went out to the barn to hitch up the open sleigh and she waited until he drove it out of the barn, and then she took the bricks and stepped outside to join him.

It had to be well past midnight, which meant it was officially Christmas Eve. Clouds had filled the sky, and snow was softly falling, adding another layer to several feet already on the ground. Everything was still and peaceful. Not an animal or person stirred within sight.

Ben helped her into the sleigh and tucked the buffalo robe around her skirts. He set the bricks near their feet, and Emmy was thankful for the heat they emanated.

Ginger led the way out of town, the bells on her harness jingling with each movement she made. The drive wouldn't take long. Usually, Emmy appreciated the short distance to and from town, but tonight, she wished the Janners lived farther away.

Neither one said a word, though there was much Emmy longed to say. She wanted to talk about the boys' departure, about Ben's newfound relationship with his father and about the rumors he might have heard concerning her and Adam. Yet, she didn't know how to broach any of those subjects, so she remained quiet.

The Janners' farm came within sight and Ben slowed Ginger until she was hardly moving. He turned and looked at Emmy. "There's something I need to tell you," he said softly. "I didn't want to say anything until everyone had had their fun tonight."

His voice was thick with emotion, making her heart pound harder.

Her eyes had adjusted and she was able to make out his features with ease. It almost hurt to look at his handsome face, knowing that she must harden her heart to the feelings he stirred within her.

"I've accepted my father's invitation to go to Montreal."

Emmy's mouth parted at the declaration, her thoughts coming into complete focus. "Montreal?"

He nodded and looked down. "I think it's for the best. With the boys leaving...and—I just think I need to move on."

She was speechless. Heartache was too kind a word for what she felt knowing that the boys *and* Ben would leave. She realized that she had taken comfort knowing she'd still see Ben on Sundays and around town—yet, the thought of never seeing him again was more than she could bear. How would she endure the grief and loneliness?

"Emmy." Ben took her hands in his. Though they both wore mittens, she could feel his warmth seeping into her cold hands.

She forced herself to take a deep breath. She would not panic. She could endure the pain of separation again, couldn't she?

"I want you to know something." His gaze was as serious as she'd ever seen it. "I love you, Emery Anne Wilkes."

His were the most bittersweet words she'd ever heard. When William had told her he loved her, she had fallen into his arms and returned his love with abandon. She wasn't at liberty to be so foolish and naive again. Giving freely meant receiving grief and loneliness in return. Tears filled her eyes and she looked down.

"I will always love you." He put his hand under her chin and lifted it for her to look at him. "It's because I love you that I'm leaving. You've made your decision clear and I respect you for that, but I can't stay here and watch you fall in love with another man—"

"I'm not in love with another man."

"Maybe not now, but someday you will be, and it would be impossible for me to watch."

She swallowed the lump of emotions that wanted to make her sob.

"I'm leaving the day after tomorrow," he said.

"Christmas?"

"It's as good a day as any. I can't stay here after the boys are gone. There's no point. I will say my goodbyes during my last church service on Christmas morning and then my father and I will leave." He ran his mitted thumb over the top of her hands. "I'm sorry for going so suddenly. I just can't stay any longer."

Ginger was about to walk past the Janners' place, so Ben let go of Emmy's hands and turned the horse into their property. They drove up the long drive and he pulled to the front of the house, stopping the sleigh near their door.

Emmy's hands had grown cold and her insides felt empty.

Ben stepped out of the sleigh and walked around to help her out. He moved aside the buffalo robe and offered his hand.

She took it and climbed out of the sleigh, though her legs didn't want to work properly.

They walked to the door and came to a stop. She couldn't look at him, for fear of crumbling into his arms. "I don't want this to be goodbye," she managed to say.

"This is the only way."

She nodded and then reached for the doorknob, but he placed his hand over hers.

The snow continued to fall, landing on her cheeks

and nose. She took a deep breath, forcing herself to look up at him.

"Goodbye, Em." He leaned down and placed a kiss on her lips, taking her breath and her heart in one instant, and then he was gone.

She watched him pull away, willing him to look back, but he never did.

The next evening, stars had started to appear as Ben paced from the front door to the Christmas tree and back. All day, he'd been on edge, wondering when Malachi Trask would show up at his front door.

After breakfast that morning, Ben had told Levi and Zeb that their father was coming to take them. The boys had cried and begged Ben to keep them, but he'd explained through his own tears that they didn't belong to him and that he had to give them back.

He took them sledding one more time, and then they had come home and packed their bags. Ben didn't know if Mr. Trask would come during the morning or the afternoon, but now, as the evening hours encroached, he wondered if the man would come on the morrow, instead.

"Why don't you go to the Christmas Eve ball?" Mrs. Carver asked as she stepped out into the front room. "The boys and I will make caramel and popcorn. As soon as Mr. Trask arrives, I'll send word to you and you can come back."

Ben had wanted to go to the ball to say goodbye to his friends and parishioners, since he was leaving the next day, but he didn't want to miss the boys' departure, either.

"I'll come and get you myself." Father sat in Ben's rocker, reading the local newspaper, *The Northern Her-*

ald, and nodded his agreement with Mrs. Carver. "You should go. You're driving all of us crazy with your pacing."

Levi and Zeb were lying on their stomachs in front of the fireplace playing a game of checkers, though he could tell their hearts weren't in the game. Zeb looked up, his sad expression making Ben's gut fill with guilt. He couldn't leave the boys, not now, not when they knew this was their last day with him.

"Go, Mr. Ben," Zeb said. "We'll have caramels waiting for you when you come back."

"Listen to the boy," Mrs. Carver said with a sweet smile. "You're making them more nervous with all your pacing. I'll keep them occupied until their father arrives."

He didn't want to miss a single moment with the boys, but he didn't want to miss one last evening with his friends, either.

"I'll go," Ben finally said. "But you must get me immediately."

"I will," Father promised.

Ben stepped into his room and changed into his evening clothes. His canvas bag sat by the door, awaiting departure. He'd packed just enough to get by on the trip. Father had said there was no need to take anything that wasn't absolutely necessary. There would be time and resources to buy everything he needed in Montreal.

He hated leaving behind his books, though he'd gotten along without them during his circuit riding days. They had been a luxury during his years in Little Falls, and he suspected he'd make a new library in Canada. But it was a shame to leave the shelf Emmy and the boys had made for him. When they had given it to him, none knew about his upcoming move, none but Mrs. Carver.

He'd already shared the news with her, telling her she could stay in the parsonage as long as she needed before traveling to her daughter. He'd already gotten approval from Abram who said it might be some time before they could find a replacement for Ben, so they wouldn't need the parsonage.

The thought of leaving his parishioners without a pastor didn't set well with Ben. He'd worked tirelessly to draw many of them to church week after week, and some had serious needs—physical, mental and spiritual—that he was meeting. He prayed fervently that God would bring another pastor to them soon, and that none would look at his sudden departure as abandonment. Pastors came and went, didn't they? Then why was he feeling so heavy at the thought of going?

He took his time getting ready, praying over each person who attended church, and those he'd been ministering to in the community who didn't. The ball wouldn't get under way until eight o'clock, though it would run past midnight, for sure, into the wee hours of Christmas morning. He planned to be home long before then to say goodbye to the boys and be rested for the morning service.

As he dressed, he thought of Emmy. Truth be told, he'd thought of her all day and hadn't slept much the night before, either. It had been foolish and selfish to kiss her one last time. If he'd had the wherewithal at the moment, he should have apologized, but he'd left her as fast as he could, afraid he might continue kissing her if he didn't.

Ben finally left his room a while later, in no particular hurry to be gone.

"My, my." Mrs. Carver raised her eyebrows. "You look very handsome, Reverend Lahaye."

Father nodded his approval, as well. "You'll be a very desirable bachelor when we arrive in Montreal." It was all his father talked about. Marrying well was something important to Phillippe, though Ben wondered why he would make such a fuss when his own arranged marriage was in shambles.

It didn't matter to Ben. He'd do what needed to be done, when the time came.

"I think I'll head out now." Ben hugged the boys and then put on his outdoor coat. "If it gets too late, put the boys to bed. We can always invite Mr. Trask to spend the night and get an early start in the morning."

"That's not a bad idea," Father agreed.

"Be sure to send for me immediately, though." Ben put on his hat and secured his gloves in place. "I still want to be here."

"Go on." Father opened the front door and Ben stepped into the cold night air. Stars sparkled across the expanse of sky. He took a deep breath and started toward the Northern, praying all the way. The boys and Emmy were out of Ben's hands, but that didn't mean he couldn't pray for them. He'd always pray, no matter how much space separated them.

When he reached the hotel, he stepped over the threshold and into the front lobby. Already, dozens of people had gathered and music was spilling out of the double doors leading into the ballroom.

Though he knew Emmy wasn't planning to attend, he couldn't help but hope that she had changed her mind. He glanced around the room for a glimpse of her blond ringlets.

"Ben." Abram waved at him from across the room and walked in his direction, Charlotte on his arm. They were a striking couple and well respected. A fine combination.

Charlotte broke away from Abram and stepped into Ben's arms, taking him by surprise as she wrapped him in a hug. "Abram told me the news. Oh, Ben, why are you going?"

Ben hugged her back, offering Abram a knowing smile over her head. He suspected the other ball guests were surprised at the gesture between them, but he didn't care at the moment. In every way, Charlotte was like a little sister to him and he suspected this was how a sister would act given the same news. "My father invited me to go to Montreal."

She stepped back and looked into his face, her perceptive gaze locked on his. "It's because of Emmy, isn't it?"

"Charlotte." Abram stepped up and put his arm around his wife's waist. "A man would never admit a thing like that to anyone. If Ben needs to go, then we will wish him well."

She wiped at the tears on her cheeks and shook her head. "It won't be the same here without you. You'll write, won't you?"

"Of course I'll write." He hated saying goodbye, but it was the right thing to do—wasn't it?

"And you'll visit us again, won't you?" Charlotte asked.

"Montreal is a long way away," Abram said, soothing his wife. "We can't make Ben promise something like that."

"I'll try," Ben said, and meant it.

"I saved a dance for you on my card." Charlotte lifted the card strung around her wrist and showed him where she'd put his name. "I'm going to try and talk you out of leaving."

"I don't think you could." Though, if anyone could, it would be Charlotte.

"Come," Abram said as he whisked her away. "I want to dance with my wife."

Ben was thankful for Abram as he watched them go. He would help Charlotte focus on something other than Ben's departure for the evening.

The citizens of Little Falls had become like family, but his love for them was not enough to persuade him to stay and watch Emmy and Adam fall in love. Nothing could make that prospect any easier to bear.

Chapter Twenty

"You hardly touched your supper," Mrs. Janner said to Emmy while she helped her landlady with the dishes. "Is something ailing you?"

The Janner kitchen felt cold and lifeless, with only the bare essentials hanging from pegs in the walls. Emmy opened the doors of a whitewashed cabinet and set the plates inside. It lacked the warmth of Ben's kitchen, and the congeniality of Mrs. Carver. The house was silent, save the sound of clinking dishes and silverware. The three men were already in the parlor quietly reading.

"I'm fine." Emmy sighed. It was easier to say she felt fine than to actually believe it. She hadn't slept at all the night before and had paced in her room most of the day. Ben's kiss had upset her more than it should—not because it made her angry, but because it felt right and pure and wonderful. It was everything a kiss should be and more.

Today was but the first day of countless others she would live without Ben, and it had been horrible.

"I know something's ailing you." Mrs. Janner wiped her hands on her apron and took the dishwater to the back door where she tossed it away from the house. When she stepped back inside she hung the pan on a hook. "Your cheeks are pale, you didn't eat all day and you're quieter than usual. I haven't had much book learning, but I'm smart enough to know lovesickness when I see it."

"Lovesickness?"

"I don't know if it's over Mr. Russell or Reverend Lahaye," the lady continued as if Emmy hadn't responded, "but I'm assuming it's one of them."

Was Emmy that transparent, or was the woman more perceptive than Emmy had given her credit for?

"I know I'm a bit cold," Mrs. Janner said with a nod, "but I used to be a young lady like you, with a lot of heartache and what I thought was wisdom."

Emmy didn't know what to say. She hardly felt like she knew Mrs. Janner, yet the woman seemed to know a great deal about her.

"I see all the signs, Miss Wilkes." She looked at Emmy almost as if she could see through her. "Something hurt you and now you're trying your best to keep yourself from getting hurt again."

Emmy nodded, unable to keep it inside any longer. "I lost my fiancé to an accident."

"I suspected something along those lines." The older woman crossed her arms and studied Emmy. "So now you've fallen in love again and you're afraid to give your heart away, in case it's broken again."

"Yes." She spoke the word just above a whisper, her heart so heavy she thought she might start to weep right there in the sparse kitchen.

"Don't do it."

Emmy looked up. "Don't do what?"

"Don't keep your heart hidden, girl. Hearts are meant

to be shared and they're meant to heal. My own heart was broken once." She looked down, her own vulnerability evident in the way she held her shoulders. "I told myself I would never love again because I'd almost lost my mind with grief. I stayed single for a while, but then life took a turn and I found myself in need of some shelter and protection. I married Mr. Janner for convenience sake—but truthfully, I married him because I didn't love him and I thought I'd be safer that way."

The grandfather clock struck eight times in the dining room and Emmy waited for her to continue.

"We've made a life together, Mr. Janner and me, but this house lacks the love and affection my heart craves. See, I thought my heart would never heal, but it has and now it wants to be given and received, but Mr. Janner and I are too far gone for romance. If I started asking for it now, he'd scoff at me."

Emmy frowned at the notion of living in a house without love. What kind of an existence was that?

"If your heart has already fallen for someone," her landlady continued, "it's too late. Even if you don't marry him, you'll be miserable for the rest of your life. Don't let fear dictate your decisions. I did, and I've regretted it for decades."

The thought of Ben leaving her for good was just as painful as the idea of marrying him and seeing him die. Either way, she would be without him. Yet, what if they both lived until they were ninety, and they had missed out on a life of love because she was afraid? She didn't want to come to the end of her life and look back on decades of loneliness.

Her heart sped up at the thought of falling into Ben's arms and telling him she loved him in return. The look in his eyes would be worth the risk of losing him, yet, if she could spend even one day as his wife, loving and being loved in return, wasn't it worth the risk?

"It looks like one of those gentlemen I mentioned is pulling in the drive." Mrs. Janner went to the stove and put a few pieces of kindling inside. It was her evening habit to make coffee and she went about it now as if she and Emmy had not just had such a meaningful conversation.

Nerves bubbled in Emmy's stomach as she went to the window. Was it Ben or Adam who had come? She longed for it to be Ben, but it was Adam who alighted from the sleigh and walked up to the door.

"I'll get it," Emmy said, her voice a bit forlorn.

"I see it's Mr. Russell who's come, but from the tone of your voice, it's Reverend Lahaye you're pining after." Mrs. Janner nodded. "He'd be my choice, too."

Emmy was too miserable to smile as she walked to the door and opened it for Adam.

"Merry Christmas Eve," Adam said, a jovial smile on his face. "I've brought Mrs. Janner a wreath." He held it up and smiled at the older lady by the stove.

"Thank you, Mr. Russell." She stepped away from the stove and took it from him. "I'll hang it on the door."

Emmy closed the door behind him, not feeling like entertaining tonight, especially since she needed to get to Ben somehow. "Adam, I'm not—"

"I've come to take you to the ball, Emmy Wilkes, and I won't take no for an answer. You're too young and too pretty to stay home."

The ball. Would Ben be at the ball? Her heart sped up again. Even if he wasn't, she could slip away to see him, couldn't she?

But was it right to allow Adam to take her to the

ball, just to get to Ben? She hesitated, yet she had never promised Adam anything but friendship.

"Do you have a ball gown?" he asked her. "Even if you don't, the dress you have on will do."

The dress in question was nothing fancy and she wouldn't be caught in it at a ball. Excitement rushed up her spine at the prospect of going to the ball and seeing Ben—but would it be too late? Had she destroyed any chance they might have with her stubbornness? Mother always said a man's pride was his worst enemy. Would Ben's pride stand in their way?

She had to find out.

"I'll be back in a moment," Emmy said to Adam. "I do have a ball gown."

"So you'll come with me?" Adam's face lit up and he grinned.

"Yes, but only as friends—you do understand?"

Adam grinned. "I'll take you any way I can."

"I'll help you get ready." Mrs. Janner left her coffee preparations and followed Emmy up the stairs to her room.

"Will Reverend Lahaye be at the ball?" Mrs. Janner whispered to Emmy.

For the first time all evening, Emmy smiled. "I don't know, but if he's not, I'll find him one way or another."

Mrs. Janner returned the smile, her face transforming into that of a young woman. "I'm happy I could help you see the truth."

"So am I."

It didn't take them long working together. Soon, Emmy was resplendent in her cobalt blue ball gown, all the hoops and layers making the skirt bell out with style. They'd curled her hair and Mrs. Janner had surprised her with her adeptness at styling it into something grand. They slipped her dancing slippers into a bag, though Mrs. Janner insisted she wear her boots until they arrived at the hotel. All that was left was her jewelry, and she chose to wear the locket with the boys' pictures inside. It went perfectly with her gown and it accented the gold earrings she'd chosen to wear. It was also a way she could keep the boys close, though they were probably already on their way south with their father.

That thought alone dampened Emmy's excitement about going to the ball and seeing Ben again. Tears threatened to fall, but she held them back, needing to keep her composure until she could be with Ben and mourn with him.

"You look lovely, Miss Wilkes." Mrs. Janner stood back and admired her. "My prayers go with you."

Emmy picked up her train and smiled her thanks as she slipped out of the bedroom and went down the steps.

Adam stood in the kitchen, clutching his gloves. When Emmy appeared, he swallowed several times and fumbled over his words. "You—you look s-stunning, Emmy—Miss Wilkes."

"Thank you, Adam."

"I have something for you to wear." Mrs. Janner excused herself and returned a minute later with a beautiful black wool cape, with intricately scalloped edges and embroidered flowers trailing up and down in a jet-black silk thread. "I wore it when I was a young lady. I hope it's not too old-fashioned."

"It's beautiful." Emmy allowed Adam to drape it over her shoulders and then she pulled on her long black gloves. Before she left, she reached over and gave Mrs. Janner a quick hug. "Thank you, for everything."

Mrs. Janner used the edge of her apron to wipe at

her eye and then turned back to her coffee without another word.

Adam reminded her of a skittish colt as he opened the door for her and helped her to his waiting sleigh. He hardly took his eyes off her all the way into town. When they pulled up to the Northern, he tied his horse to a hitching post and came around to help her out. "I can't believe I'm the man who is walking in with you tonight."

She tried to smile at his attempt at flattery, but all she could think about was Ben. What if he wasn't inside? What if—her heart almost stopped beating when she considered that he might not want to see her at all. Yet, she had to try.

Emmy allowed Adam to whisk her up the steps and across the hotel porch. He opened the door, his eyes still on her.

"Miss Wilkes." Charlotte Cooper stood visiting on the other side of the lobby with a gaggle of ladies, but stepped away when Emmy entered the lobby. "You look lovely tonight," Charlotte said. "I'm so happy you decided to come."

Emmy longed to ask her if Ben was at the ball, but Adam was beside her and she didn't want to make him uncomfortable.

"I'll get a dance card for you." Charlotte led her to the front desk where a young lady had a stack of dance cards ready. "You'll be a welcome addition to the ball."

The lady handed her a card while Emmy tried to look around the lobby for Ben. She didn't want to appear overeager, but she also didn't want to waste another moment.

"Will you allow me the pleasure of the first and last dance?" Adam asked.

It was only right and fair, so she nodded and allowed him to write his name on her dance card. Several dances had already commenced and been marked off, leaving a dozen or so. When she pulled the card back, she saw that he had taken a third dance, right in the middle of the evening. Three dances were only reserved for couples who were courting or engaged—neither of which described them, but she didn't have time to discuss that now.

The clerk behind the counter took her cloak and hat, and Emmy slipped into a dressing room to change from her boots into her slippers. She looked in the mirror, smoothed down her curls and pinched her cheeks, then stepped out again, hoping and praying she'd see Ben soon.

"Shall we?" Adam appeared at her elbow, ready to take her into the ball.

She held her breath and let him escort her, not knowing how this evening would end.

The ballroom was warm and filled with the scent of mulled wine and gingerbread. A large Christmas tree had been set up behind the orchestra and the candles were lit, offering a glow to the room. Ben stood near the refreshment table with two elders from the church, explaining his decision to leave. No one had taken his announcement well and he'd been second-guessing his plans to leave so suddenly—yet, he needed to get away, the sooner the better.

From where he stood, he had a good view of the ballroom, especially the main doors. All night, he'd kept his ears on his conversations, but his eyes had been searching for Emmy. He didn't think she'd come, but if she did, he wanted to see her.

"Do you know of anyone who could take your place, at least temporarily?" Mitch O'Hare asked Ben.

"Abram would be a good replacement until a preacher could be found." Ben took a sip of punch and set his glass on the table, smiling at the Northern's cook, Martha, who bustled about behind the refreshment table refilling the platters and bowls. "He might disagree, but he's a fine preacher and knows the Word of God inside and out."

A movement at the door caught Ben's attention, making his breath catch and his heart pound.

She'd come.

Emmy stood in a stunning blue gown, with long black gloves extending up her slender arms. Her curls were piled in a becoming style, with ringlets teasing her neck and shoulders. From where he stood, the overheard chandelier caught the gold locket resting on her chest, making it shine.

There was an anxious look in her expression as she scanned the ballroom, her eyes not resting as she looked from face to face.

Adam Russell stood beside her and spoke into her ear, stealing her attention. Soon, he had her in his arms, twirling her around the dance floor with the other couples.

She'd told both men she didn't want to come to the ball, yet here she was in Adam's arms. Obviously, she'd changed her mind, and Adam had been the one to get her to come.

It felt as if Ben had been punched, square in the gut, and he knew when he was beat. Emmy had made her choice, just as he knew she would, and here was proof.

"If you'll excuse me," Ben said to Mr. O'Hare. "Goodbye."

"You're going so soon?" Mr. O'Hare frowned. "But we haven't finished our conversation."

"I'm sorry." Ben was already moving away, his voice trailing behind him. Anger, embarrassment, grief—it was all mingling inside, and he hoped Emmy didn't see him. He didn't want her to know that he knew she was with Adam. A part of him wanted to save her from her own embarrassment over the whole situation.

He'd kissed her, just last night, when she'd already been in love with Adam. At least he'd never kissed Charlotte or Elizabeth—that was one regret that they didn't share. Emmy, on the other hand— He just needed to leave.

"Ben." Jude Allen stood by the door with his wife, Elizabeth. "I just told Lizzie the news."

Elizabeth was a beautiful woman, with dark hair and sparkling blue eyes. Her eyebrows came together in dismay. "We're going to miss you, Ben. I never thought we'd have to say goodbye."

Ben didn't want to be rude, especially to such dear friends. But here was yet another reminder of a happy couple he had been forced to watch over the years. Their growing family was a testament to their love and affection for one another. He wasn't bitter or envious, just tired of being alone and seeing other people have what he wanted.

"Life's like that." Ben stood in front of the Allens, his back to the dancers. He couldn't handle seeing Emmy look upon Adam with adoration. That would be too much.

Jude frowned at Ben, his gaze going over Ben's shoulder. Realization dawned in his brown eyes and he gave Ben a knowing half smile. "I always told Lizzie you were too passive. Even when I wanted you to pursue her, you refused—which, I suppose, worked out for me."

Elizabeth didn't look shocked at her husband's statement. Apparently they'd discussed this before. It gave Ben permission to speak freely.

"What would you have me do, Jude? I already made my feelings clear." Clearer than he'd ever made with anyone else. "She's made her choice."

"Has she?" Jude lifted his eyebrows. "Then why is she scanning the room, even while she's dancing with Mr. Russell?"

Ben didn't want to turn and see. She wasn't looking for him.

"Make me one promise before you leave," Jude said to Ben. "Ask her to dance, just one more time, and tell her how you feel again. If she says no, then you have your final answer. If she says yes…well, you'll know what to do then. Don't be passive."

"I have no desire to be humiliated again."

"Ben." Elizabeth stepped away from her husband and put her hand on his arm. She looked up at him with respect and admiration. "Jude and I were in love a long time before we admitted it to one another. I almost left Little Falls, but Jude had the courage to tell me he loved me one more time—and that time it was exactly what I needed to hear. Don't be afraid to share your heart with her. At this point, you have nothing left to lose and everything to gain." She smiled at him. "If nothing else, do it for Charlotte and for me. We want you to be happy."

His chest filled with hope. She was right. Even when it came to Charlotte and Abram. They'd been in love for a long time before either one had the courage to speak up just one more time.

He turned, looking for Emmy. Jude was right, too. He's been too passive in the past, so he made a decision now without further thought. He wouldn't wait until the song ended to speak to her. She was in the middle of the dance floor, twirling with Adam. Ben stepped through the crowd of dancers, weaving this way and that to avoid collision. When he finally arrived at his destination, he didn't hesitate, but tapped Adam on the shoulder. "May I cut in?"

Adam and Emmy came to a stop and Emmy's beautiful blue eyes filled with surprise, and then complete and utter joy.

That look alone was enough to make all else fade away. He didn't even wait for Adam's approval, but took Emmy into his arms, and led her away.

"Ben." Her voice was breathless and heady—a sound he longed to hear.

"I couldn't let you go without a fight, Em."

She nibbled her bottom lip in a gesture he'd come to know and love.

"Do you love him?" Ben asked, his voice low and guarded, afraid of what she might say.

"No."

"Do you think you'll fall in love with him?"

"I will never love Adam."

He continued to waltz with her, twirling and spinning her around the floor, as if they'd done it together a hundred times before. He needed to know more—longed to hear her say the words. "Why won't you love him?"

Her eyes looked bluer than usual this evening, and they shone and sparkled when she gazed upon him. "Because I love you, Ben, more than I ever dreamed possible."

He wanted to scoop her into his arms and take her

away from curious eyes to show her how much her words meant to him, but the waltz continued, and all he could do was smile—yet he knew her heart had been broken and she needed reassurance and hope in this moment. "Are you willing to take a risk and let me love you like I want to love you?"

"That's why I came tonight." Her shoulders lifted in a way that told him she'd been set free from her fear.

He leaned his head down to touch her forehead with his, speaking softly. "I would have waited a lifetime for you, Em."

"And that's exactly what I didn't want to happen." They had come to a stop on the dance floor, while everyone waltzed around them, and she placed her gloved hand on his cheek. "I don't want to waste a lifetime being afraid—I'd rather spend a lifetime loving you—even if that lifetime is shorter than we want. God has ordained our days, Ben, and He's offered us a beautiful love story to enjoy for as long as He sees fit. Who am I to question His sovereignty?"

He put his hand over hers. "Then let's not wait another day. Let's get married tomorrow, on Christmas."

"But what about your father and your plans to go to Montreal?"

"I'll simply explain to him that my plans have changed."

"Do you still want to go to Montreal?"

He knew the answer, even before she finished asking her question. "I never really did. My heart is for ministry. If it suits you, I'd like to stay in Little Falls and continue serving right here."

Her smile was big and bright. "It suits me just fine." She slipped her hand up to the locket, her smile dimming. "It will be strange living in the parsonage without the boys. How did they take the news? Did they warm to their father? Were they sad to go?"

"They haven't left yet."

Emmy's eyes grew wide. "They haven't?"

"Malachi didn't come today."

"Can we go to them? Wake them up if we need to? Tell them our news? Give them hugs and kisses and hold on to them for as long as possible?"

Ben laughed and took her hand, loving that he could do so without any reservations. "Let's go now."

The waltz had come to an end, and the other dancers had stopped to watch Ben and Emmy, a few with knowing smiles on their face.

Ben caught a glimpse of Elizabeth and Jude. He winked at them as he stepped out of the ballroom, and Elizabeth's smile couldn't be missed.

Charlotte and Abram stood in the lobby, visiting with other guests. When Ben entered the room with Emmy at his side, he received happy smiles from them, too.

Ben asked for their coats and hats and turned just in time to see Adam's approach.

"I see you're running off with the young lady I escorted here this evening." Adam's voice was neither happy, nor angry. There was a resigned acceptance in his tone.

"I'm sorry, Adam." Emmy put her hand on his arm. "If it's all right with you, Ben will take me home this evening."

"I should have known as much." Adam shook his head, giving her a sad smile. "But a man can hope, can't he?"

"I wish you all the best, Adam." Emmy stepped away from him and allowed Ben to slip her cloak around her shoulder.

Ben put on his own coat, not sure what to say to Adam, if anything.

In the end, he simply nodded at Adam, and then stepped out of the hotel without another word to anyone.

They stood on the porch, the stars sparkling overhead, but Ben only had eyes for the woman he loved. He wouldn't take another step until he had kissed Emery Anne Wilkes.

And that's exactly what he did.

Chapter Twenty-One

Emmy was breathless as she clung to Ben. She had given him her heart and she would never take it back, no matter what life handed to them.

The streets were quiet, though the orchestra music seeped out of the hotel, wrapping them in a sweet haze. She could have stood in Ben's arms for hours, but the sound of the stagecoach brought both of them to their senses.

Ben pulled away as she turned to watch its approach. His arm stayed around her waist and he held her tight, making her smile. She suspected Ben had no intentions on letting her leave his side for a long time, and she didn't want to go.

"Malachi might be on the stage." His simple sentence felt like ice sliding though her veins.

She tightened her hold on him, ready to face whatever may come.

Andrew pulled the horses to a stop with a whoa. "Merry Christmas," he said. "Stage is late tonight, on account of some merrymaking down at the St. Cloud saloon."

"Your merrymaking, or some others?" Ben asked

with a hint of a smile in his voice, though Emmy knew he was only trying to hide his worries with a joke.

"Well, now." Andrew cleared his throat and nodded at Ben. "I won't be going to confession anytime soon, Reverend Lahaye, if that's what you're getting at."

Ben chuckled, though his back was stiff. "Did you bring anyone?"

"No one is on the stage tonight." Andrew reached into his pocket and leaned forward. "But you happen to be just the man I'm looking for. I have a letter for you."

Malachi wasn't on the stage? What did that mean?

Ben stepped away from Emmy long enough to take the letter and then he came back, examining it by the glow of the window behind him. "It doesn't have a return address."

"If no one is planning to get on the stage, I think I'll be heading out." Andrew clicked the reins and waved his hat. "Merry Christmas."

"Merry Christmas," Ben and Emmy replied.

"Who do you think it's from?" Emmy asked Ben.

"I don't know. But let's go home and read it there."

Home. Emmy's chest filled with warmth at the sound. She hoped the boys were still awake so she could hold them close.

They walked to the parsonage, hand in hand, and Emmy could do nothing but smile.

When they arrived, Ben pushed open the door and let her enter first. The tree was still aglow with candles, and the fireplace was crackling. Mr. Lahaye sat in the rocker, a book in hand, though his chin was resting on his chest and his soft snores filled the room.

Mrs. Carver was in the kitchen, the sound of pots and pans rattling around, but there was no sign of the boys.

Ben helped her remove her cloak and hat, hanging them on the hook, and then he took off his coat.

Emmy waited for him to open the envelope and pull out the letter. He read to her.

"Dear Reverend Lahaye,
It is with a heavy heart that I write this letter. It has taken me days to get up the courage to say what needs to be said, though I was tempted not to write at all.

When I went home to Katrina, I discovered that she had packed all her things. The next day, she left me to return east to her kinfolk. I plan to head out myself, make something of my life in Colorado or California. Maybe one day, when I am better, I will go after Katrina and do right by her. Until then, I will work hard and try to stay sober.

Please find a good home for my boys. I don't want them to know what kind of a man their father is. If you ever need to speak of me, please do it with kindness. Give them hope for their own futures, even if I couldn't.
Sincerely,
Malachi P. Trask"

Ben folded the letter and looked up at Emmy, his countenance heavy. "I will never cease praying for that man as long as I live."

"Neither will I."

He put the letter on the table next to the lantern, which was lit for passersby, a warm beacon of hope that had welcomed her the first night she blew in with the storm.

"Do you know what this means, Em?"

She nodded, tears already sliding down her cheeks. "Levi and Zebby need a home."

"Would you—"

"You don't even have to ask."

His smile was beautiful as he pointed at the stairs. "Shall we go wake them?"

Mrs. Carver stepped out of the kitchen and held the door open for the two little boys who followed, one holding caramel, the other a bowl of popcorn.

"Miss Emmy!" Levi's face lit up and he handed the caramel to Mrs. Carver. He raced across the room and jumped into her arms. "You came back."

Emmy hugged him tight and bent down to reach for Zeb, who was right behind Levi. She lifted both boys, a feat unto itself, but she wouldn't have it any other way. "Merry Christmas."

"Why didn't I get that kind of welcome?" Ben teased.

Zeb reached for Ben and Ben took him into his arms.

"Now isn't this a pretty picture?" Mrs. Carver asked, holding both the caramel and the bowl of popcorn.

"Is it Christmas yet?" Levi asked.

Emmy glanced at the clock. "Just a couple more hours."

"I have a present for you, boys." Ben looked from Zeb to Levi. "Miss Emmy has agreed to marry me."

Zeb's smile was colored with pink cheeks and Levi frowned, as if he'd had plans to marry her instead, but both boys looked happier than they had in a long time.

"And," Emmy said, placing her cheek against Levi's as she looked at Zeb, "we want to make you our little boys, forever."

"Forever?" Levi asked. "What about our pa?"

Ben touched Levi's cheek and smiled, though there was a hint of sadness behind his eyes. "Someday, you'll understand a little better, but your pa asked us if we'd find a good family for you. He's moving west and decided it would be better for you to stay here. He loves you and wants the very best for you."

Levi wrapped his arms around Emmy's neck and hugged her tight. "Miss Emmy is the best for me."

Ben and Zeb grinned, and Ben nodded. "She's the best for all of us."

"I hear congratulations are in order." Mr. Lahaye stood and set his book on the chair. "If my old ears don't deceive me, there's to be a wedding real soon."

Ben stood a little straighter as he addressed his father. "Tomorrow, I hope."

"A Christmas wedding." Mrs. Carver had set down the treats and was hugging her middle, happy tears in her eyes.

Mr. Lahaye walked across the room and extended his hand to Ben. "Congratulations, son."

Ben shook his hand, his eyes searching his father's face. "I'm sorry if I've upset you."

Mr. Lahaye turned to Emmy, acceptance and love in his handsome face. "I have always wanted what's best for Benjamin, just like Mr. Trask wants what's best for Levi and Zeb." He smiled at Emmy and reached out to wrap her and Levi in a hug. "I couldn't agree more with these three gentlemen. You are what's best for my son, so I welcome you into the family with open arms."

Emmy returned the hug, happiness and joy filling every inch of her. "Thank you, Mr. Lahaye."

"Call me Père, as Ben does."

She nodded as he stepped back.

He took a deep breath. "I suppose this means I'm returning to Montreal alone."

"I'm afraid it does," Ben said. "But I would like to take my family to visit you very soon."

"I would like that."

"Will you stay for our wedding?" Emmy asked.

"I wouldn't miss it."

"Come and eat up," Mrs. Carver called. "We have a lot of planning to do, if you're going to be married on Christmas."

The boys wiggled out of their arms and raced over to the popcorn and caramel, Père close behind.

Ben reached out and took her hand. She entwined her fingers through his, and together they walked over to join their family, which was no longer a temporary arrangement, but soon to be a permanent union.

A hushed silence filled the evening air as if signaling the beginning of something special.

Ben led Zeb and Levi from the kitchen door of the parsonage to the back door of the church, their feet crunching over the hard-packed snow. The sun had already set and the stars were shining overhead as they made their way in their Sunday best.

When they reached the church, Ben squatted down in front of them, adjusting Zeb's tie and smoothing Levi's hair, his breath puffing out in a frozen cloud. "Remember, I want you to be on your best behavior while we're in the church."

"Yes, sir," they both said in unison, their eyes filled with the excitement of the moment.

"Will we be a family after the wedding?" Levi asked.

"Yes."

"Can we call Miss Emmy our mama?" Zeb asked.

"She'd like that."

"Will you be our pa?"

"For the rest of your lives."

The boys grinned at each other and Ben smiled.

"Are you ready?" he asked the boys.

They nodded and Ben opened the door, entering in behind them.

Charlotte had outdone herself. The church was filled with dozens of candles, filling the room with a flickering glow. Pine garland had been strung along the pews, dripping with red ribbons and silver bells. And the church was full of dear people who had chosen to give up their Christmas evening plans to witness Ben and Emmy's marriage vows.

He smiled at several now. Abram and Charlotte sat just behind Mrs. Carver and the boys, all their children filling in the rest of the pew. Ben had gone to them earlier that day to tell them the news, and Charlotte had instructed him to leave everything to her. If they were willing to wait until evening, she said she would have everything ready—and that's exactly what she had done. He smiled his thanks to her now and she nodded.

Emmy had gone out to the Janners' place and spent the day there, getting her things ready to move back to the parsonage. She had missed the morning church service, but everyone understood why. Father had gone out to pick her up after supper and would have her at the church any minute.

Ben stepped up to the front where old Judge Barnum stood, a smile on his wrinkled face. It would have been nice to be married by another pastor, but there was no time to invite one to come, and the judge was an old friend who was honored to perform the ceremony. Ben had given him the book of vows he used for every wedding he'd ever performed, and asked the judge to do what he thought was best.

Everyone smiled at Ben from their places around the church. Jude and Elizabeth were there with Elizabeth's little sister Rose, and their brand-new baby girls. The Ayers had come in from the mission, their presence a wonderful and unexpected gift. The Hubbards were there with their four children, the Morgans with four, as well. Other church families had come to celebrate, and though it wasn't a big crowd, it was everyone he had hoped to see.

The main door opened and the congregation rose to their feet. Mrs. Carver stood and went to the piano where she waited to play the wedding march for Emmy to walk down the aisle.

Mr. and Mrs. Janner entered and scurried around the back pew to find their seats, meaning Emmy wasn't too far behind.

Ben took a deep breath, his pulse ticking in his wrists as he waited.

Finally, Father stepped into the church with Emmy on his arm, and all else faded away.

She wore her ball gown again, the dark blue fabric shimmering under the candlelight. Her hair was done up in another beautiful bouquet of curls, and she wore her locket again. When she saw Ben, a glorious smile filled her face and he knew, in that instant, that all the times God had said no to his pleas for a wife, had been because of His sovereign plan for this one final yes.

Mrs. Carver played the march and all eyes turned to Emmy.

He could hardly believe that after the dozens of weddings he'd performed in this church, the bride was finally walking down the aisle to join him and not another groom.

Mrs. Carver finished playing and took her seat with

the boys. Their excitement couldn't be contained as they bounced on the pew beside her. She had to put her hands on their knees to still them.

"Who gives this woman away in marriage?" Judge Barnum asked.

"It is my honor to give this bride to my son, on her father's behalf," Phillippe said with a hint of pride in his voice, his French accent thick.

Ben smiled at his father and then gave his sole attention to Emmy. He took her hand, drawing her gently to his side, and hoped his eyes conveyed how lovely she looked.

She smiled back at him, already nibbling on her bottom lip as tears of happiness filled her eyes.

Soon, very soon, he would kiss those lips every time they started to tremble, though he would do all in his power to prevent her tears from shedding.

"Dearly beloved," the judge began. "We are gathered here today in the sight of God and these witnesses to join together this man and this woman in holy matrimony. Marriage is commanded to be honorable among all men, and therefore it should not be entered into unadvisedly or lightly, but reverently, discreetly, advisedly and solemnly. If any person can show just cause why they may not be joined together, let them speak now or forever hold their peace."

Ben held Emmy's hand confidently, knowing that no one or nothing could come between them now.

"Benjamin." Judge Barnum smiled at Ben and nodded. "Do you take Emery Anne Wilkes to be your wedded wife, to live together in marriage? Do you promise to love her, comfort her, honor and keep her, for better or worse, for richer or poorer, in sickness and health, and, forsaking all others, be faithful only to her, for as long as you both shall live?"

He couldn't wait to make this promise. "I do."

"And do you, Emmy, take Benjamin Lahaye to be your wedded husband, to live together in marriage? Do you promise to love him, comfort him, honor and keep him, for better or worse, for richer or poorer, in sickness and health, and, forsaking all others, be faithful only to him, for as long as you both shall live?"

"I do." She squeezed his hand, looking deep into his eyes. "With all my heart."

"Do either of you have a token of your commitment?"

Ben took his mother's ring out of his pocket. It was the one his father had given to his mother, though they'd never legally married. It was a beautiful ruby with diamonds on either side. Phillippe had kept it on a chain around his neck all these years and had given it to Ben just before leaving the parsonage to pick up Emmy. Ben handed it to the judge now.

The judge took it and admired it for a moment before saying, "May this ring be blessed as the symbol of this affectionate union. These two lives are now joined in one unbroken circle. May these two find in each other the love for which all men and women yearn. May they grow in understanding and in compassion. May the home which they establish together be such a place that many will find there a friend, and may this ring on Emmy's finger symbolize the touch of the Holy Spirit in their hearts."

Ben had spoken the same words at every ceremony he officiated, but this evening, with the holy season of Christmas upon them, the words felt intimate and personal, as if they'd been written just for Ben and Emmy.

Judge Barnum handed the ring back to Ben and said, "Put this ring on your bride's finger and repeat after me, 'Emmy, with this ring you are now consecrated to me as my wife from this day forward.'"

Ben faced his bride, the words memorized in his mind and sealed in his heart. He didn't need the judge to tell him the rest. He slipped the ring on her left ring finger and repeated his vows, then added the ending. "I give you this ring as the pledge of my love and as the symbol of our unity, and with this ring, I thee wed."

Her eyes were filled with such love, and such hope, Ben almost didn't wait for the judge to finish before kissing her.

"By the power vested in me by the state of Minnesota," Judge Barnum said. "I now pronounce you man and wife. You may kiss the bride."

Ben took Emmy into his arms and placed a kiss on her soft lips. She wrapped her arms around him and met his kiss, giving the congregation cause for goodhearted laughter.

They pulled apart and Emmy smiled up at him. After she composed herself, she whispered, "Thank you for choosing me, over all else, Ben." Her smiled dimmed just a bit. "You really don't mind not going to Montreal?"

Not only did he not mind, he was grateful for a reason to stay. "'Therefore shall a man leave his father and his mother, and shall cleave unto his wife: and they shall be one flesh.'" He quoted the Scripture from Genesis and shook his head. "I couldn't imagine being anywhere, but right here with you and the boys." He motioned for the boys to join them, taking Levi's hand as Emmy took Zeb's. "I can't wait to bring all three of you home, once and for all."

He walked them to the main door where they would receive their guests before going to the Northern Hotel for a Christmas wedding feast.

The door opened and Mr. Samuelson walked in, his eyebrows drawn together in a frown. “So it’s true.”

Ben’s laughter rang throughout the church, the irony not lost on him. “I’m sorry, Dennis. I was just as adamant that we hire a male teacher as you, so we wouldn’t have to look for another one so soon—but I’m the one who went and married the one sent by mistake. I’ll personally take it upon myself to find her replacement.”

Others joined in on the laughter, though Mr. Samuelson only scowled.

“It wasn’t a mistake,” Emmy said to Ben with just as much humor in her voice. “It was exactly as God had planned.”

He put his arm around her waist and nodded. Emmy was right. Hiring her was not a mistake—it was the best thing that could have happened to all of them.

* * * * *

Dear Reader,

When I research the history of my hometown, I'm always amazed at the little nuggets of information I find. One of those nuggets is about Miss Ellen Nichols. She arrived in Little Falls in 1855 and served as the first schoolteacher in town. She and her husband, C.S.K. Smith, also have the distinction of celebrating the first wedding in Little Falls soon after her arrival. In a town known for its large male population, it's no wonder the schoolteacher married quickly. This historical information was the idea that sparked and grew into the third story in my Little Falls Legacy miniseries.

This story is especially dear to my heart because I modeled the twins, Zeb and Levi, after my own twin boys, Judah and Asher, who were six at the time I wrote *The Gift of Twins*. I tried to imagine how Judah and Asher would react if put in the same situation as Zeb and Levi. Some of the scenes were hard to write when life wasn't fair to the Trask boys, but other scenes were a lot of fun. I especially enjoyed watching Ben and Emmy fall in love with them.

I hope you've enjoyed this story as much as I have.
In His name,

Gabrielle Meyer

COMING NEXT MONTH FROM

Love Inspired® Historical

Available January 2, 2018

MONTANA GROOM OF CONVENIENCE

Big Sky Country • by Linda Ford

If Carly Morrison doesn't find a husband, her father threatens to sell the ranch she loves. So when Sawyer Gallagher arrives in town hoping to give his orphaned little half sister a home and family, a marriage of convenience is the answer to both their problems.

ACCIDENTAL COURTSHIP

The Bachelors of Aspen Valley • by Lisa Bingham

Women are forbidden at the secluded Utah mining camp where Jonah Ramsey works. When an avalanche strands a train full of mail-order brides nearby, can he avoid clashing with the newly hired—and female—doctor, Sumner Havisham?

HIS FORGOTTEN FIANCÉE

by Evelyn M. Hill

When Matthew Dean arrives in Oregon Territory with amnesia, Liza Fitzpatrick—the fiancée he doesn't remember—needs his help to keep the claim a local lumber baron covets. But will he regain his memory in time to save the land and give their love a second chance?

A MOTHER FOR HIS FAMILY

by Susanne Dietze

Faced with a potential scandal, Lady Helena Stanhope must marry, and with John Gordon in need of a mother for his children—and not looking for love—he's the perfect match. But their marriage in name only just might force them to risk their hearts.

SPECIAL EXCERPT FROM

Hoping to make his dream of owning a farm come true, Jeremiah Stoltzfus clashes with single mother Mercy Bamberger, who believes the land belongs to her. Mercy yearns to make the farm a haven for unwanted children. Can she and Jeremiah possibly find a future together?

Read on for a sneak preview of
AN AMISH ARRANGEMENT
by Jo Ann Brown,
available January 2018 from Love Inspired!

Jeremiah looked up to see a ladder wobbling. A dark-haired woman stood at the very top, her arms windmilling.

He leaped into the small room as she fell. After years of being tossed shocks of corn and hay bales, he caught her easily. He jumped out of the way, holding her to him as the ladder crashed to the linoleum floor.

"Are you okay?" he asked. His heart had slammed against his chest when he saw her teetering.

"I'm fine."

"Who are you?" he asked at the same time she did.

"I'm Jeremiah Stoltzfus," he answered. "You are…?"

"Mercy Bamberger."

"Bamberger? Like Rudy Bamberger?"

"Yes. Do you know my grandfather?"

Well, that explained who she was and why she was in the house.

"He invited me to come and look around."

LIEXP1217

She shook her head. "I don't understand why."

"Didn't he tell you he's selling me his farm?"

"No!"

"I'm sorry to take you by surprise," he said gently, "but I'll be closing the day after tomorrow."

"Impossible! The farm's not for sale."

"Why don't you get your *grossdawdi*, and we'll settle this?"

"I can't."

"Why not?"

She blinked back sudden tears. "Because he's dead."

"Rudy is dead?"

"Yes. It was a massive heart attack. He was buried the day before yesterday."

"I'm sorry," Jeremiah said with sincerity.

"Grandpa Rudy told me the farm would be mine after he passed away."

"Then why would he sign a purchase agreement with me?"

"But my grandfather died," she whispered. "Doesn't that change things?"

"I don't know. I'm not sure what we should do," he said.

"Me, either. However, you need to know I'm not going to relinquish my family's farm to you or anyone else."

"But—"

"We moved in a couple of days ago. We're not giving it up." She crossed her arms over her chest. "It's our home."

SPECIAL EXCERPT FROM

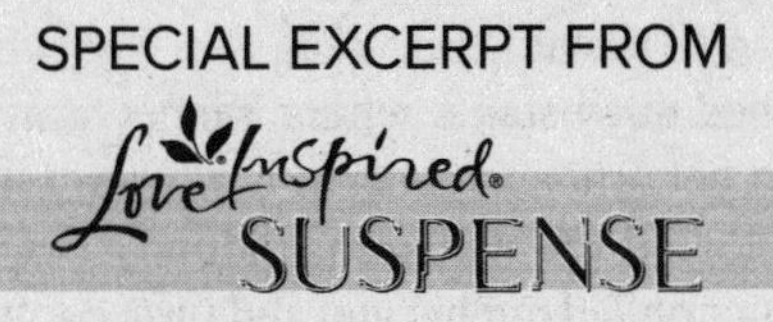

Special Agent Tanner Wilson has only one clue to figure out who left a baby at the Houston FBI office—his ex-girlfriend's name written on a scrap of paper. But Macy Mills doesn't recognize the little girl that someone's determined to abduct at any cost.

Read on for a sneak preview of THE BABY ASSIGNMENT by Christy Barritt, *available January 2018 from Love Inspired Suspense!*

Suddenly, Macy stood. "Do you smell that, Tanner?"

Smoke. There was a fire somewhere. Close.

"Go get Addie," he barked. "Now!"

Macy flew up the steps, urgency nipping at her heels.

Where there was smoke, there was fire. Wasn't that the saying?

Somehow, she instinctively knew that those words were the truth. Whoever had set this fire had done it on purpose. They wanted to push Tanner, Macy and Addie outside. Into harm. Into a trap.

As she climbed higher, she spotted the flames. They licked the edges of the house, already beginning to consume it.

Despite the heat around her, ice formed in her gut.

She scooped up Addie, hating to wake the infant when she was sleeping so peacefully.

LISEXP1217

Macy had to move fast.

She rushed downstairs, where Tanner waited for her. He grabbed her arm and ushered her toward the door.

Flames licked the walls now, slowly devouring the house. Tanner pulled out his gun and turned toward Macy.

She could hardly breathe. Just then, Addie awoke with a cry.

The poor baby. She had no idea what was going on. She didn't deserve this.

Tanner kept his arm around her and Addie.

"Let's do this," he said. His voice held no room for argument.

He opened the door. Flames licked their way inside.

Macy gasped as the edges of the fire felt dangerously close. She pulled Addie tightly to her chest, determined to protect the baby at all costs.

She held her breath as they slipped outside and rushed to the car. There was no car seat. There hadn't been time.

Instead, Macy continued to hold Addie close to her chest, trying to shield her from any incoming danger or threats. She lifted a quick prayer.

Please help us.

As Tanner started the car, a bullet shattered the window.